What people are sayi

PROVIDENCE

"Chris' first work of fiction is a showcase for his incredible talents. He brings to this book the same quality and creativity I have seen in him for years."

Michael W. Smith, singer/songwriter

"In his first novel, *Providence*, my friend Chris Coppernoll unfolds the wonder of a God of second chances—a God who brings beauty from ashes in the lives and relationships of those that trust Him. It's a book I wholly recommend to the ever hopeful romantics among us."

Rebecca St. James, Grammy Award-winning Christian singer/best-selling author

"Chris Coppernoll's novel is perfect for those of us who love to curl up and read a great story in our pajamas."

Kerri Pomarolli, comedian/author, *If I'm Waiting on God, Then What Am I Doing in a Christian Chatroom?*

"Chris Coppernoll has written a tender and heartfelt story that illustrates the transforming power of the gospel and its ability to reflect the truth about our lives."

Jill Phillips, singer/songwriter

"In *Providence*, Christopher Coppernoll reminds us that if we allow Him, God can use anything, even our past and the memories it holds, for good."

Donna VanLiere, New York Times best-selling author, *The Christmas Shoes* and *The Angels of Morgan Hill*

"In *Providence*, Chris Coppernoll explores the tensions we all feel between our own plans, and the mystery of God's unfolding will."

Chris Rice, singer/songwriter

"Emotionally charged and intriguing! *Providence* invites you into Jack Clayton's world and allows you to feel his frustration and heartache along with his joy. The beauty of this novel is that it leads us all to the positive message of redemption and hope no matter what life brings."

Karol Ladd, best-selling author, *The Power of a Positive Woman*

"Chris Coppernoll is an apt student of the Human Experience. He has keen insight into the motivations that drive people to succeed–and the ultimate cost of fame. In *Providence*, Chris proves he is equally adept at translating reality into compelling fiction."

Mike Parker, contributing editor, LifeWay.com

Gabriella

PROVIDENCE

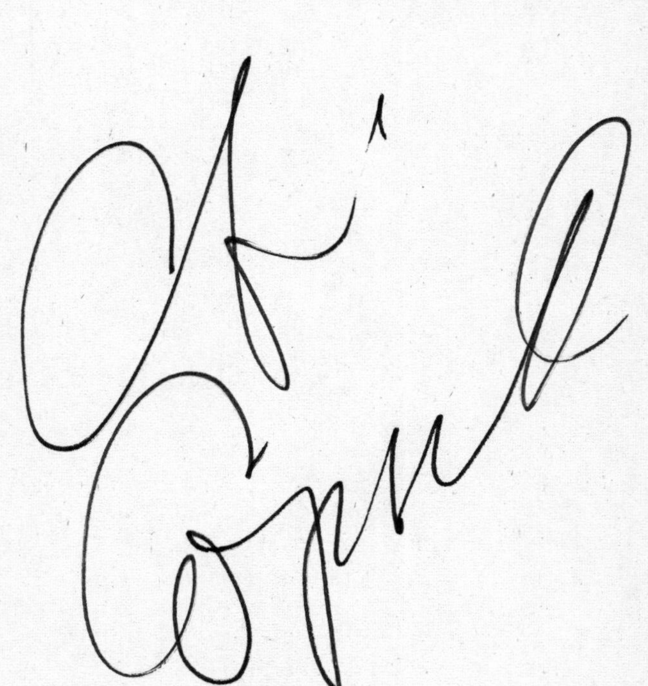

a novel

PROVIDENCE

Once Upon a Second Chance

Chris Coppernoll

PROVIDENCE
Published by David C. Cook
4050 Lee Vance View
Colorado Springs, CO 80918 U.S.A.

David C. Cook Distribution Canada
55 Woodslee Avenue, Paris, Ontario, Canada N3L 3E5

David C. Cook U.K., Kingsway Communications
Eastbourne, East Sussex BN23 6NT, England

Mass Market ISBN 978-1-4347-6442-3

The author is represented by MacGregor Literary.

Cover Design: The DesignWorks Group, Jason Gabbert
Interior Design: Karen Athen
Cover Photo: iStock; Shutterstock
Author Photo: Allen Clark

Printed in the United States of America
First Edition 2007

1 2 3 4 5 6 7 8 9 10

062707

To the Giver of second chances,
and to everyone who needs one

~ One ~

Christmas is the time to say "I love you"
Share the joys of laughter and good cheer.

—Billy Squier
"Christmas Is the Time to Say 'I Love You'"

Midwinter's bleak shadow had fallen upon Providence, Indiana. That morning a curtain of paste-and-gauze clouds doused the sun's brilliant light, robbing its rise to full glory. Though Christmas was nearing, my house was absent of a decorated tree or colored lights. Every corner of the room felt like how C. S. Lewis described Narnia: always winter, but never Christmas.

In the living room downstairs, I turned on the floor lamp next to the sofa and flipped up all the light switches on my way to the kitchen. This helped warm up a chilly house. Awake since early morning, even earlier than normal, I had already consumed half a pot of coffee. By the time I heard my neighbors warming up their cars for the cold city commute, caffeine had begun to iron out the wrinkles that come with being up half the night. The root cause of my insomnia? Two unanswered questions: "What have I gotten myself into?" and "Why can't the past stay buried?"

At seven thirty, I telephoned my book publisher. Arthur Reed had been there at the beginning of all this mess. He'd witnessed the pandemonium that entangled my life these past three years. He'd even done his part to make the mess grow bigger, fanning the flame, jubilant at seeing it burn out of control. At some point during the long night, I'd decided to call Arthur and deliver the worst news he could imagine.

On the kitchen table, a toasted bagel covered with melting cream cheese cooled on a plate. I leaned inside the kitchen doorway, the phone pressed against my ear. As I listened to it ringing, I remembered Arthur's antics. How he'd worked so hard at selling me on the idea of writing about my side of the phenomena. I knew the reasons he wanted another book from me, all eighteen million of them, just as I knew this phone call would rock his world. What I didn't know was how it would kick off an extraordinary new journey.

Across the breakfast table lay the book responsible for everything. A 220-page hardcover bearing a small black-and-white photograph of me on the inside back cover. Above it an italicized paragraph summarized to my satisfaction everything anyone ever needed to know about me:

> *Jack Clayton serves on staff at the Campus Missions Office through the auspices of Providence College in Providence, Indiana. He has authored two books*

> *about CMO's ongoing ministry work in the three-and-a-half-square-mile area of Providence known as the Norwood community, Providence's poorest neighborhood. For twelve years Jack has encouraged, coached, and recruited hundreds of student volunteers to recognize the needs of the world around them, and to work for change.*

I'm not a writer, but five years ago I began scribbling down stories of the people impacted by the Norwood ministry for our city newspaper, the *Providence Appeal.* Those stories raised awareness and much-needed funds for the ongoing work in Norwood. They also captured the attention of Arthur Reed, who asked to publish those stories in book form. My first book sold roughly four thousand copies, mostly in Providence and to alumni who blindly support anything associated with the college. A second book was released the following year, and partly due to a story on National Public Radio, it outsold the first by more than nine thousand copies. My third and last book in the series was called *Laborers of the Orchard.* In a single year it sold over eighteen million copies and landed my face on the cover of *People* magazine.

When you write a book that goes to number one on the New York Times Best Seller List and stays there for twenty-nine weeks, everything in your world changes. *Laborers of the Orchard* was labeled a "hot ticket" in media circles, and suddenly every magazine editor and cable-television news producer wanted to interview the "Pastor to the Poor." I made an enormous mistake refusing to sit down for any of those interviews. I had good intentions: to insulate myself from life's inevitable fifteen minutes of fame. However, my plan backfired, sparking a brush fire of media interest in my private life. It's also what prompted a now-wealthy Arthur Reed to daydream about publishing the inevitable follow-up. My personal story. My memoir.

Just when I thought it was too early for Art to be in, he picked up the phone.

"Arthur Reed." His voice trumpeted through the speakerphone.

"G'morning, Art. It's Jack."

"Jack, good morning, and Merry Christmas!" he said, though the actual day was still weeks away. "How's the writer doing?"

"Well, I'm digging up bones, and some of them are rattling," I said. I could hear Arthur's hearty laughter. It sputtered like the sound of exhaust escaping a frozen Mercedes-Benz.

"Sounds interesting. I take it you've finally started writing your memoir?"

"Yeah, last night. I worked on it past midnight, and again this morning, which brings me to why I'm calling you."

"Brilliant," Arthur said.

I heard the sunburst sound of his computer booting up, his ADD already kicking in. By the sound of it, Arthur had just stepped into his office. If his Starbucks hadn't jolted him awake yet, what I was about to say would.

"Art, this isn't going to be easy to hear, so I'm just

going to come out and say it. I've decided I'm going to let this one go. I'm going to pass on writing the memoir."

I paused—not for dramatic effect, but to let the words sink in. Arthur was convinced my memoir would be another best seller; he'd said it many times. It would be another blockbuster for Arthur Reed Publishing and would further establish his firm in the industry. But the book was more important to Arthur than I knew.

"I don't understand," he said, sandbagged by the news. "You started writing, right?"

"Yeah," I repeated. "Last night."

"But now you've stopped?"

"Right."

Like a cork pulled from a genie's bottle, uneasiness filled the phone line, turning our conversation suddenly thick.

"I'm confused," Arthur said. "What in the world's gotten into you since last night?"

This is where I should have come clean. I should have just told Arthur about the memories. How they'd come knocking when I pulled the Christmas decorations out of the attic and saw that photograph stashed inside one of the ornaments. How they'd come back to me again while I was sitting at the computer screen trying to remember what I'd tried so hard to forget.

"I started thinking it over, that's all. About whether I have it in me to go through with writing another book, especially now. Is this really what I'm supposed to be doing over Christmas? Writing books, avoiding interviews? It's easy to lose focus, Art, and before you know it, the train's coming off its tracks."

"What on earth does that mean?"

Arthur hates metaphors.

"It means I've had doubts all along about writing this book. I've been forcing it out of friendship, Arthur, trying to write a follow-up book for you because there may be a market for it. But I've decided I'm not going through with it."

Arthur's talent as a never-say-die negotiator was booting up alongside his computer.

"Oh, there's a market for it, Jack. My desk is littered with evidence to that very fact, and you promised to write it."

"I promised to take a crack at it, that's all. You pitched, I swung, broken bat."

If the tumblers wouldn't open spinning the dial to the right, Arthur would simply spin them to the left.

"So don't write it. I'll hire someone to ghostwrite it for you," he said. "All you have to do is remember and talk. You can do that, right?"

He had an answer for everything. Maybe that was the secret of his success—relentless persistence. I imagined myself sitting in my living room across from some freelancer. He wouldn't know what questions to ask, and I sure wouldn't know how to answer.

"That wouldn't work," I said.

Outside the snow began falling again onto an already frozen landscape. Inside, the old furnace kicked on, and I could feel its muted heat blowing up through the floor vents.

My long-forgotten past tapped against the door in my mind, showing me faces again I didn't want to see. Jenny's face, bright and lovely, edged in a halo of summer sunlight. Her smile, radiant; her lips full and red.

I turned the lock on the door.

"Arthur, we need to put this issue to rest. For the sake of our friendship. Try seeing things from my point of view."

"Forgive me if I ask you to try and see things from *my* point of view. I'm not asking you to write *War and Peace;* I'm asking you to turn in two hundred pages. Give me whatever you've got."

An elusive best seller—that's what *Laborers* had been. An eighteen-million-to-one shot. The success, Arthur's standing with the big publishing firms back east. His tiny Indianapolis organization wasn't in the same class, but *Laborers* had at least put it in the same school. He coveted their acceptance. How could he say to his colleagues, "Yes, we could have had another blockbuster, but my author just didn't feel like writing it"?

"At first they laughed behind my back," he'd confided to me over dinner one night at his house in Waterbrook. "Podunk publisher. They laughed at your success like it was nothing more than a fluke." Arthur had stared into his drink as if it were a deep well.

"They're not laughing anymore, Jack. Your sales numbers go up faster than the clicker board on a TV telethon. And every time they do, another New York agent calls me with a new book idea attached to a best-selling author."

"I'm sorry," I told Arthur. "You have to accept that this book isn't going to happen. I won't be writing it."

I was never more relieved that I hadn't signed a book contract—or accepted the lucrative advance Arthur had offered.

"Look, Jack, it's not that simple. You said you would. While you've been getting your ducks in a row, I've been setting up contracts with all the major retailers, greasing the wheels for another Jack Clayton best seller. Your new book is already sold in. People are counting on it. We've got advance orders for over three million books."

I shouldn't have been surprised that Art was selling a book I hadn't even officially agreed to write. But I was.

"Not a day goes by without a request for a Jack Clayton interview," he continued, unaware of my dismay. "People are suspicious about why you've never done one. They want to know how someone claiming affinity with the poor has made so much money writing about them. And what are we saying to those in the media? That the story they've been chasing for three years is finally being penned by the author himself! Don't you see how perfect this is?"

Art was playing a game of chess, advancing his army of pawns. "What do you think they'll write about you once they hear you've backed out of your project? How do you think they'll fill in the blanks? And Jack, they *will* fill in the blanks."

"I never signed a contract …"

Art wasn't listening. "Wake up, Jack," he said. "People want to know why you're so private. They're interpreting your … introversion as hiding secrets. Everyone has questions about your history, questions about your finances. They want to know why a man who does so much good for the poor feels like he has to hide. Are you thinking about all the people genuinely interested in what you're supposed to be writing about? Or the kind of influence you can have for good? Readers *want* this book, Jack. Booksellers want it; journalists and, yes, even us little people at Arthur Reed Publishing who have worked for twenty-five years with writers who can't even sell five thousand books. Just like you used to be, Jack. You can't just take your ball and go home because you don't feel like playing anymore."

The December sky looked like miles of dark cotton stretched across the sun. My head ached as I listened to Arthur, reminded of the people affected by the decisions we make, and more aware than ever how my elusiveness had created suspicion. I was a "best-selling do-gooder" who might just have something to hide. That's what the press was saying. The problem was, they were right.

"Arthur, you have to understand something. I'm not complaining about deadlines or about writing late at night until the coffee burns the taste buds out of my mouth. It's about delving into ..."—I paused. In my mind I saw a picture of Art and me engaged in a tug-of-war, my flag being pulled across his line—"into areas of my past I'm not comfortable with." The moment I said it, I wished I hadn't. Friend or not, Arthur would push through my excuses like a linebacker finding a hole in the offense.

"What's the big deal, Jack? Everyone's got a couple of skeletons hiding in their closet!"

"I don't have a few skeletons, Art," I blurted out. "I have enough to build a whole skeleton army, and I'm not about to parade them down Main Street."

Then it happened. A stroke of genius so obvious I

wondered why I hadn't thought of it in the first place. "Listen, Art, there's something else. I've got a staff meeting at the Campus Missions Office this morning. I haven't mentioned this book to anyone at CMO. You know I'll need the full support of my colleagues before committing to such considerable time away from CMO."

Immediately Art saw through the strategy I was employing. "Jack, listen. This book means more than you realize. You're taking this far too lightly."

That was an understatement, and for the first time I heard fear in Arthur's voice.

"I'm heading over to the office now," I said. "I'll call you this afternoon and let you know the outcome."

It was all over, and he knew it. Aaron and Peter would support me in whatever I thought was best. Nancy would follow suit.

"Jack, I need you to give this serious thought—"

"I will, Arthur, I will."

I cut off the phone with my finger, ending our conversation. Round one had been messy, but I'd won. Round two would be easy. Aaron, Peter, and Nancy would surely agree that I couldn't be spared from CMO's work, especially during a demanding Christmas season. The memoir of Jack Clayton would be laid out flat. A two-round knockout.

~ Two ~

You can listen as well as you hear.

—Mike and the Mechanics
"The Living Years"

An eighties song was playing at the BP station when I pulled in to gas up the Jeep. Not everyone had switched over to wall-to-wall Christmas music. I knew the tune right away. I didn't like it much as a twenty-year-old college student here at Providence, but as a forty-year-old, I found myself humming it as I drove off into the steady downpour of a thick, wet snow. *"Say it loud, say it clear; you can listen as well as you hear."*

The song had faded from my mind by the time I shut off the engine in the lot behind the Campus Missions Office. Jenny's countenance, which had surfaced for the third time in less than twenty-four hours, thankfully faded with it.

Stopping for gas made me late. I climbed the icy stairs at the rear entrance of the building, darted past Mrs. Burman, our receptionist, and then bounded up the staircase to the second-floor conference room, nearly running into CMO's fifty-three-year-old founder, Aaron Richmond. The man who'd hired me to work at CMO more than a decade ago was setting a full box of Krispy Kreme doughnuts in the middle of the conference table.

"Krispy Kreme," I said. "What's the occasion?"

"We're officially in Christmas mode now," he said. "In other words, I felt like it."

Aaron is, not surprisingly, thick in the middle. Friends say he couldn't be any smaller and still contain so much good humor and genuine compassion for others.

Peter Brenner came in after me, carrying a very large cup of something from Starbucks and looking like an advertisement for J.Crew. Tall and thin, sporting a short goatee, and round-framed glasses, he wore his trademark red flannel shirt, blue jeans, and a Duckhead cap. Peter looked casual because he was.

This probably accounts for some of his success teaching the hugely popular Crosswise Bible study on Tuesday nights. Peter has a gift for teaching, and even students who don't identify themselves as Christians feel comfortable filling the seats in Warren Auditorium to hear him speak plainly and compellingly about the gospel.

"Krispy Kreme and Starbucks, oh yeah. Breakfast of champions."

Nancy Arcone entered after Peter, trademark notepad and pen in hand. She took her seat next to Aaron. Nancy is CMO's chief administrator and smartest teammate. She's a married mother of three (two of them in college). She brought a master's degree in nursing and a University of Wisconsin MBA to CMO with which she bridles what would otherwise be a disorganized organization.

"Has anyone heard the weather report? It's starting to look pretty nasty out there."

"They predicted three to four inches last night, and we got almost a foot," Peter laughed. "Today it's supposed to clear up. What was it doing when you drove in Jack?"

"Uh … snowing," I said.

"Thank you for your brilliant analysis, Jack. You know as much as the guy on TV."

"Jack, thank you for sending your book to my dad … and for calling him," said Nancy. "I talked to him on Sunday, and I could tell he really thought that was something."

"No problem. I only wish he were closer than Green Bay. I'd love to visit him."

"Well, it did him a world of good. I wanted you to know that."

Peter opened the meeting with prayer, then Aaron wrapped up a few loose ends from the fall semester, which felt more like winter. When he finished, he opened the floor for new business. I took my cue.

"Good morning again, everyone. There's a small, simple matter I need to discuss with you. This shouldn't take too long, but I do feel it's necessary to bring up what's happening in my life and ministry." I glanced at the faces around the conference table, hoping to gauge their receptivity. There was no indication, so I went on.

"Arthur has asked me to start a new book. Don't laugh, but he wants this one to be about yours truly." I chuckled, giving them permission to laugh too. Nobody did.

"Anyway, this has been an unusual season for CMO, as I'm sure you'd agree. The commotion from the last book … well, you all know what that was like. This office was turned upside down, and there were times when the chaos got in the way of the real work that's supposed to go on here."

It was true. The attention lavished on *Laborers* was both a blessing and a burden. At its peak, tourists would stand in front of our building snapping pictures or knock on our front door asking for tours. One early morning Aaron had pulled into the parking lot to find a reporter from News Channel Five ready to pounce on him with a surprise interview as he climbed out of his Ford Taurus.

"Arthur will want to market this book in a big way. He hasn't said it yet, but I'm sure that's his plan. This would mean pulling my energies away from the office over Christmas when things will be at their busiest, and even into the first part of next year. So you can see why I wanted to discuss this with you before I commit … *if* I commit to this project."

We were already overworked and understaffed. Even with just one person out, like when Peter had the flu the month before, the workload could feel crippling. The Christmas season was already upon us, and our student volunteers were up to their sleep-deprived eyeballs cramming for final exams just when the need for service was at its peak. This wasn't merely a lousy time to make special requests, it was the absolute worst.

Aaron, Peter, and Nancy listened attentively, offering no clues on their faces as I finished my opening remarks. I suspected each was deliberating how to phrase a gentle letdown, something about how a less-hectic semester, like summer, would be a better time for me to write a book.

"I don't know what anyone else at this table is thinking, Jack," Aaron finally said, breaking the silence, "but I think you need to write the book."

I was stunned. Across the table Peter nodded his head in slow agreement. This didn't make sense. I turned to Nancy and asked her what she thought.

"I think you should do the book, Jack. Why wouldn't you want to?" Nancy's expression was calm, but her words shot their own kind of caffeinated stimulant into the meeting.

Peter and Aaron turned in unison to catch my reaction.

"It isn't that I don't want to write the book," I said, hoping to sound convincing. "*Part* of me wants to write it."

Nancy's words had blindsided me. It hadn't even crossed my mind that my three closest friends would agree with Arthur. The reality left me scrambling for cover.

"I'm very aware of how this … I'm trying to be sensitive to …"

In front of my friend's knowing eyes, I wrote, erased, and rewrote excuses until Aaron mercifully stepped in.

"Jack, I'm going to speak candidly. What's

happened with your book over the past year or so has been remarkable. It's something only God could have done, and through it, I believe He's allowing millions of people to reconsider their faith and reflect on how they should serve the poor. But it wouldn't surprise me if God is up to something more, Jack, something specifically focused on you."

Around the table there were confident nods of agreement. There was also an odd burgeoning energy that made me uncomfortable. I began to squirm in my seat.

"Everyone who comes in contact with your book seems to benefit: the college, the Norwood community, and Arthur Reed, I'm sure. But I don't think God's done with it yet, Jack. I really don't. There may be something in all of this He's saving just for you."

"You've got to be joking!" The words left my mouth before I could rein them in.

"No, I'm not joking. I've worked with you for twelve years. There are a lot of things about you *I* don't know."

"Never gives interviews," Peter interjected, his face propped up against one open hand, his eyes studying me.

"I've read your books." Aaron held three fingers in the air. "Hardly a word about yourself in any of them. Why is that?"

"Well, they're not about me. They're books about Norwood," I said, sounding more defensive than I intended.

"Fair enough, but you found space in those pages to talk about everyone who lives in Norwood, and most of the students who've volunteered here. You even wrote a paragraph or two about those of us around this table, but never so much as a word about yourself."

"Yeah, I've thought that too, Jack," Peter said. He tugged at the white plastic lid on his Starbucks cup, a Cheshire-catlike smile appearing on his face. "Maybe this is God's way of getting you to write your story." He let out a slow laugh, and I heard something in it that scared me: truth.

With the three of them sitting on the opposite side of the table, the meeting felt like a parole-board hearing. I didn't like how this was going. I'd already fought a tug-of-war with Arthur. Now Peter, Aaron, and Nancy were grabbing hold of the rope too.

I wanted to say something to change their minds, but before I could find the words, Nancy spoke.

"Jack, God may be giving you not so much a book to write as a course to take. Maybe He has something for you to discover about Him or yourself, something you can't learn any other way."

"That's possible," Aaron said. "He may even want to heal something from your past you're not aware of."

"I don't know about anyone else," said Peter, "but I don't think you have much of a choice. You need to write this book." He seemed awfully chipper about the whole thing.

"I don't doubt this will be challenging for you, Jack," Nancy added, "but look at the positives. It could be an incredible adventure."

And there it was. My three friends spoke as if God Himself were speaking through them. I knew then that

I had to write this book. I felt it in the core of my being just as surely as I feel this plastic keyboard beneath my curled fingertips. I'd raced in looking for a way out. What I found was a trio of voices to accompany Arthur's self-assured solo.

There was a fifth voice, too. One that came from inside me. Until that moment it had been silent. I could say no to Arthur, even to my coworkers, but not to this inner voice.

"You're not concerned about our work?" I asked.

"The students will come back in January ready to handle a lot more than when they arrived here last fall," Peter said. "I can take on more."

The four of us sat in silence.

"Jack, the work we do here is service based," said Aaron. "It's not just assistance to the college but serving any needs we see the Lord directing us to. If you're asking for our counsel—which I'm not sure you wanted when you came in here—my suggestion is to take time off, to think and pray, to remember, and especially to write."

Nancy pushed in the stinger. "Jack, have you considered taking a leave of absence?"

"No, I haven't." *But I can read the writing on the wall.*

"I think that's an excellent idea," Aaron said.

Downstairs the office phone rang, and I heard Mrs. Burman pick it up. "Campus Missions Office."

Aaron stood, and Nancy and Peter followed suit. Our meeting was over. The most trusted people I knew on earth had just cut me loose from the tether that held me to it.

"You've had an incredible year, Jack," Aaron said. "Don't be afraid to take some time off."

"Yeah, Jack, unwind a little." Nancy smiled.

"We're not trying to get rid of you!" Peter quipped, prompting laughter from Nancy and Aaron and lightening my somewhat dour mood.

As Aaron walked through the conference-room doorway where I'd nearly knocked him down twenty minutes earlier, he turned and issued a decree. "Use this week to get your things together, and then take off the rest of December and January—even February if you need it."

I spent the rest of the morning in my office answering e-mails, canceling appointments, and wondering what had just happened. I'd walked into the building intent on ditching the book. Now, as the heaviest snowfall of the year fell outside my office window, I was clearing out the desk I'd known as my home away from home for the past twelve years. It didn't take a week to get my things in order. By ten thirty I'd scratched all the upcoming events off my day planner.

"Doesn't do interviews," Peter had said.

"There are a lot of things about you *I* don't know," Aaron had said.

Welcome to the club. I've been walking around in these shoes for forty years, and there's plenty I don't know either.

Around noon Mrs. Burman knocked on my open door. She handed me mail she normally would have left in a box downstairs.

"A little birdie told me you're gonna be leaving us for a while," she said, making it sound like I was a kid about to be dropped off at summer camp.

"Yes. I've been hearing that too, Mrs. B. You want to join me? We can make it a twosome."

She laughed, ever guileless. "Oh-ho, I can't do that. But I'm going to miss you when you're gone."

I knew she meant it. I got up from my desk and gave her a hug, not something I normally did, but it felt natural just the same. I thanked her for her thoughtfulness and took it all as a sign the office would find a way to adjust to my departure.

I called Arthur and told him the news. I'm certain he tried covering up the phone, but I could still hear him squealing with delight. He was a lucky jackpot winner hitting it big the day his house almost got repossessed.

"The Lord works in mysterious ways, Jack!" he told me. I wondered how he'd ever wipe the grin from his face.

After twelve years at CMO, my last official day ended with Peter and me stepping out for a quick bite at Oscar's, a popular on-campus deli. We grabbed seats in the first open booth. A busboy cleaned off the vinyl red-and-white-checkered tablecloth, and I scanned the mini-jukebox mounted on the wall between us. We gave the waitress our order without looking at menus. Over the noise of the bustling lunch crowd, Peter asked how I was doing.

"I'm fine," I said, not wanting to admit to either of us the trepidation I was feeling. "It's going to take transition time, that's all."

"Sorry if we were a little brusque with you. We could have eased you into things a little better," Peter said, mending fences that didn't really need mending.

"It's fine, Peter. I'll get into the swing of things."

"That's the spirit. You really do need a break. What'd you sell? Something like a billion books? After that kind of earthquake, I'd think anyone would want to step away for a while, nail their cupboards back on the walls."

The waitress returned and dropped off two oversized Reubens with dill pickles and chips and two Coca-Colas in large red plastic cups. We asked the Lord for His blessing, then dug in.

"I'm not against taking time off, Peter," I said. "I just haven't figured out what I'm in for."

"All the more reason to take a break. Have you thought about going somewhere? An exotic writer's retreat, or whatever you best-selling authors call it. Go somewhere and just write and relax."

Did those two words go together? Write and relax?

"I can't say it's crossed my mind," I said, suddenly distracted by a twenty-something female student a few tables away, who reminded me of someone I knew a long time ago.

A customer in the booth behind me dropped a quarter in the jukebox and punched in a song. Even with the deafening crowd noise, I could hear the faint melody from an era ago.

"This is the sound of my soul, this is the sound . . . "

"You're writing the book, right?" Peter took a long pull from his Coke.

"Yes." I said for the official record.

"So, fly out of here. What's keeping you? We're

in the middle of the coldest winter in memory, and Jamaica is eighty degrees with blue waters and white, sandy beaches. I thought you were rich, Jack." He shook his head. "I wouldn't even be here now."

I took another bite of my Reuben. "Jamaica, huh?"

"Why not? You haven't taken a vacation in … how long has it been?"

"Twenty years, give or take a decade."

"So go. Who knows, the future Mrs. Clayton may be waiting for you on one of those beaches." Peter smiled, a subtle tease at my being forty and still single.

I didn't need to remind him that he was single and nearly forty too. I wouldn't remind him, of course, how there'd almost been a Mrs. Clayton. That was a memory I kept private. As close as Peter and I were, I could never tell him about Jenny. Where would I start? And just how would I end, with her tears or my own?

"Well, I hope she doesn't burn easily," I said.

After lunch we drove back to the office and said our good-byes in the parking lot, the relentless snow temporarily switched to off. I climbed into an ice-cold Jeep and fired up the engine. Sitting in the frozen cab with the windows frosted over, my mind wandered to dreams of tiki huts, resting my bare feet on a crate of fresh papaya, reading in a lazy netted hammock, the setting orange sun warm on my face.

Driving out of the parking lot, I thought about those boxes of memories sitting unopened in the far reaches of my mind, most having not seen sunlight for twenty years.

I got home around two o'clock, exhausted, and managed to switch on CNN before falling asleep on the sofa in front of the TV. Two hours later I awoke feeling disoriented and went upstairs for my second blistering-hot shower of the day. By the time I was dry, I felt a state approaching normal again. Across the bedroom the phone-message light was blinking red. I walked over to the nightstand and pressed the playback button.

"Helloooo, Jack!" the caller said in a tone crackled and low. "This is a voice from your past. Does the name Howard Cameron ring any bells for you?"

Oh my gosh …

Howard's good-natured laugh trailed after the question like the twinkling tail of a kite. "You're probably at work right now, but since this is the only number we have—without tracking you down through the FBI—we'll just have to leave a message."

Had it been twenty years?

"By now you've probably received the postcard Angela and I sent you."

Postcard?

"We're back from England as of the seventh, and as I wrote on the card, we'll be passing through Providence this Saturday. We both read your book by the way and are delighted to see you've finally come to some good!" More hearty laughter. "Hope you're free 'cause we'd love to see you, Jack. Anyway, we'll try you again later in the week."

The machine shut off, and the little red light began blinking again. For all these years, Jenny's parents had been in England working as missionaries. The last time I'd seen them, they were leaving to *go* to Europe. I'd always liked Howard and Angela, especially Howard. He acted as if he thought the world of me, even though I never did a thing to earn it. Now they were on their way back to Indiana.

"Well, I've got the day off," I said to the empty room, a sure sign of my impending crack-up.

I finished dressing and went downstairs. It was five thirty and already dark outside. I set a fresh pot of coffee to brew in the kitchen and returned down the hallway to the office. I switched on a small lamp and lit a scented candle I'd found in the back of a drawer. Nothing wrong with a little atmosphere.

Soon the room was aglow with light and the scents of vanilla and cinnamon. Fractured frost painted the windowpanes in front of my desk. Outside, Indiana was a winter icebox, the wind whistling her subzero carols.

When the iMac finished booting up, I double-clicked the document icon I'd planned on tossing out just twelve hours earlier. It was time to write—but first, time to pray.

Lord, You're here with me. I know You're doing something. Let my work be in line with Your plans. Make me fit to serve You. I needed God's blessing, and His company, on whatever journey I was about to take. I needed to hand Him the book before I wrote a single word.

The iMac greeted me like C-3PO from *Star Wars.* "Master Jack, how good of you to return! I knew you wouldn't leave us!"

"Leave you? No, I wouldn't do that, C-3PO. I've got a story to write. And I need your help to travel back in time, to the year 1985."

~ Three ~

These dreams go on when I close my eyes
Every second of the night I live another life.

—Heart
"These Dreams"

I bolted upright in bed. A cool breeze whispered through the open window after a day as hot as a summer greenhouse. I could hear the rumble of a storm tumbling from the far side of Collinger County. Awakened from a bad dream, I lay back in my bed, counting the seconds of silence between the flashes of light and the booms of distant thunder. I listened for sound coming from the other side of the upstairs hallway where my mother, Marianne Clayton, slept, but I heard only the raging of the storm outside. There was no noise loud enough to wake my dad, George Clayton, since divorce had transported him to Southern California eight years earlier.

His departure left my sister, Ruth Ann, and me alone with our mom in a three-bedroom country home in Overton, Iowa—the only home we'd ever known. I'd spent the last eighteen years of my life there.

Bright and early in the morning, my best friend, Mitch McDaniels, would pilot his navy blue Cutlass Ciera up our long gravel driveway, past the bountiful, sweet-smelling farms. I'd load two bags into the trunk, and we'd fly over the Cloverlane bridge, leaving Overton for college.

For good.

I'd waited eight years to blast off from Overton, to leave for college or anywhere else. On nights like this when the bad dreams came, I'd learned to close my eyes and remember the good times. And there *were* good times, like the last vacation we'd all taken together as a family. But remembering them had gotten harder over the past few years.

Ruth Ann died when I was sixteen. She was killed by a drunk driver only a few miles from our house. That driver was her best friend, Patricia Dunwoody. Patricia had been sitting behind the wheel of her dad's 1980 Chevy Caprice, with Ruth Ann buckled in next to her. The two eighteen-year-olds were driving around Overton enjoying some postgraduation fun when Patricia missed the turn at Archer's Farm and plowed into a hundred-year-old oak tree. Patricia received a cut across her forehead just below the hairline. Ruthie died instantly.

There are some things in life we just have to deal with. If we don't, then those things get stuffed inside like laundry in a canvas bag with the cords pulled tight. Ruth Ann had been accepted at Providence College in Indiana, a school I'd never heard of at the time. A good student, she'd been awarded their prestigious Hensley-Drumons Science Scholarship at Overton High School's honors banquet during graduation week.

I saw my dad for the last time at Ruthie's funeral. Two years before I would head out on my own. Two years before the door would finally close on that tragic era. Two years before I'd leave my mother standing in the yard, wondering how we'd become such total strangers.

In the years following Ruthie's death, Marianne and I lived in relative silence. We'd gotten used to the steps of three dancers when Dad left, but with only the two of us left, we didn't know how to move. We lost the rhythm.

During the fall of my senior year, I got it in my head that I wanted to go to college, and not just to any college, but to Providence College, where Ruthie had been accepted. Standing with Mitchell at our lockers between classes, I tried to convince him we should *both* go to Providence, though months earlier he'd applied to the University of Iowa. After weeks of persuasion, he finally caved in and applied to Providence.

Our last season in Overton was a whirlwind. It was 1985, the summer of Live Aid; "We Are the World" was still playing on the radio. That time was as much about celebrating our freedom as saying good-bye to childhood. I had an unshakable confidence that things could only get better at a place called Providence College. It became for me a shimmering oasis far from the barren desert Overton had become.

There was another low rumble of thunder, this one followed by a strong breeze that chilled the room and shook the trees outside my bedroom window. I rolled over in the twin bed I'd outgrown years before and told myself to think about the good times just around the corner. I was certain, as sure as I'd been of anything up to that point in my life, that Providence College would mend all the broken pieces inside me. It just had to be so.

Marianne woke me at eight o'clock with a shout from the foot of the stairs. The radio alarm clock had already gone off. Like so many other mornings that summer, I'd slept through it without hearing so much as a riff from 92 K-Rock.

"Honey, you've got to get up. It's already past eight!"

I could hear the music now, and it was the perfect sound track for my day—"I Ran" by A Flock of Seagulls. My eyes opened to posters of rock stars: John Cougar Mellencamp, Journey, the Blasters.

"I ran so far away ..."

And then the reality hit me.

I was leaving home for good. My exit would be less devastating than my dad's, less catastrophic than Ruthie's, but it would complete the final chapter in my family's personal book of exodus. George Bailey may have stayed in Bedford Falls to save the old building and loan, but not me; I was leaving. I showered and dressed, then transported my already-packed bags downstairs.

The screen door opened to a perfect August day. I glanced out hoping to see Mitchell's car—the promise of a quick exit and avoidance of a long good-bye—but there was no Mitchell. Only the sun and sky and two acres of freshly cut green grass between our front porch and West Baxter Road.

"Jack, breakfast is ready."

Marianne's voice and the smells of a country breakfast and brewing coffee drew me to the kitchen, where eggs and bacon sizzled in a large pan. Two glasses of orange juice sat on the table. A stack of buttered toast rested on a plate. I looked to Marianne for an explanation, but she stood with her back to me, cooking at her post in front of the stove.

"Coffee?" she offered.

"Yes, thanks." I settled in at the table. She poured me a cup and placed a carton of half-and-half on the table.

"I spoke with your Aunt Nancy last night."

"Really?"

"She wanted me to tell you how proud she is … you going off to college and everything. She says you're getting the kind of education *she* always wanted."

I poured the cream into my coffee, watching it marble and tumble in the black pool. "That's nice. Tell her I said thanks."

Marianne set a plate of eggs and bacon in front of me. Then she shut off the burners on the stove and leaned against it.

"Are you excited, Jack? I know how you've been looking forward to this."

"I think so," I said, uncomfortable with the thought of the conversation shifting to anything remotely emotional.

She remained there against the stove, her slight frame and sandy hair painting a picture of someone I used to know well—someone I used to call "Mom."

"Did you get everything packed?"

"Packed up yesterday before Mitch and I made the rounds," I said between bites of bacon. I hoped Mitchell would show up soon.

"Who'd you say good-bye to?"

"Scotty," I said. "Bruce Tinsdale's already left for Iowa State. Eric and William won't be around much longer either. We said good-bye to those guys and stopped by some of the old haunts. I saw Frank Willis in town. Saved me a trip to his farm."

"You've had some good friends here, Jack." She laughed. "I can still remember all you boys camping out in the woods behind the house. All the mosquito bites … And wasn't someone covered in leeches from swimming in the pond?"

"Yeah," I said. "Those were the days."

The clock above the stove read 8:45. "It's hard to imagine where all the time's gone."

She was right about that. Mitchell would dock the Cutlass no later than nine o'clock. I had just fifteen minutes remaining before takeoff. Marianne and I were already running low on conversation. We hadn't been like the typical mother and son for years—all of us Claytons divorced our traditional roles years before.

"Jack, have you got enough for everything … for school, I mean?"

I nearly choked, but I bit my tongue instead. It was nice of her to ask, but a little late to be playing the part of the involved, concerned parent.

I thought about money. Working for Bubba's Subs through the school year. How Frank Willis had asked me to work summers at his farm that first year after Ruthie's death. Every dollar I made on the Willis farm I saved—every penny, too.

"You gonna put all that money in a Firebird, Jack?" Frank would tease me, passing my paycheck across his work desk in the mudroom every other Friday. I'd just smile back, making jokes of my own and folding that gold paper into my pocket. For two years I walked those checks down to the bank. He didn't know what I planned to do with the money, but I think even Frank might have fallen off his chair if he'd known just how much my nest egg had grown.

While I casually sipped my orange juice that morning, I was resting in the knowledge that I had more than $24,000 sitting in the Iowa State Federal Bank awaiting transfer. Hard work had taught me the value of hard dollars. Still, her question touched a nerve that was hard to conceal. Maybe it had something to do with growing up too fast, or remembering the four of us together on our last vacation. Mom, Dad, Ruthie, and me eating in the restaurant at the Weststar Hotel in Virginia Beach, innocent of all that lay ahead.

"Yes," I said at last. "I think I've got enough."

We heard Mitchell's car pulling up the long gravel drive. I wiped my mouth and hurried from the table, heading to the screen door where I'd dropped my duffel bags. I picked them up and used one to push through the door. Marianne laid her hand on my shoulder from behind, and I turned around. She looked as if she wanted to say something but remained silent. All except her eyes. I leaned into the door, again hearing it smack against the side of the house.

Marianne trailed me beyond the cover of the aluminum awning and into the hot morning sun.

Mitchell cut the engine and stepped out of the Cutlass. "You look like you could use a four-year education. G'mornin', Mrs. C."

"Good morning, Mitchell."

Tall and athletic, wearing cropped brown hair and dark sunglasses, Mitchell looked like he was headed for Top Gun flight school, not Providence College. It was no wonder he'd had girlfriends to spare since the seventh grade.

"Mitchell, you're a Swiss train," I said. "It's nine o'clock on the nose."

"I would've been here earlier, but you know Hank and Blanch," Mitch said, rolling his eyes, acting excessively put out by his perfect parents. "First it was 'Did you make sure to get the oil changed?' Then it was 'Are you sure you have the directions to Providence?' I'm lucky I got here at all."

Mitch walked over to open the trunk.

"I haven't had much of a chance to catch up with you this summer, Mitchell," Marianne said. "How are your folks doing?"

"They're good. They still wish I was going to the University of Iowa, but I think overall they're excited to get me out of the house." Mitchell grinned. "They're happy I'm not sticking around here for Jack's old job at Bubba's."

Marianne laughed. She loved Mitchell, had always been at ease with him. I tossed my things into the trunk and walked to the passenger door. Marianne stood a few feet away talking with Mitch, her arms locked across her chest like there was a chill in the air.

Maybe there was. I wondered if part of her was wishing she could come along on our adventure, or at least have one of her own.

"Mitchell, I've got a hot breakfast inside if you're interested," She tempted him.

"I'm not sure that's a great idea," I interrupted, drawing looks from Mitchell and Marianne. There was every chance Mitch would take Marianne up on her offer, and I couldn't risk it. Closure loomed so close now, it hummed like electricity in the air between us.

"We'll catch something on the road," Mitchell said, covering for my curt response.

"Hey," Marianne said, "Let me get a picture of you guys!" She headed back toward the house.

"There isn't time," I called out, a little too abruptly.

Marianne turned. "Jack, I'm not going to paint your portrait."

She disappeared into the house. I gazed at Mitchell to check his demeanor. He was in excellent spirits.

"Good morning, Mr. College Man," he said.

"Good morning, Mr. Cutlass," I replied, greeting him in that adolescent style exclusive to friends of a certain age. Eighteen seems a lot younger now.

Marianne must have planned this photo op because she returned in a flash with her camera, ready to pose Mitch and me. She had us stand next to each other in front of the passenger door of the navy blue car. My arm around his shoulder, his around mine, Marianne snapped the photo I still keep on the bookshelf in my office.

"We're leaving now," I said seconds after the shutter clicked, as if all manner of business was closed. "We'll call you when we get there. Daylight's burning, and we've got a lot of traveling to do."

I pulled on the door handle, but Marianne reached out as fast as a ninja. She took hold of my sleeve, preventing me from getting in the car. We stared silently at each other on the gravel driveway next to the house where we'd both grown up fast and far apart.

"So that's it, Jack? You're just going to leave? You don't want to say good-bye? You don't want to hug me?"

I should have embraced her, but immaturity got the best of me. "That's the picture I have," I said.

Marianne's face fell. I wished I could take the words back, but words can't be reeled in again. Her face became transparent. Suddenly it was crystal clear to her what a total stranger I was. The breakfast, the questions, the camera—all an attempt to make an impression that despite everything we'd been through, Marianne still cared.

I get that now, but on that day, I wasn't even close to getting it. I tried backpedaling. "Mom, you know we've got to get going if we're gonna be on time."

"Oh, right, Jack. I don't want you to not be on time." Her face pulled tight and red. Her eyes were puffy.

"What do you want me to say, Mom? It's been nice seeing you come in from your shift while I go out on mine? It's not your fault, but I don't want to do this anymore. All I want is to get in this car."

Tears fell from her eyes. Marianne began to slowly step backward, stiffening her backbone as the physical space between us grew to match our emotional chasm.

"Then good-bye, Jack." She wiped tears from the corners of her eyes.

A distance had cropped up between us like weeds in the front yard that neither of us had skill enough to pull. She would offer no more hugs. No good-bye kisses, or any "Call me when you get there." She walked back up the porch steps and went inside, watching us through the screen door.

I climbed inside the car, my eyes never leaving Marianne's, and Mitchell started up the engine. The car rolled backward, cutting into the grass, then he shifted into first gear and rolled back onto the drive. In the rearview mirror I watched the house, the porch, and Marianne get smaller and smaller, until we turned onto West Baxter Road and all was gone.

Mitchell and I looked at each other and burst out laughing. Minutes later we were climbing the Hamilton Overpass. I looked out the window at Overton, Iowa. The first chapter of my life had ended, its hard grip already weakening. I was emerging from a two-year ache. I felt the winds of change as tangibly as the thick summer breeze whipping through my fingers outside the car window.

There would be no more tractors to drive, no more turkey subs to microwave. No more walking past Ruthie's empty room. My past and my future were being separated like the parting of Siamese twins.

The Cutlass tilted suddenly sideways as we accelerated through the wide curve that merged with the highway. Mitchell pushed a cassette into the car stereo. "How 'bout a little music?"

Bruce Springsteen's "Born to Run" thundered over

the noise from the open windows. Every digit that turned on the odometer represented one less degree of hold the past had on me. Its grip loosened, melting like pieces of a snowman on a hot spring day. We sped onto the highway. Mitchell reached over to boost Bruce's volume. The highway was already jammed with broken heroes, and Overton was giving up two of its own. I closed my eyes.

The thrill of escape was ecstasy, super-powered by four hundred horsepower and the revving guitars of the E Street Band. On a hill overlooking the highway, a sign in the window of Bubba's Sub Shop said it all: CLOSED.

~ Four ~

When some cold tomorrow finds you
When some sad old dream reminds you
How the endless road unwinds you.

—Steve Winwood
"While You See a Chance"

Tuesday morning I awoke to the smell of bacon and immediately thought back to what I'd written the night before. As I lay in bed upstairs, feeling a surprising sense of peace and comfort, I finally shook off the cobwebs enough to realize that Mrs. Hernandez had let herself in. In my groggy state, having stayed awake writing until three, I'd thought at first it was Marianne.

Mrs. Hernandez comes by a couple of times a week to cook and clean. It's a ritual she's repeated now for eight years. A proud first-generation Mexican American, Mrs. H has three grown children and five grandchildren all living outside Providence. Long before I was earning the kind of money that comes to best-selling authors, Mrs. Hernandez was helping a bungling bachelor run his household. The thought of a single man cooking and cleaning for himself was totally unacceptable to her. We'd met through the church and soon adopted each other. She's been a blessing ever since.

I heard her downstairs singing in Spanish. I put on my robe and made my way to the kitchen. "*Buenos días,* Mrs. Hernandez," I said, squeezing her shoulders.

"*Buenos días,* Jack. I thought this might wake you."

"Woke me to a dream. Nothing says 'I love you' like a hot breakfast," I said and grabbed a strip of bacon.

"You are up late again last night?"

"Yes, writing again."

"Oh, that's good, and so you have an appetite this morning?"

"I'm starved," I said, in the mood for some of Mrs. H's homemade food.

She switched off the stove, scraped the eggs onto a plate, and picked up a few slices of bacon with her fingers, dropping them beside the eggs.

"Come, eat."

I poured myself a cup of coffee and carried my plate to the table. The house was filled with an incredible wash of light, as if there were two suns, one shining from the heavens above and another from the snow below.

"Do you have time to sit down and have breakfast with me?"

"No, busy day. I'm finishing here. Then I'm cleaning Mrs. Delaman's house. Do you know her?"

"No, can't say I do."

"Well, I hope to finish here and Mrs. Delaman's this morning. Oh, I brought your mail in. It's on the table."

"Thank you, Mrs. H."

She rinsed the pan in the sink and left for the other room. I put on my glasses, digging into the morning mail and my breakfast. Among the utility bills, junk mail, credit-card offers, and coupons was one piece of mail that sent chills through me: a picture postcard from London, England. On the front, a nighttime photo of London Bridge strung with colorful Christmas lights. On the back, this neatly written message:

> *Dear Jack,*
>
> *Angela and I read your very fine book. You should be proud! We'll be in Providence before Christmas and would love to see you! Keep up the good work!*
>
> *The Lord is a rewarder of faithfulness.*
>
> *Howard and Angela Cameron*

Five sentences. Three exclamation points. Classic Howard Cameron. The card had been mailed weeks earlier.

I tossed the postcard back on the stack. Two decades had passed since I'd seen any member of the Cameron family, though their impact on my life remains to this day. Jenny's parents were returning to Indiana after twenty years of missions work in London. Strange how we hadn't seen each other in all these years, but the book had reached faraway places. It had found its way to nightstands around the globe. The postcard threw me off kilter. Everything that had happened since Sunday night left a trace of strangeness. My life had been dipped in liquid uncertainty, and I'd come up dripping with it.

One thought pushed to the forefront of my addled mind: Would Jenny be with them? The last I knew, she'd been working alongside her parents in London. I doubted they'd leave out such an important detail.

The Jenny of twenty years ago was somewhere in the memory box Arthur wanted me to crack open. Our story had begun in a euphoric corner of Eden—and had ended much as the original, with angels barring reentrance to paradise.

Mrs. Hernandez switched on the vacuum in the back hallway. I picked up the portable phone in the kitchen and took it into the living room to call Arthur. He always worked Tuesday mornings from his home in North Indy, part of his clock-wound routine. I knew he'd be interested in how the writing was coming along. And I wanted to know if he wanted the pages sent to ARP. Normally, I wouldn't hand him a thing until the last period had been punched on the final sentence. Then I'd print two copies from the hard drive, bundle one in cardboard and string, and ship it overnight with CDs to Arthur and his editor, Judith Raines.

But this was different. I *wanted* Art to see what I was writing. There was an outside chance it would be so different from what he was expecting, he'd halt the project. A *very small* outside chance. I could probably write the book in haiku, and Arthur would still publish it. I dialed his number.

"Hello, Jack Clayton." The wonders of caller ID.

"Hi, Arthur. I did some writing last night," I said.

"What did I tell you, Jack? I knew you could do it." Arthur's voice shimmered like an oiled penny. "When can we expect to see a manuscript?"

"I can fax over early drafts later this week. By the way, what's the due date for this history-making yarn? Six months?"

"How does July sound?" Arthur said, giving me my first break. The last thing in the world I wanted was to be rushed to meet a deadline.

"July sounds manageable. I think I can get it to you by summer."

"Not finished—have it in stores," he said. "We'll need the completed first draft no later than March 31."

I waited for Arthur's laughter to rip through the receiver but realized it wasn't coming. "You're kidding, right?"

"Jack, you've got twelve weeks. All you need to do is remember and write. Judith will shape whatever you send. I've already told her what we're up against, and she's ready for anything. It's top priority."

"What makes you think I can write a book in three months when everything else I've written has taken ten?" I asked.

"We're going to release excerpts by June to give readers a taste. And we'll need full chapters for publicity and marketing, endorsements, and review copies, all of which have to happen by early spring if we want people happily reading your book while they tan at the beach over their summer vacations."

"Why not wait until Christmas next year when they can enjoy it just as much in front of their fireplaces, sipping eggnog in their robes and slippers?"

"Jack, your book is red-hot *right now*. We've never seen interest like this before. It's selling into *all* the big chains—Costco, Wal-Mart, Sam's Club—and it's selling into major retailers all over Europe who've been contacting *us* because of the rumors and early buzz. But this market's fickle. We can't expect the same level of interest twelve or eighteen months from now … which reminds me, we'll need to shoot a cover photo of you. I'll have Judith or Andrew call to schedule it. Are you able to come up to Indianapolis after the first of the year?"

"Art, don't make promises for me to keep," I said. "If the book doesn't get finished, you're going to be in deep water."

"You'll finish it, Jack. You'll finish it."

"Yesterday, I wasn't sure I'd be writing it, and to be honest, I'm still having moments of doubt." *I wasn't even close to knowing how this would come off.*

"You're making way too much of this, Jack. Just scribe us a book. Two hundred pages; that's just two pages a day," Arthur said, sounding like a third-rate used-car salesman shining up the deal. He didn't seem to care what I gave him. He just needed my life printed, packaged, and shrink-wrapped in quickie-mart time.

After our conversation I was agitated. Each event in this saga seemed to take more control out of my hands. I went back into the kitchen to refill my coffee mug and felt like a man adrift in an ocean of sharks. Arthur had no idea what was going on inside the mind of his million-dollar author. He didn't have the first clue about the anxiety prickling under my skin.

My life was beginning to implode. For the next twelve weeks, I'd wade into mysterious waters and submerge into the wreckage of a shipwrecked past. And I'd stay there, grappling with emotions that, like shark fins, were only now beginning to surface.

~ Five ~

Bermuda, Bahama, come on pretty mama.

—The Beach Boys
"Kokomo"

It was eleven thirty when I emerged from my office Tuesday night. The inside of the house had taken on the quietness of an empty church. Outside I could hear the muted sounds of fireworks popping in the night sky, signaling that Christmas break was close at hand. It was a welcome nuisance.

I walked the long hallway downstairs, stretching every aching muscle, breaking my body free from the mad hours spent working in the same seated position.

Ten mad hours of writing. I'd done this before, lived it while working on my last three books. But that writing was part-time, absent the pressure of a twelve-week deadline.

Being single all these years, I'd gotten used to long stretches of flying solo. Somewhere in my thirties, I'd finally recognized that my singleness wasn't just a phase

I'd outgrow. I'd had dreams once of being married. I certainly never imagined living alone year after year. Yet here I was, a forty-year-old man who'd learned to take the love he had for one woman and break it into a thousand pieces to give away to the poor.

I switched on the stereo with the remote and pushed the shuffle button. A moment later Chris Eaton was singing "Wonderful World."

I have shouldered the blame for too long, I have hidden my light under a cloud…

Two of Mrs. Hernandez's Christmas burritos wrapped in green cellophane caught my eye on the top shelf of the fridge. I stuck them in the microwave and grabbed a cold can of Coke.

It was snowing again, the graceful snow of angels. The hypnotically slow rhythm of white flakes falling through the black sky. I remembered the weatherman saying something about accumulation. Had it been today or the day before? I carried my plate to the living-room sofa. My eyelids grew heavy, and I was too tired to eat. Another song came on. A Taylor Dayne love song from the eighties.

Love will lead you back
Someday I just know that
Love will lead you back to my arms
It won't be long
One of these days
Our love will lead you back

I fell asleep with the lights on, drifting off and wondering what it would feel like being brought back by love. Thoughts and words melted together beneath the firm press of unconsciousness. "The Lord did it," I whispered. "Led me back by love."

Early the next morning, I dressed in two layers of sweats and jogged through five inches of fresh snowfall. Covered in the fresh powder, the Providence campus looked brand new, untouched by traffic and footprints.

Twenty minutes later I pulled open the heavy glass door of Liberty Deli, a greasy spoon a block off South Campus. It was one of the first restaurants Mitch and I had claimed as our own when we'd gotten to Providence. The place is run by three Middle Eastern brothers named Quaddi, and it's loved in Providence for its unique … character. Orange-cushioned booths, a Formica counter with red swivel chairs, and cartoonlike paintings of food depicted in a mural on the wall. A long hot griddle ran the length of the counter where the Quaddi brothers cooked and shouted at each other. It's the kind of restaurant where the waitresses are rude, the floors are filthy, and the food is perfect.

Liberty Deli was half-empty due to the snow and the early hour. I sat in a booth along the wall.

Debbie Holms shouted from behind the counter, "What'll it be, Jack? The usual?" and I gestured back.

A few moments later, Debbie brought me a plate of eggs and sausage and a cup of joe. "Didn't think we'd see you in here this morning," she said, making friendly talk.

"I'm out of my normal routine," I told her, "but better late than never."

I gave Debbie a friendly smile. She was pretty. I'd always liked her because she worked hard, though she had little to show for it. She was smart, too. Not college smart. *People* smart. No one could fool her. She was a thirty-one-year-old unmarried mother of a preschooler. A girl. I wondered how she got by on the money she made serving college kids and the downtown crowd.

"I guess even superstars have to eat," she said.

Her comment seemed out of character. Or out of time. My book had been out for three years, and we'd already done the "Hey, aren't you that guy?" bit.

"Yes, Debbie, even we superstars need a little grease in our works." I returned her gaze, not sure where this was going. We'd joked enough mornings to be at ease with each other. This seemed different. "Are you looking for an autograph or something?"

"I may be." Debbie held out a magazine she'd hidden behind her back, then tossed it on the table. It was the most recent issue of *Time* magazine, and I was on the cover. The headline read: Person of the Year.

"You've got to be kidding."

"'Fraid not. You're an actual big shot now, Jack," Debbie took a step closer as we stared at a black-and-white photograph of my face. "You've seen this, right?"

I picked up the magazine and held it in front of me. "Can't say that I have."

Did Arthur know this was in the works?

"I'll take that autograph now." Debbie pulled a pen out from her work apron and laid it down by my coffee cup. "You can make it out to Jessica, my daughter. Even she knows what *Time* magazine is."

I signed my name and asked if I could keep the copy awhile. I promised to return it before I left.

"No problem," she said. "Just don't get anything on it, okay?"

She walked back to the grill, and one of the Quaddi brothers smiled at me, waving his greasy spatula in the air.

At first I thought the magazine cover story was a gag, that someone was playing a trick on me. But it wasn't. The story focused on "the seismic cultural-paradigm shift" that had occurred in the United States since the release of *Laborers.* It had been written by a freelance journalist named Thom McCay. Included were sidebars and charts and graphs. It also gave statistics on the rising number of Americans involved in some kind of "goodwill work" and evidence that charitable donations were at an all-time high. And a story specifically on the Norwood program, featuring before-and-after photographs of houses students had rebuilt through CMO. There were even profiles of Norwood residents, including Beverly Williams and her two kids, Derrick and Nicole.

McCay's article reported that as many as fifty other charter programs inspired by the Norwood model were sprouting up on college campuses and through faith-based initiatives. He traced it all back to *Laborers of the Orchard*. The article was refreshingly positive, but I took issue with this claim. I hadn't started a movement to care for the poor; God had. Nor did I inspire people to suddenly have an interest in the suffering of others; God did. McCay's efforts to give me credit for the "seismic shift" made me squeamish.

I dug my cell phone out of my hooded sweatshirt and called Arthur. Shirley Dawson put me through.

"Jack, where have you been? I've left twenty messages on your home phone."

"I shut the ringer off when I'm writing, Art. Sorry. I must have forgotten to turn it back on."

"You're sorry? I've been going crazy here! Do you know what's happening this morning?" Arthur spoke as if he might at any second explode from overheating.

"I'm looking at *Time* magazine," I said. What's going on?"

"Everything is going on, Jack. It's a madhouse here. The phones haven't stopped ringing. We've been getting congratulations from the governor's office, the mayor. I've been giving out quotes to the press. You wouldn't believe it!"

"Did you know this was about to happen?"

"We had *no idea* this was about to happen. They don't tell you when you're going to be named Person of the Year. The media tosses a few names around, but no one really knows for sure until the issue hits the newsstand. You weren't even on their short list."

"So no one knew?"

"Do you think I could have kept a lid on something like this?" Arthur said, reclaiming instant credibility. "I've been on the phone with *Time,* thanking them for their story. I spoke with their editor, Jeff Tinorin. He said they respected your stance on not giving interviews. It's the first time we've heard that one from the media.

That's partly why they gave you the cover. It's more authentic, real. Something like that."

I covered my closed eyes with my hand.

"It's nice that they've highlighted CMO's work, but I'm not behind all this, Arthur. It isn't right giving me credit."

"Then who, Jack? Who wrote your book? Who worked all those years in Norwood, pounding nails, recruiting kids? Who did all that, Jack?"

"Arthur, giving to others isn't the highest pinnacle of human goodwill; it's the ground floor. As far as who's responsible, that would be God. He's the One who calls us to do good, and when we obey, everyone gets blessed. Haven't we had this conversation before?"

I could hear Arthur's ADD spinning his mind in a new direction. Around the half-vacant restaurant, diners were beginning to stare. I lowered my voice.

"Thom McCay, the author, did a pretty good job with this. He picked up the Holy Spirit part, inviting people to serve others, but he's missing the point when he aims this all back to me. It's God's doing, not anyone else. Can we get him to print that?"

"The magazine is already on newsstands. How do you think we found out about it in the first place?"

"I don't mean this issue, Art. What about a reprint or something? A correction?"

"Jack, *Time* magazine just named you their Person of the Year. I don't think the best way to say thank you is by telling them they got the story wrong. They may not understand what you're saying anyway. I'm your friend and publisher, and I'm not sure *I* do. If you want that story told, you'll have to tell it yourself."

"Would you give me the number for that editor at *Time*?"

"You're not going to give them an interview, are you?" Arthur said, strutting his brand of dry irony.

"No, I just want to track down the author."

Arthur gave me the number. "Listen, Jack. If you talk to McCay or anyone over at *Time,* you might want to get a plug in for the new book. Perfect follow-up to the story. Don't say anything that leaves an unfavorable impression. We want to keep them in our corner."

"Arthur, just when did we become the center of the universe? Do we need to constantly put our shoulders to the grindstone of self-promotion, inflating egos and bank accounts? Is this the highest thing to which we can aspire?"

There was silence on Arthur's end of the line. I'd lost him.

"Jeff Tinorin."

"Hi, Jeff. This is Jack Clayton. I wanted to call and say thanks for the cover story and the Man of the Year thing."

"You're welcome, of course. It's great hearing from you, Jack. You're sort of an enigma to most of us in the news business. But after all that's happened with your book, I can't think of a better cover for our Person of the Year issue."

I could feel my interview phobia rising. "I'm actually

calling because I want to speak with Thom McCay. Does he work out of the office there?"

"No, Jack, he doesn't," he said. "But listen, while I've got you on the phone … what's the likelihood of you consenting to do an interview? I think you can see we'd be fair."

"I don't decline interviews because of fairness," I said, hoping to get this conversation back on point. "That's what I want to talk with Thom about."

This got his attention. I didn't intend for it to sound as though I was calling to arrange an interview, but judging by Jeff's reaction, he clearly took it that way.

"Thom lives in Boston. If you'd like to leave me your number, I'll make sure he gets in touch with you."

"Actually, I was hoping to speak with him this morning. Would he mind if you gave me a number where I could reach him?"

Evidently he didn't mind, and a moment later I was listening to Thom's phone ringing in the Beacon Hill area of Boston.

"Hello."

"Hi … Is this Thom?"

"Yes …"

"This is Jack Clayton. I wanted to talk to you about the *Time* magazine article."

"I hope you aren't calling to tell me you didn't like it." He laughed.

"Oh no, I liked it. Thanks, by the way. You wrote some very encouraging things. I did have a clarification though …"

"Hey, no problem. It gave me an opportunity to research your program in Norwood, and frankly, I was very impressed. Of course, I'd have loved to have had the chance to talk to you in person." He sounded honestly disappointed, not hinting. "What sort of clarification?"

"Well, the attention surrounding *Laborers of the Orchard,* and all the things you wrote in your article aren't my doing, Thom. It's nothing I take credit for."

"Who would you credit … God?" Thom asked, his voice amplified by a God-given understanding.

"To give credit where it's due, yes."

"I thought you might say that. I would have been disappointed if you hadn't. I consider myself a devout Catholic. What's happening up here in Boston is exciting, Jack. Both Harvard and Boston College are chartering volunteer programs based on your Norwood model. They've worked on a dozen houses or more in Roxbury and South Boston. We've seen significant changes up here."

"That is exciting," I said, pushing away a plate of cold eggs, "but there's more to it than repairing houses, as important as that is."

"What do you mean?"

"Do you remember 1 Corinthians 13:2?" I asked. I didn't ask these sorts of questions often because I didn't like putting people on the spot.

"Ah … something, something, if I have the tongues of angels but speak … er … what's the verse?"

"You've got it. 'If I have a faith that can move mountains, but have not love, I am nothing.'"

"Right. So you're saying you'd like these college students to serve and love the poor."

"God draws us nearer to Him, Thom, when we see Jesus in those who suffer or who are in need. We're saved by His act, not our own good deeds. I get a little uncomfortable when service to others is connected to a fad, or seen as just another chance to name one of the ordinary among us Person of the Year. The roof repairs and trash pickups are all good things, but the spiritual reward is learning to love."

"Okay, I'm sold. Will you allow me to put some of this conversation in print? I'm certain *Time* will run it."

"I did call you hoping you'd be able to get this message out. Yes. You have my permission."

I thanked him again, and we said our good-byes.

My world had felt disjointed the past few days, and even the grease from Liberty Deli couldn't ease all the pieces back where they belonged. I'm not big on changes, and my least favorite are the *sudden* kind. However, the conversation was a turning point. From that moment forward, I approached the writing with less groaning and more intent. I knew it would be painful at times, tearing open those strongboxes and not knowing if the contents would be bitter or sweet, or would jump out and cut me at the end of a taunt spring. But I clearly felt God's hand in this. I would step where He blew leaves from my path, even if the path He cleared pointed me into a haunted wood. Something good would come of it all.

"Hi, Jack. It's Howard Cameron once more. If you're in, please pick up.... Oh, all right. I guess we're two for two [laughter]. Hey, I hope you got our earlier message ... we

still haven't heard back from you. It looks like we'll roll into Providence on Friday. Wanted to see if you might be available for lunch on Saturday. When you get a chance, will you call us? Angela and I are up in Bean Town at the moment, staying with very good friends, Pat and Terry Oslander … But leave us a message …"

There were four messages from Arthur in addition to the one from the Camerons. Hearing Howard's voice for a second time that week wasn't any less surreal than the first time. Yes, Saturday would be fine. I dialed the number Howard had left for the Oslanders, a nervousness fluttering underneath my skin. I'd never met the Oslanders, and when their answering machine clicked on, I realized I wouldn't be meeting them today either. I waited for the beep.

"Hello, this is Jack Clayton," I said, getting it on record that I was, in fact, alive. "Howard Cameron said I could reach him here. Howard, I'm sorry I haven't gotten in touch with you sooner; it's been quite a week. I'm available Saturday for lunch and recall your fondness for the Schneider Haus in Germantown. Unless you have another place in mind, I'll meet you and Angela there around twelve."

The weekend promised to be eventful. As I sat the phone down, it rang. I picked up with a rush of nervous glee. It wasn't Howard but Arthur's top-notch editor, Judith Raines.

"Hi, Jack; it's Judith. I wanted to give you a call and see how things are coming with the new book."

"It's coming along fine," I said, switching gears between two worlds.

"I also wanted to congratulate you on being named

Time's Person of the Year. That's extraordinary. Are you pinching yourself yet?"

"Only when I fall asleep writing," I said.

She laughed. Judith is an extremely intelligent thirty-something woman, six years married, no children. Professionally, there's no literary problem Judith can't solve. It was no wonder Arthur relied on her the way he did. She could have gone off to work at Simon and Schuster if she'd wanted to live in New York. She didn't, and Arthur was able to keep his all-star on the ARP team.

"Are you getting my faxes?" I asked.

"Yes. That's why I called. I like what I'm seeing, Jack. This is excellent. You're lifting up the veil and letting us peer inside. It makes for a compelling read."

I listened to her feedback. I needed it. I wasn't sure about the stories I'd written the past few nights.

"Arthur's probably mentioned to you the tight deadline. We're already behind the eight ball on this one. We could get a big jump on editing if you would e-mail your pages to me instead of faxing them."

"Sure, Judith. That's not a problem. I'll resend what I've already faxed."

"That's all I need for now," she said.

"So, is Arthur pushing you as hard as he's pushing me?" I asked, searching for a little *esprit de corps*.

"Oh, you know Arthur. These have been the best two years of his life. You can't blame him for wanting to get the next chapter started."

"I guess not. Is he still in the office?"

"No. We haven't seen him since Monday. I think the office is forwarding calls to his cell."

"I just spoke to him this morning."

"Yep, me, too. But he left for Las Vegas last night."

"Las Vegas? Another book convention?"

"No, the next one's not for another month. I think he's talking to retailers. You know they have to pay us in advance to get this one, right?"

"No … What do you mean?"

"If retailers want to have the sequel to Jack Clayton's best-selling book in their stores on release day, they have to cough up 50 percent up front."

"Before they even get the book?"

"That's right. It's never done that I'm aware of, but chains are lining up to pay. It's a pretty big deal, Jack. If they don't get in on the initial order, stores have to wait another ten days to get the book in stock. Arthur's been selling this strategy to retailers since July."

No wonder he'd been so unrelenting about my writing the book. He'd already collected payments.

"Do you think Shirley can track down Art?"

"She should be able to. Do you want me to transfer you to her when we're done?"

"Yeah, that's not a bad idea."

Judith and I talked for another minute, and then she put me through to Arthur's assistant.

"Arthur Reed Publishing. Shirley Dawson."

"Hi, Shirley, it's Jack."

"Well, hello there, stranger. When are you coming up to see us again? It's been forever."

"I'd love to come up, but Arthur's got me chained to a desk here. Until he comes back to change my food and water, I'm afraid I'm stuck."

She laughed. Shirley always laughs at my jokes.

"I hear Arthur's in Vegas. Could you transfer me to his cell number?"

"I don't think he's picking up anymore."

"Is he in meetings?"

"Probably. He flew into Las Vegas last night, but he's flying to the East Coast later today."

"East Coast?"

"Uh-huh. New Jersey, I think."

"Didn't you create his itinerary?"

"Not this time. When he has to leave quickly, he usually makes his own arrangements. He checks in later to tell me where he is and when he's coming back."

"Do you know any other way to get in touch with him?"

"I should hear from him later this evening or tomorrow, Jack. Do you want me to have him call you?"

"Yes, please ask him to contact me ASAP."

"I will, Jack. And oh, by the way … congratulations on being *Time*'s Person of the Year. We're all just thrilled!"

I thanked Shirley and pushed the Off button on the portable phone. Arthur Reed had been selling my book for five months—and taking 50 percent of the proceeds from retailers even before I'd agreed to write it. Arthur could be aggressive, certainly ambitious, but this seemed out of character. Dark secrets on the other side of the writing world?

The bedroom TV was tuned to CNN, but with the sound muted. I meant to turn it off before I dozed but never got the chance. I fell asleep in minutes.

~ Six ~

My heart is old, it holds my memories
My body burns a gem like flame.

—Mr. Mister
"Kyrie"

Mitchell and I talked in a frenzy for the first two hours of the trip, but as we settled into the rhythm of the road, we chose music over talking, the Welcome to Providence sign still hours away.

Mitchell and I had become best friends on a middle-school playground fighting over a green and blue stocking cap that eleven fifth-grade boys were chasing. He got a bloody nose that day, and I got a friend for life. His parents were well-read Republicans who valued public education above everything except University of Iowa football.

The McDaniels' home was like a natural-history museum. An old stuffed fox perched on the fireplace mantle in a basement that smelled like cherry-balsam pipe smoke, an aroma that wafted in from his father

Hank's workshop. Mitch's room featured a working model of the human nervous system that lit up inside a translucent man. On summer nights Mitchell's dad would set up the Celestron telescope, and the three of us would stay up late gazing at the stars. They loved astronomy, so I learned to appreciate it too, swept up by something I would never be exposed to at home.

The McDaniels' house was open and breezy, in contrast to the literal and figurative darkness of my own. Mitch's mother, Blanch, was a redheaded beauty who sometimes fried homemade potato chips for us to snack on after school.

One Friday night Hank took all the guys to the drive-in to see *Night of the Living Dead.* We were thirteen. The movie scared Scotty Levett so much, we couldn't hear the chomping of human flesh over his screaming. Robert Dullis choked down a whole stick of bologna during the movie and promptly threw it up over the front seat after witnessing more acts of zombie cannibalism than his stomach could take. We left soon after. I still haven't seen how the movie ends.

School fights, tree heights, dog bites. In sickness and in health, Mitchell and I grew up together. We played basketball through tenth grade, we dated girls together, we sang in the senior chorus, and we camped out at Indian Falls with the gang. But one day stands out above all others: the day Mitchell bought the classic 1976 navy blue Cutlass. It was his sixteenth birthday. There's no feeling in the world that compares to riding in your best friend's navy blue Cutlass through Overton, Iowa, on a Saturday night.

Through high school Mitchell was popular

and good-looking, while I was neither. The closest I'd come to a high-school romance was a brief on-again-off-again relationship with a girl named Maria Lambert. We'd dated through my junior year, and then she dumped me to go to the senior prom with James Whitford.

Mitchell, on the other hand, experienced at least one serious infatuation every year of high school. All of them ended in an emotional mess. Mitchell fell head over heels for a girl named Heather Howell at a football game our senior year. Her name always made me think "feathered owl," and I never saw in her what Mitchell did. The two were combustible. They'd fight and make up, fight and make up, all of us riding the roller coaster along with them. It all came to a head in March. They'd had words yet again, only this time Heather threw something—a can of Coke, an ashtray, a brick—at Mitchell while he was sitting in the Cutlass. She nailed the backseat window. *Hasta la vista,* baby. That was the end of Heather. I reminded Mitchell of that story as often as I could.

Providence, Indiana, appeared before us as bright as the moon and fantastically different from the small planet we'd traveled from five hours earlier.

Up Brighton Avenue, through the Mercer Mall, we drove the east-side marketplace, where recent city expansion gave evidence that Providence was indeed a college town. There were rows of student housing—renovated Victorian houses painted purple or bright orange. There was the fraternity mansion district—giant homes with giant porches filled with twenty-one-year-olds holding giant plastic cups of beer. We passed the Holloway Ice Arena, where the Badgers play ice hockey, and Briggs Stadium, where seventy-five thousand football fans camp out every Saturday when the Badgers play at home.

"Directions, please."

"We're going to ..."—I pulled a folded sheet of paper from my shirt pocket—"1740 Wilshire Avenue. We're meeting a rental agent named Margaret Shiner at four o'clock."

The Providence College housing policy normally required freshmen to live in on-campus dorm rooms their first two years. But because of overcrowding from a peak year in admissions and woefully behind-schedule dorm renovations, there was a historic shift in college housing policy: Freshmen were allowed to live off campus. Mitchell and I were happy to take advantage of this change.

We met Mrs. Shiner at her office after grabbing lunch at Taco Bell. She showed us two apartments within walking distance of West Campus, and we took a semi-furnished two-bedroom on the corner of Alder Street and Thatcher. We moved in thirty minutes after handing over a cash deposit and signing the lease.

On Monday I wired my twenty-four-thousand-dollar nest egg from home, and Mitch and I set up shop. That summer of 1985, we would drink about a million bottles of Pepsi because something called New Coke had elbowed real Coca-Cola aside, and finding it was like finding treasure in Al Capone's vault. McDonald's Fry Guy glasses cluttered our kitchen shelves, and paper

Kentucky Fried Chicken barrels filled the back of the fridge.

Mitch soon found a part-time job at Providence Athletics, a sporting-goods-and-school-supply store still in business on Broadway. I was hired at the famous City Club Restaurant and Bar, a downtown eatery on Fifth Avenue, simply known to patrons as City Club. It went out of business after I left college, but in its prime in the mideighties, it was *the* place to be. I worked there every Friday and Saturday night through football season, and a couple of lunches during the week. For this I made two hundred and fifty dollars a week. In student terms, a small fortune.

We became friends with Brian Aspen, Reggie Moehler, and Kim Prang, the guys in the apartment directly above ours. We all flirted with the two girls across the hall, especially the blond with movie-star good looks, Jennifer. But Jennifer left college before the end of our second semester. We didn't know the reason until later. Turned out she was pregnant. Amy, her roommate, was the first girl Mitchell pulled into his magnetic gravitational field.

Each weekend brought carloads of new freshmen and returning upper classmen. Dorms became an unloading zone. The apartments, a daily ritual of lifting two-ton sofas up three flights of stairs. The streets and cafés of Broadway, the campus's main drag, filled with rowdy undergrads and beautiful Providence College girls.

The last days of summer are blurred snapshots now. Mementos, once textured to the touch, now time smoothed of distinctive details, their essence blended together: Mitchell grilling steaks on the terrace, the girls next door playing the same Go-Go's album over and over, Mitch and I watching the Cincinnati Reds playing well late into August. All was right in our world. If only we could have frozen that season of life. It was preseason for Providence football and preseason for Mitch and me.

I turned out the bedside lamp and wondered why I'd come here. Was it because of Ruthie? Was it all those pictures in the college catalog of happy students wearing their silver Providence College sweatshirts and maroon baseball caps? Or had Providence simply sprung up like an oasis, a cool place to rest and shelter my soul?

I thought about the yearbook pictures from Overton I kept in the drawer next to my bed. Every dime I earned had paved another inch of asphalt to Providence. Ruthie had disappeared, but Providence College remained.

~ SEVEN ~

Do you ever dream of me
Do you ever see the letters that I write?

—ELTON JOHN
"Nikita"

One appointment remained on my work calendar—a lunch date I'd refused to cancel with my friend Raymond Mac. Raymond has lived in Norwood most of his adult life. Back when the majority of Norwood's residents weren't sure they could trust us, dismissing our efforts, Raymond took our commitment seriously, championing our cause.

Raymond stands five feet seven inches, though he swears he was over six feet tall in his prime. He has silver hair on the sides of his head and, since he stopped driving, walks with his cane wherever he wants in Norwood, when the weather allows. We celebrated his sixty-fifth birthday together a couple of years into our friendship and his seventy-fifth in July this year.

Marvin's is a rib joint on the edge between

two worlds—Norwood and the rest of Providence. Raymond, like a lot of the people who live in Norwood, doesn't venture outside the neighborhood much. I never met Ray's wife, Ella. She died of cancer a few years before I arrived. They had one son, Roger, a Marine Corps sergeant killed in action in 1991 while serving our country. Ours is a mutually beneficial relationship: Ray tells me what he remembers about his life, and I bring him things he likes to eat. Beef jerky, fried chicken, chocolate-covered raisins, Little Debbie snack cakes. Raymond doesn't worry too much about cholesterol or heart disease, but then again, neither do I.

"Boy, you look like dirt. Don't you have sense enough to go to bed at night?"

"I don't have sense, Ray. They've got me writing another book. It keeps me from doing the things I like, such as sleep."

Raymond and I sat at one of ten white plastic tables. This place isn't the Ritz. Marvin's doesn't only serve food; it serves gasoline to thirsty cars. The gas-station shelves are empty except for a case of pork and beans, enormous bags of road salt, and odds and ends like children's balloons and decks of playing cards. They sell lotto tickets, cigarettes, beer, and … the best pork barbecue this side of Memphis.

"Oh, I see. They *made* you write it. They own you now." Raymond focused his attention on the plastic fork he was using to eat his coleslaw.

"It's a long story. Anyhow, I'm writing again, so I don't sleep much. That reminds me, I'm not working for the ministry anymore, for the time being, that is.

So if you need anything, call me at home. I won't be at the office."

Raymond looked up at me as if I were certifiable. "What? You done quit everything now? Who's going to take care of people out here when they need help?"

"Peter Brenner. And the college will be out here again the second week of January." I slid a rib out of a red and white paper basket and bit into it. The taste of molasses and honey was instantly familiar and instantly incredible.

"I don't trust him," Raymond said.

"Why wouldn't you trust Peter?"

"He talks on that phone too much."

"Peter's a good guy and you know it."

"If he's such a good guy, how come he never takes me to Marvin's?"

"Are you saying I'm a good guy, Raymond?"

Ray lowered his ice tea, refreshed to continue. "Yeah, you brought me here, and I need to talk to you. How come you never get married? Don't you know what God can give a man in a godly woman?"

He removed the lid from his Styrofoam cup and poured back a mouthful of sweet tea while I thought of how to answer a question that comes up at lunch with Raymond as predictably as dandelions pop up in my front lawn each spring.

"I'm ready when He is," I said.

"Ready when He is! You need to be more than ready. You need to be ready, willing, and able." Raymond let out a belch. "Ready, maybe. Able, I don't know. Willing, I doubt it."

Ray never minces words; such is the case with old

people and children, they say. That's one of the things I like best about Raymond.

I tried nudging our conversation to something more amiable. "Is that how you met Ella?"

"Don't you change the subject on me. Boy, your problem is that you're hiding all the time. Hiding at work, hiding out in your house. Hiding out in some fancy book you're all about writing. When you gonna come out and be a man? That's what I want to know. When you gonna come out and be a man?"

Raymond's words fired out between mouthfuls of pork barbecue and beans. This kind of exchange would have been insulting from anyone else, but not from Raymond.

He studied the pile of rib bones stacked on his plate while I scrutinized the horizontal lines running across his forehead like black lightning. Was he right? Was I hiding? Something moved in me to tell Ray what I'd yet to confess even to myself.

"Ray, I'm in love with a married woman. She lives with her husband in London, and I haven't seen her in years."

Ray's expression remained unchanged. I don't know what I expected him to say, if anything.

"Why do you love this woman?" Ray asked. His voice was composed and strong, not the trembling mutter of the tottery and aged, but the voice of a father.

I leaned in closer and quieted my voice so only Ray could hear. "Because I've never met anyone before or since who so moved me, stirred me to the core, and made me feel blessed just to be in the same room with her." The tension in my voice surprised me. I relaxed into my seat. "She was a great woman, Ray, and I miss her."

It was the first time I'd said it out loud. Even though Jenny and I hadn't spoken to each other in nearly twenty years, hearing just how strong my feelings ran for her unnerved me. I'd dealt with losing her the only way I knew how, by putting everything about her out of my mind. What else could I do? She was in love with someone else, married to someone else.

Ray nodded his head. I don't remember Ray ever having accepted a statement from me without commenting. I can't count how many times he's told me how full of baloney I am (though he doesn't say "baloney"). But not this time. This time Raymond was quiet, and when he spoke a moment later, it wasn't about my shortcomings but about Ella, the woman he loved.

"Ella was a great lady too. I met her in Memphis in 1961. She was working as a maid at the Century Hotel, and I was in the army." Raymond chuckled. He gave me his Bill Cosby grin, laughing a contagious and irresistible chuckle I couldn't help but join.

"She was friends with Darrell Robertson's wife, Dolores. Darrell, he was *my* best friend. We'd come down together on leave out of Fort Campbell, Kentucky. It was April, and Darrell's mother and Dolores threw a welcome-home party. That's when I first saw her. I asked Darrell to introduce me to her after dinner, and he did."

Ray wiped his mouth with a paper napkin. "We wrote each other for seven months before I saw her again, but the next chance I had, I rode the bus to Memphis and asked her to marry me … which she did."

"You were married for thirty-five years."

"I was in love with that woman for thirty-five years. I loved her, watched her raise my son, watched her make us a home. And I watched her get the cancer, taking her through all the radiation and the chemo. I watched her get frail, and I watched her pass away. But I had her life, because she gave it to me. Do you see that? She gave me the best part of her, and I gave her the best part of me. She gave me her secret heart, the one a woman only gives the man she loves."

Raymond closed his eyes and rolled his head back, swept away in the swell of memories that wash you down below the waterline. His face looked ragged and tired. His seventy-five years descending back upon him like a heavy, wet coat.

"What do you have, Jack Clayton, other than your world of regrets?" he asked, opening me up like a can of beans.

"I don't know what you mean, Ray." I said, but his eyes rolled long. They said, *"We're making progress here; don't go back to being a jackass."*

"There was no other woman for me," Ray said. "Never could be. I never broke her heart, and I never broke her trust. You may have the same love, but you don't have the *life*. She gave that to her London man."

I opened up my hands and pasted a smile on my face. He was right, but I didn't want to hear that truth.

"So where does that leave me?" I asked, not really expecting an answer. Not really wanting one.

"Alone, I'd say."

I dropped Raymond at his place after lunch. His energy had drained quickly. After our good-byes and his expression of gratitude for the meal, he set his wooden cane on the sidewalk and made his way to the front door, warmed by memories of his wife and his trademark red and black plaid coat.

He unlocked the front door of his small white house with bold black shutters the students had painted last summer and vanished inside.

I was tired too. The caffeine from my lunchtime tea got me home, but I crashed on the sofa in the den. Around three, I woke up feeling off-kilter. Midday darkness was extending its twigged fingers over the city skyline. Car lights arched their beams across the living-room walls, and I realized I didn't want to be alone.

I drove to CMO and parked out back. The lot was empty and white, the yellow lines already erased by snow. As the mercury descended, the rain that had fallen at lunch became snow, turning Providence into a frozen ice village.

I climbed the slick metal stairs and entered the building through the kitchenette. I had planned to spend a couple hours answering phone messages, something that would give me an excuse to hang around and catch up with Peter and Aaron. But the building was empty, the only light coming from the gold table lamp Mrs. Burman left on in the downstairs lobby.

I climbed the ornamental wooden staircase to the second floor and switched on my desk light. Everything was just as I'd left it on Monday. No new phone messages, faxes, or memos. The room felt less like an office and more like a storage space for a large desk and my reading sofa. I reached for my Bible and lay down. Most mornings I'd go through a similar routine, spending time on the sofa reading and praying. Sometimes I'd take ten minutes, but more often that time would stretch to forty-five when I would hear the doors open downstairs and a second CMO staffer arrive.

The Word of God is my sanctuary. It's where I turn to unscramble the world. When I'm reading and praying, the Lord had my complete attention. It's a lecture hall, a private counseling session, a daily check-up with the All Knowing Physician. I hoped He would show me what He expected me to do with this book, which too often felt like a heavy weight pulling me asunder. I didn't blame God for difficult situations, and I wouldn't complain, but I needed His strength. He had a plan, and my job was to find out what He was doing, let His power work it out through me, and work it out in lives of others around me.

The slow-motion snow was stealing color from the world. And my home was threatening to steal what was left of me with its unopened boxes full of tangled memory wires, each of them in desperate need of untwisting. I craved an experience with the Word.

After prayer I found a sticky note from Peter on my computer screen. It read: "To: Jack Clayton, From: Peter Brenner—If you are reading this message, GO HOME! Love, Peter."

The phone rang, and I saw my direct line light up. After hours I always let the machine pick up. But I wondered if it was Peter calling and clicked on the speaker phone.

"Campus Mission's Office."

"Hi, is this Jack Clayton?"

"Um … yes," I didn't recognize the voice.

"Hello sir! My name is Bud Abbott, and I'm with the Chicago Tribune. How are you doing today?"

I couldn't believe on the one day I decide to answer an after-hours phone call, I found myself talking to one of the people I'm so famous for avoiding. Before I could answer his benign question, he rolled ahead with a few that promised to be less benign.

"I'm working on a story about you for our Sunday edition and I just wanted to know if I could ask you a few questions?"

I wondered how he'd gotten the number for my direct line. "Bud, it's rare that you got through to me. Usually my secretary answers the phone. But I'll just say what she would have told you: I don't give interviews." I wasn't trying to be rude. He certainly knew this before he called.

"Yeah, I'd heard that. But I wanted to know if you'd make an exception?"

"Why would I do that?"

"Well, Mr. Clayton, I've run across hospital records from New Mexico that say you were admitted with gunshot wounds in 1988. So … what do you think? Would you like to answer a few questions …?"

~ Eight ~

If I go there will be trouble
An' if I stay it will be double.

—The Clash
"Should I Stay or Should I Go?"

I locked the back door of CMO and walked into the cold winter. The pavement was frosty white and crunching beneath the weight of my footsteps. The temperature had taken a severe midwestern nosedive, and I wished I'd remembered my gloves. This was the gloomy onset of *real* winter. Not the fickle cold of November, which could still surprise with warm days awaiting their turn in the queue, but the deep-freeze winter cold, which isn't afraid to drop a few feet of snow and doesn't care if you've remembered your gloves.

I drove out of the CMO parking lot not knowing when I would be back. Massey became Second Avenue, and I hit a red light at Broadway. I was quickly learning to dread being alone inside my house, listening to a louder silence and pouring over the storage spaces in my mind. This writing assignment was like beginning a long trip with only a quarter tank of gas. Here it was, just days later, and the warning lights on my dashboard were starting to blink. The last thing I needed was one more unexpected surprise to throw this uneasy rider into a ditch.

Like a phone call from Bud Abbott.

I hadn't expected this day to end with a threatening phone call from Bud any more than I'd expected my week to start with an involuntary three-month sabbatical. My conversation with the reporter didn't last long. I'm sure he didn't expect it to. He just wanted to get my attention. Well, he got it. And my anger. What right did he have investigating my personal life? My medical records? And how did he get my unpublished phone number?

He had the facts, but he lacked the story. They're not the same thing. The facts only sketch the lines, like a sidewalk chalk drawing. Facts are two-dimensional. They can't describe depth or intensity, or mystery; and that is, of course, where all the action is. Where the story lies. Life is what happens when the skies roll dark and the daylight burns away. It's what happens when we mesh our lives with others' until they are so intertwined they're practically the same. That's why ordinary folks don't get their information from the facts but from the in-betweens. Sure, we listen to facts, but we watch the eyes of the fact teller. We realize intuitively that the facts are little more than mortal promises. Stick men in a flesh-and-blood world.

Before the light turned from red to green, I decided I wasn't going home. I'd begun feeling like Paul Newman's character in *Cool Hand Luke,* a man repeatedly sent to solitary confinement because of his nonconformist attitude.

"What we've got here is failure to com-mu-ni-cate."

Maybe that was my problem. I'd failed to communicate with the world around me. I'd burrowed my head in the sand, and now the French Foreign Legion—I mean the *Chicago Tribune*—was coming to help me with my *com-mu-ni-ca-tion* whether I wanted it or not. I could hear it in the frankness of Bud Abbott's questions.

"Mr. Clayton, you were hospitalized for two weeks in the Albuquerque Medical Center, recovering from gunshot wounds. I have the name of one doctor, Dr. Gerald DeWhitter, the names of a couple of nurses who treated you, hospital records. Wouldn't you like to take this opportunity to set the record straight on the circumstances of your injuries?"

"Opportunity? Thanks, but no comment."

"Mr. Clayton, if you won't speak up and tell your story, someone's going to tell it for you," the reporter had said, trying to coerce my cooperation. He was right, but what he didn't know was I'd already been beaten into a confession by my publisher, who was at this moment selling my life story to the highest bidders in New Jersey.

The light turned green. Just before I pulled through the intersection, two students wrapped in dark coats darted across the street. Their faces were pink from the razor-edged wind. The sky gave birth to a billion snowflakes, swirling in downtown Providence like a ticker-tape parade. Directly in front of me, a light green minivan veered left on Wilson. I wondered what it would be like to pick a car at random and follow wherever it led. Perhaps my little green friend would take me to sunny Daytona Beach, where I could drive the Jeep onto the sand and sleep beneath the stars. Who would stop me? Certainly not the wife and kids. Bud Abbott would miss me, but I'd get over it.

All along the streets giant candy canes hung from the lampposts. Christmas lights blinked in shop windows. The minivan turned left down Fulton, and I followed it. But what I was really following was a strange feeling. An impulse to break free from the pressures and uncertainties and loneliness. Another two blocks, and the Providence campus framed by my rearview mirror faded into the distance. Good-bye frozen students in wool hats and gloves.

Past Fifth Avenue, the minivan turned down Carter, probably toward the I-74 feed, but I didn't follow. I switched to a kind of instinctive driving, just going wherever seemed like the most fun. I found myself in a winter migration away from my snowy address on Sycamore, avoiding drive-time traffic trying to beat home the weather. I followed *the nudge*. The nudge didn't want to go home. The nudge didn't want to sit in traffic. The nudge wanted to escape. I turned down Ellison Parkway and found the destination I didn't know I was looking for: the Hyatt Regency Hotel. I turned onto the horseshoe-shaped drive and stopped the Jeep at the revolving doors. A uniformed doorman opened my driver's side door.

"Good evening sir! Checking in?"

"Yes," I told him. And no, I didn't have any luggage. A minute before, I didn't even know I'd be here. I grabbed my book bag and climbed out. A valet hustled my Jeep away to underground parking.

This was all new to me. I knew next to nothing about the high-end hotel experience. I pulled out three one-dollar bills, handed them to the doorman, and walked through the rotating doors into the hotel. Floor to ceiling, the grand lobby was a splashy, extravagant world of excess, a far cry from the dreary winterland outside. An enormous Persian rug covered most of the marble floor, and the sound of splashing water drew my attention to a huge, intricate fountain in the center of the cavernous room. Near the lounge, businessmen and women in suits mingled sociably, waiting to be seated for dinner. I approached the front desk.

"Welcome to the Hyatt Regency, Mr. Clayton" the man at the front desk said. "Will you be staying with us this weekend?"

For a moment I didn't know how he could have known my name. Then I remembered that my face was on the cover of *Time* magazine. This kind of recognition could only happen downtown, miles from the campus, where any novelty of fame had worn off, mellowing into friendly, aweless greetings from students and visitors.

The clerk's recognition didn't signify to me any sense of my own importance, far from it. Instead, it perpetuated a mild sense of paranoia, one that had been building all week and had spiked that afternoon with Bud's phone call.

"I'll be staying the night," I said, handing over my driver's license and credit card.

While he typed my info into the computer, I wondered what he might think about local guests who check in with no luggage. Perhaps he thought I was planning a clandestine rendezvous for the evening. A little dalliance to help the writer write. He rang the desk bell twice, and a bellhop appeared out of nowhere.

"Suite 704," he said, handing the bellhop my plastic card-key and wishing me a pleasant stay.

When we reached the seventh floor, the bellhop walked ahead of me to the room, unlocked the door, turned on the lights, and explained the switches that controlled everything from lights to window shades inside the luxurious suite. I tipped the only other bill in my wallet, a five. When he was gone, I bolted the room's heavy door and peered out the fish-eye lens at the middle-aged man shrinking as he walked back down the hallway.

I sat on the edge of the bed, kicked off my shoes, peeled off my socks, pulled off my damp parka and clothing, and crawled into the most comfortable bed in America. So this is what money can buy: a sumptuous night of sleep behind a locked door on the top floor of a fancy hotel, where no one knows how to find you.

~ NINE ~

I have a picture pinned to my wall
an image of you and of me
And we're laughing, we're loving it all.

—THOMPSON TWINS
"Hold Me Now"

Twelve weeks had passed since Mitchell and I had left Overton. The days of autumn were growing progressively cooler. But Indian summer brought a June-like heat wave to Providence, and the campus morphed into a beach with students sunning themselves on blankets spread across fallen maple leaves.

Mitchell had been "Joe Athlete" in high school. I guess he missed the ache-inducing workouts and brutal team practices, so on this extraordinary day, we dug out running shorts and T-shirts and hit the campus trails.

We ran for forty minutes across north central, over the bridge from the Jeffrey Brown Arts and Sciences Building, and then to the hilly west side, where dorms house a third of the students. Racing up a grassy slope, we found ourselves at the doorway of a women's dormitory, Lillian Hall. We were bent over at the waist, our lungs burning from lack of oxygen, our shirts damp with sweat. West Campus was practically unexplored territory. The view from the summit was sensational.

Lillian Hall was one of three women's dormitories at Providence. An impressive three-story expression of midwestern Ivy League distinction and modest old money. I sat on a stone bench in the courtyard while Mitchell pressed his face against the glass door.

"I think window peeking is still illegal, Mitch."

"Very funny," he said, his hands cupped around his eyes to block the light. "I know a girl who lives here."

"Really? What's her name?" No sooner had I asked than a cute blonde opened the front door and leaned out.

"Mitchell? Hi!" The young woman pushed a runaway strand of yellow hair behind her ear. "What are you doing here?"

Mitch stepped backward, drawing the mysterious Lillian Hall girl outside. The two of them lit up like diamonds.

"We were just out for a run," Mitch said, gesturing toward me. "I thought I'd tempt you to enjoy this awesome day."

I was quickly getting the picture that our run was merely an excuse to get to Lillian Hall.

"Jack," Mitch said, gesturing, "this is Erin Taylor. She's in my sociology class. Now behave yourself, she's decent."

I stood and approached. She was only twenty, but

her eyes were those of an old soul. She glowed when Mitchell introduced her.

"Hey, Erin," I said, taking her hand. Her grip was firm and confident like she'd known hard work.

"Mitchell has told me a little bit about you," Erin said, the corners of her mouth rising into a smile. Her teeth were perfect and white. Her shoulder-length blond hair curled up pertly at the ends. She gazed up at me through piercing sapphire eyes.

"You seem like a nice person, Erin. How do you know a skunk like Mitch?"

"Oh, Mitchell is not a skunk!" Those same eyes sharpened, and her voice took on a gentle defensiveness.

"Just kidding," I said, but I wouldn't joke like that around her again. She was too sweet to make irksome.

"We're in the same class on Tuesdays and Thursdays."

"It's a very intimate group," Mitch said.

"About sixty people!" Erin laughed again—a nice laugh.

Mitch smiled, she smiled, then I smiled. These two were in love. Or destined for it. Where had she come from? How could Mitchell meet someone and fall in love so quickly?

A steady stream of young women moved in and out of Lillian Hall while the three of us chatted in the courtyard. Without fanfare, another delicate and beautiful young woman slid into our conclave as if she already belonged. She entered my life unannounced, but over the next few years, she would overturn every stone I was.

"Looks like somebody's making friends."

"Hi, Jenny," Erin said. "You know Mitchell, and this is Jack ..." She squinted.

"Clayton," I said, turning to look at Jenny for the first time.

"Jack is Mitchell's roommate."

Mitchell's roommate? Funny, I'd always thought of it the other way around.

"And this is my roommate, Jenny. We've only been friends since about the sixth grade, so I hardly know her."

They giggled. Mitch, Erin, and Jenny started talking about Indiana's unseasonably warm weather and unsympathetic class schedules that prevent poor college students from enjoying it. Their conversation buzzed around me, sweeping in and out, hushing their voices and slowing the seconds into a slow-motion film. *Who is this girl? Who is this incredible girl?*

The striking twenty-year-old junior exuded a presence like no one I'd known. She was sharp as angel's eyes, stunning in her beauty, elegant in her demeanor. A calm surface concealed a passion for life in the waters below. She was confident, fearless, and yet peaceful and content. I wondered what kinds of dreams she dreamed. I wondered if I'd ever have the chance to hear them.

"Mitchell and I were thinking of catching a movie tonight," I heard Erin say. "I won't be back before nine thirty or ten."

"Sounds like a good time," Jenny said.

"You guys are free to tag along," Erin added.

For a moment I was excited by the thought of

spending time with Jenny, but my nervous thrill was short lived.

"No, that's all right," Jenny answered, shifting the bag she held from one small hand to the other. "I'd love an excuse to play, but I've got a meeting at the library in an hour. I'm just here to pick up something."

"I'm going to buzz Mitchell in for a second," Erin said. "I have some notes upstairs he needs. We won't be long."

Erin and Mitch walked through Lillian Hall's stately doors, leaving Jenny and me alone. I hadn't spoken to her yet. She walked a few steps to a mailbox and opened it with a key. She removed colorful envelopes and smiled wide like a schoolgirl who's just been handed a box of valentines. I wondered if one of the cards or letters was from a boyfriend. Women as attractive as Jenny always had at least one; it's practically federal law.

I needed to say something before Jenny disappeared into Lillian Hall, but I didn't have a clue what that something should be.

She glanced up from her letters. "It was nice meeting you, Jack." She stepped closer to the door and reached for the handle.

"Is it your birthday?" I asked.

"Tomorrow," she said. "These are cards from friends, my mom … you know." It seemed obvious she'd been loved all her life.

"It's a bummer not having your family here to help celebrate your birthday," I said.

"I'll see them at Thanksgiving, and besides, I've got Erin. She's as good as family."

No mention of Mr. Boyfriend. From the top of her

chestnut hair to the soles of her patent-leather shoes, Jenny's beauty shimmered in the light of the afternoon sun. As I write this today, I am back there with her in that moment. Time hasn't erased what it felt like to meet her.

"Good," I said. "No one should be without loved ones on their birthday. Nineteen?" I asked.

"This one makes twenty," she said, unrushed. Perhaps she was flattered by the attention.

"Well, Jenny …"

"Cameron. Jenny Cameron."

"Well, Jenny Cameron," I said, taking a step back. "Happy birthday. And have a great meeting."

"Thank you, Jack," she said. Her eyes turned to the door, her body followed, and then she was gone.

I didn't wait for Mitch. I ran down the hill, my drive intensifying with every step. I sprinted a mile to the North Campus athletic complex and raced around the quarter-mile track until I'd burned my adrenaline back down to a manageable level.

After my run I walked through a grassy field to cool down and stretch my muscles. The sun's slow descent resembled the last embers of a beach fire, our November gift of a summer's day succumbing to the earth's slow revolution. The light became dazed and delicate, and I allowed myself to daydream about seeing Jenny again. I guess some daydreams come true, because right then Miss Jenny Cameron herself walked up in blue jeans and a beige sweater. I wondered if there was a certain something to this life, a certain something that lined events up just the way they ought to be lined up. She looked up and saw that our two sidewalks would soon cross, and if we maintained our current paces, we'd collide.

"Still running? You must be in good shape."

"I think it's the weather. I didn't plan on being out this long." We stopped in the centermost point of North Campus. "But bumping into you again makes me glad I stopped to run a few laps," I said, too flirty but true. She ignored it.

"Listen," Jenny said, "I'm glad I ran into you. I wanted to say I'm sorry if I was short with you before, back at the dorm."

"You weren't short. You were fine."

"I've been looking for a check in the mail, and it hasn't arrived. I guess I'm sort of preoccupied."

We smiled, signaling that if any infraction had been committed, all was right now. We walked side by side, both of us headed in the same direction. At first we strolled in silence, but I wanted to hear her speak.

"So, Jenny Cameron, what are you planning to do for your twentieth birthday?"

"I don't have any big plans. Erin and I will probably just have dinner in the dorm and go to bed early for a change." She shrugged off my question like the birthday was no big deal.

"So I guess you and Erin are really close?"

"She's my best friend. We've been roommates here for two and a half years too. I'd say we're pretty close. How well do you know Mitchell?"

"He's been my best friend all my life. I couldn't leave him back in Iowa, so I made him come with me to Providence."

"So you're the brains in the operation."

It must have sounded like I thought I had the world in my pocket.

"I don't know about that. Sometimes I think Mitchell lives in a world all his own. Had you met him before?"

"Once. The three of us had lunch at that little pita sandwich shop on Broadway last Friday."

We walked along the winding sidewalk to the central library, the night air rapidly cooling.

"He's a pretty good guy."

"Erin wouldn't give him the time of day if he wasn't."

"And yet maybe you should keep your eyes open just in case." I smiled.

"I'm sure Erin can take care of herself."

As we approached the Tillman-Aubry Center, Jenny's body began to blend in with the dusk, mellowing it with her presence.

"I'm going to have to make another quick exit, Jack. This is where my meeting is."

Jenny climbed the first of the wide cement library steps and turned around. Behind her the building's facade was lit by yellow light shining through tall rectangular windows. The smell of smoke from a campfire drifted in the air as Jenny said good-bye to me for the second time that day.

"Good-bye again," I said. "I hope you have a great meeting and a great birthday. Um … I already said that, didn't I?"

She offered a sweet smile.

On impulse I added, "Well, if you'd like to have dinner with someone who'd love to make your birthday special ..." The words met the air sounding brash and forward. They hung precariously until Jenny replied, instantly turning my awkward words into a friendly invitation.

"That's very nice of you, Jack," she said. She paused for a moment, processing the request, I suppose. "Actually, I'm sure Erin and Mitchell will be in the mood to see each other. Would you and Mitchell like to come over for cake tomorrow night?"

I had my answer ready before she'd finished her question.

"Yes. We'd love to come over for cake. We'll bring the ice cream."

"I'm sure Erin will approve." We stared at each other in the final moments of twilight. "Good night, Jack. I guess I'll see you tomorrow."

She walked up the steps into the building, and I turned for home. I don't recall wondering if I'd made an impression on her. But the impression she'd made on me was transformational. I felt there was something significant about the way we'd met, and then met again. About how Jenny had invited us over to watch her blow out the candles on her birthday cake. About how lucky I was to be one of only two men on campus, or in the entire world, with such an invitation.

As I walked back to the apartment in my sweat-damp running clothes, I replayed everything that happened over and over again in my head. I barely noticed the chill in the air or the lingering smell of burning campfires.

~ Ten ~

At night I wake up with the sheets soaking wet
and a freight train running through the
middle of my head.

—Bruce Springsteen
"I'm on Fire"

The next morning I opened one eye to find myself in a strange world. A magnificent clear blue sky filled the enormous hotel window. I climbed from the king-size bed and pressed against the glass for a better view. I'd never seen Providence from so high up before, and the city below looked as quaint as a snow village. But it was a quiet village, shut down by a blanket of fresh wet snow. Nothing moved on the streets.

I looked around my room by the light of day.

My suite was amply stocked with every comfort from Pellegrino water to toothbrush and toothpaste, deodorant, and Hershey bars. A yellow legal pad and black-felt pens invited me to sit down and write at the work desk. I ignored them and called room service, ordering eggs, bacon, and a pot of decaf. No one knew I was here except the front-desk clerk, and if he wasn't talking, neither was I. I'd checked in feeling as taut as piano wire. But what a way to unwind.

While waiting for breakfast, I called Peter's cell phone.

"This is Peter."

"So I'm not fired, right? You're going to let me come back to work when the book's finished?"

"No, you're fired," he said, kidding, I hoped.

"In that case, maybe I *will* consider moving to Jamaica. I could get used to a little relaxation."

Peter Brenner grew up fifteen miles south of Providence. He'd come on board less than two years after I did, and we'd hit it off straight out of the box. Peter has been like a brother, calling on weekends, checking in on me. He drove me home from the doctor's office once after a minor outpatient procedure. And he helped me move in when I bought my house.

"Aaron said he thought you were down at the shop yesterday afternoon. You aren't going to make these stopovers a habit, are you?"

"No, I'm done for good, Peter. I needed to get CMO out of my system, but I won't be back." I'd meant during the sabbatical, but the words sounded more emphatic, and perhaps prophetic, than intended.

"Where was everyone? I thought I'd at least see Mrs. Burman."

"Don't you watch the weather where you live, Jack? Aaron closed the shop at two thirty so we could all beat the blizzard home. We got more than a foot last night. Everyone with any sense left Dodge by midday."

"No kidding." I took the phone over to the window and looked down to the street again. I could see only the whitewashed concrete and huge drifts that, upon further study, turned out to be buried cars. "Anything new going on?"

"The office isn't the same without you, if that's what you wanted to hear. Aaron's asked Nancy to go back to a five-day workweek."

"What'd she say to that?"

"She doesn't want to do it, but we're down one man. I mean, I'm glad you're taking this time off … I am … but January is going to be a real challenge if we don't stay on top of stuff right now."

"I don't think she should do it. Aaron should hire someone else, someone new." I caught my reflection in the mirror. Even ignoring my bed-head hair, I looked ragged.

"He hasn't said anything, but I'm sure he's thinking about it. I've hinted too, not that we're replacing you, old buddy. I mean, is that even possible?" He smirked.

"I'll talk to Aaron," I told Peter.

"Enough shoptalk. Why don't you tell me how the book's coming?"

"I'd almost forgotten about it for a second." I picked up the remote and clicked on the Weather Channel.

"That bad, huh?"

"The words are going on paper, Peter, but I'm not the superstar people believe me to be. This is definitely not the book Arthur's expecting."

"What kind of book is that?"

"You know, 'I did it the right way, I care about people, my life is perfect, go and do likewise.' Your basic inspirational pep talk."

"You're not trying to please people are you? That can't be done, you know."

"Maybe." Wandering into the kitchenette, I opened the fridge looking for other surprises. "Peter, you've known me for ten years. What do you think I'm writing?"

"You're from Iowa—might want to leave that part out. You graduated from Providence College, left for a number of years to do something, possibly chase wild women and work the rodeo circuit. Then you came to your senses and helped inspire a nation to love their fellow man and serve the poor. The end."

"An inspiration?"

"Well, listen, in all seriousness, Jack, you are. It doesn't mean you don't have faults. I can write that chapter if you like. But you've done enough. People are going to be inspired. What's wrong with that?"

"What's wrong is sometimes people don't tell even their best friends what they've been through."

"What haven't you told me?"

The fridge was empty. I headed back into the living room. "Just everything, that's all."

"What'd you do … kill a guy?"

I was silent.

"Jack, listen, I've got no idea what you're writing, no idea whatsoever, but if it's what you believe God wants you to do, then tell your story. Something good will come of this. And if it just so happens you've …"

His voice trailed off. He was thinking about what I might have been capable of in my younger days. He was thinking about what it must be like having your shadows flooded by a public spotlight.

"You see, Peter, that's the problem," I interrupted, rescuing him from the uncomfortable silence. "I thought I could sketch a story of my life—where I grew up, my years as a Providence student, what happened when I returned, and how I wrote *Laborers*. But that's not the story God wants me to tell, and I want to run away like Jonah."

"And look what happened to him."

"Do you know how scary it is standing up in front of the world and telling them the truth about yourself?"

"Oooh," Peter groaned.

"I don't expect you to be able to solve this," I said.

"I'm not trying to solve it, but at least I have a better grip now on your hesitancy in the meeting. Aaron thought you were just being humble."

I laughed. "Will you pray for me? I could use your support."

"You've got it. Always. Say, where are you, man?"

"I'm out at sea in my little boat, whale watching."

"Don't get lost out there."

"I won't. I hope I won't."

Peter and I hung up, and I made a second call. This one to the concierge.

"Good morning, Mr. Clayton," said a voice on the other end of the line.

"Good morning. Can you recommend a men's clothing shop downtown that might be open today?"

"If you can give me your measurements, Mr. Clayton, I'll call Duroth's Menswear. If they're open today, I'm sure they can deliver whatever you need."

"It's all right," I said. "I can stop by."

A moment later room service knocked at my door.

A young man rolled in a breakfast cart. I was out of cash, so I asked him to add a 20 percent gratuity to the bill. He thanked me and left. I was on my second cup of coffee when the concierge called back with the news that Duroth's was open. He gave me walking directions that gave purpose to the black-felt pen and the pad of yellow paper.

Charles Duroth is a stout man in his midfifties with a full head of black hair. He looks every bit a tailor in his silver and white houndstooth vest over a crisp white starched shirt, his sleeves rolled up to midforearm. He greeted me at the door. I stepped out of the frozen cold into one of the warmest greetings I ever recall receiving.

"Mr. Clayton!" Charles Duroth clapped his hands together, accentuating my name. "I hear you're looking for some new clothes." The concierge had obviously mentioned my name.

"Yes," I told him. "Just a few things … pants, a shirt."

"Mr. Clayton," Mr. Duroth shook his head. "A man like yourself … you ought to look your very best. What you need is quality clothing. Am I right, sir?"

Something told me Mr. Duroth had a subscription to *Time* magazine. I had a sneaking suspicion he was glad he'd battled the weather and opened his store that Saturday morning. He'd surely sell me his most expensive suit, and a shirt and tie to go with it. I suspected the warmth of his greeting had been heated by the thought of a big sale.

"I'm really just looking for a new suit."

"And that's just what I'm going to help you with. Do you mind if I get a few measurements?" He lifted his tape measure inches off his shoulders and held it, awaiting my answer.

"No," I said.

With the open palm of his small hand, Mr. Duroth gestured me over to a tailor's stool set in front of three angled mirrors.

"Step right up here, Mr. Clayton. You probably know your measurements already, but I like to take them anyway, just to be 100 percent."

"No problem," I said, stepping up on the stool while he went to work quickly and efficiently. "You work fast, Mr. Duroth."

"You're a busy man, Mr. Clayton. I understand that. In fact, I understand people. You don't spend thirty-five years in this business and not learn something about people."

Mr. Duroth kneeled to take a pant-length measurement. The snowstorm had kept other customers away, and when we didn't speak, it was completely quiet in the room. My eyes roamed the displays. I spotted a rack of specialty jackets Mr. Duroth must have rolled out in anticipation of my arrival. There were at least fifteen separate articles of clothing, jackets of different styles and colors for all occasions, business and pleasure.

"Please don't go to a lot of trouble, Mr. Duroth. I don't need much. My stay downtown this weekend was unexpected, and I didn't bring a change of clothes."

He didn't look up from his work. "That's my business, Mr. Clayton. That's exactly what I provide. A change of clothing, a change of style."

I had to admit, I was impressed by Mr. Duroth's legerdemain. He wasn't about to let me tell him what I needed.

"What are you … a thirty-eight regular?"

"Forty, actually."

"No, I think you're more of a thirty-eight. Here, try this on." Mr. Duroth stood and rested the tape measure back across his narrow shoulders. He pulled a brown-checked sports jacket off a hanger and slipped it up my arms. "Take a good look at this jacket in the mirror, Mr. Clayton, and tell me it's not a beautiful coat."

I turned back to face the mirrors. I had to admit it was a gorgeous sports jacket. While I adjusted and admired my new look, Mr. Duroth brought me two pairs of pants, olive and tan. He gestured to the curtained dressing rooms.

"Why don't you try these on, Mr. Clayton?"

I stepped down from the stool, still wearing the jacket, and took the pants inside the tiny dressing room. There was a lot to like about Mr. Duroth. He was pushy, but like Debbie Holms at Liberty Deli, he worked hard and clearly knew what he was doing.

I stepped into the olive pants and walked back outside. I looked again at my reflection in the trifold mirrors. I didn't know if I'd ever looked this good. Chalk up a win for Mr. Duroth.

"I'll take them," I said.

"If you like the fit of the olive pants, take the tan

slacks as well—they're identical. This way you can vary the look. You're also going to need shirts."

I had to smile. "Mr. Duroth, you're quite a salesman," I said, genuinely complimenting him. "I'll take the pants, the shirts, and the jacket."

"What about shoes? Please don't tell me you're one of those men who wears tennis shoes with a sports jacket," he said.

"I repent, Mr. Duroth. Show me some brown shoes in a size ten."

Almost immediately he was lifting a shoebox and rustling the tissue paper as he took out a pair of dark burgundy handsewn leather loafers. The kind you don't see for less than two hundred dollars.

"These are *the* shoes for that jacket, Mr. Clayton. You'll feel like a million dollars when you wear them," he said. I hoped he wasn't hinting at the price.

Mr. Duroth looked at me from behind the counter, and now it was my turn. He'd shown me his best, now would I take it or leave it? I asked the Boss, the One I ask all questions. The One who tells me to go backward or to move forward. He answered immediately.

"Wrap 'em up. I'll take 'em."

I returned my new jacket to the rack and changed back into the clothes I'd walked in wearing, shabby by comparison. By the time I'd returned from the changing room, everything had been bagged, except for the dress slacks, which Mr. Duroth was hemming at a sewing machine behind the counter. I reached for my wallet.

Charles Duroth carefully folded the dress pants onto wooden hangers, using the same fluid strokes of an artist brushing watercolors onto parchment. His black-framed tailor's glasses slid down on his face as he worked.

"I wonder if you know my son, Mr. Clayton. He's a graduate of Providence College, and he went through your … what do you call it … training program?"

"Really?" I said. I didn't recall anyone named Duroth. "What's your boy's name?"

Looking at me over the top of his bifocals, Mr. Duroth looked like an old-world craftsman. "Justin," he said. "He's a good-looking, tall kid. Six foot two. Brown hair."

"I can't place him … That's odd."

The craftsman continued his work.

"He's always said nice things about you. He gave us one of your books—I think it was for Easter, or maybe Christmas. Signed. It was very nice," he said, because it was a gift from his son, not because it was my book.

"I'm glad you enjoyed it. What's Justin up to now?" I asked, hoping more information would help jog my memory.

"He's a missionary in London. Works with World Missions Outreach. Ever heard of a guy named Howard Cameron?"

The expression "small world" took on new meaning as chills prickled the skin on my neck. Goose bumps the size of goose eggs rippled up the back of my arms. *Mr. Duroth, you're stepping into my cellar. You're standing near my unopened boxes.*

"Yes," I said.

"He and his wife started a missionary church over there. Justin's been on board for about a year now. He works with the Camerons. They got their whole family over there. The daughter works with them too."

Tiny beads of sweat appeared at my temples.

"What do you hear from Justin these days?" I wondered if God was about to send me a telegram.

"Oh, he's doing great. He got married right after graduation, and he and his wife moved right over there. They love it. We have two grandchildren now—twins. My wife and I took a vacation to see them this past August."

What's that like? Having a family, I mean.

"I'm sure you and your wife had a wonderful time."

He smiled, and I knew that they had.

"Yes, we certainly did. We all went to see Buckingham Palace. Well, not the twins. Howard's daughter Jenny looked after them."

I can't believe I'm here, Mr. Duroth.

I stepped closer to the counter, held on to it so I wouldn't fall over from the shock. I'd come here for a change of clothes. What I was getting was the first report on Jenny in more than a dozen years.

"So she watched the twins, huh. Must have had her hands full," I said.

"Well, she's got a couple of boys herself. Cute little guys."

Did you know I was the girl's first love back in college? I never got over it. Was she wearing the silver necklace I bought her? Did she speak of me?

"How long did you say you've been in business?" I asked.

"Thirty-five years I've been here, rain or shine,

snowstorm, ice storm, economy good or bad ... whatever. It's not easy to stay in business here when everybody wants to shop at the mall."

"No, not easy. But I don't think they have service like this in any mall."

"I like to think they don't have service like this anywhere else in the free world, Mr. Clayton." He smiled a warm, peaceful smile as he stuck the last item in the garment bag.

"What do I owe you?" I asked, bracing myself for an astronomical total.

"Nothing, Mr. Clayton. Your money's no good."

I studied the tailor's face. The peaceful grin had been replaced by weathered, rougher features. His face revealed deeply etched worry lines, like a rug that's been paced on for years.

"Now why would you say something like that?"

"Mr. Clayton, in all these years, you've never stepped inside my store. I don't know why that is ... Maybe you get your clothing at the mall like everybody else. Maybe you don't get downtown much. But if you'd have come in here anytime before today, I would have told you then what I'm going to tell you now." Mr. Duroth pulled his glasses from the bridge of his nose and wiped at his face with a handkerchief slipped from his front pocket.

"Justin was always a good kid. But he got in trouble with drugs when he was in high school. Dropped out. Got busted for selling and had to go to juvenile detention for ten months. While he was in there, you came to speak at the detention center."

"Ah ..." Finally I remembered a piece of this story.

"He read your book, and that's when he decided he wanted to come to school here and be a part of the program. It turned his life around."

"God turns lives around, Mr. Duroth," I told him, hoping I didn't sound like I was correcting.

"You're right, Mr. Clayton. But then God doesn't need new slacks, and you do, or you wouldn't have come in here today."

I asked Mr. Duroth again to let me pay for the clothes, but he refused.

"Mr. Clayton, I hope you will enjoy your new clothing. You know, every man should dress his best."

"Thank you. And please tell Justin I said hello the next time you speak with him."

On the walk back to the hotel, more downtown businesses were opening up. Lunch with Howard and Angela was set for 1:00 p.m. at the Schneider Haus, a German restaurant west of downtown. There was a good chance they'd be open now. Whether or not Howard and Angela would be there, I wasn't sure. However, I was sure I'd left the Oslander's number back home.

Howard loved the Schneider Haus. At least he did twenty years earlier when he and Angela had taken Jenny and me there for lunch while visiting Providence. Howard had an affinity for all things European, a quality that sustained his work in England over the years, I'm sure.

Seeing myself in my new clothes back in my hotel room, I was pleased I'd taken this detour from my usual mall-based clothes-shopping routine. This was just the sort of impression I wanted to make with Howard and Angela. And in general.

Howard and Angela loved their daughter. Like so many parents, they were keen to protect her from the dangers that can accompany first loves. I thought about the stories they must have heard years before, wondered if they felt any lingering bitterness toward me. Howard mentioned that my book had made a positive impression. Why would they bother seeing me after so long?

I shut off the bathroom light and put on my coat. It didn't match the new sports jacket, so I left it in my room and caught a cab in front of the Hyatt. In less than twenty minutes I was going to have lunch with two of the most important people in my life. Not this life, but the one I lived in 1985.

As the taxi pulled away from the curb, I tried to think of another situation where the characters from a book come to life. And the writer, dressed finely in his new wardrobe, drives off in a taxi to meet them.

~ Eleven ~

Ooh baby, do you know what that's worth?

—Belinda Carlisle
"Heaven Is a Place on Earth"

Mitchell and I stood at the front entrance of Lillian Hall. This time we weren't dressed in running clothes but in sports jackets without ties. In the cool evening air, we'd walked from the apartment in a state of excitement, thinking about how to properly celebrate Jenny's birthday. The mood was reminiscent of the complex blend of naïveté and sophistication that accompanies prom night.

Earlier in the day we purchased fancy ice cream from a shop called I LUV MOO. We played Billy Joel's *An Innocent Man* album—music that's more about falling in love than it is about innocence. I pressed a pair of khakis and a white oxford to "Uptown Girl," assembling my best party attire from a closet full of blue jeans and sweatshirts.

We were buzzed in at Lillian Hall by a girl reading a

magazine at the front desk. She knew Mitch, so we were granted permission to head upstairs without an escort or chaperone.

On the third floor we drew wide-eyed stares from women in sweats while we walked past their open doors. I suppose we did sort of stand out. We were, after all, the only men on the floor ... and we were carrying a half gallon of ice cream and an oversize bottle of sparkling grape juice.

Mitch knocked on the door at the end of the hallway, room 335. Jenny opened the door, and we immediately launched into an off-key rendition of "Happy Birthday," the only preplanned event of the evening. The faces of envious women popped out of doorways all along the corridor, followed by loud applause and unrestrained squeals.

"Come on in, guys. That was *wonderful.*"

Their dorm room was small compared to our apartment. In fact, it was small compared to a Volkswagen. They'd utilized every square inch like sailors sharing quarters on a ship. A birthday banner hung above the dressing mirror, and a bouquet of white and purple balloons sat on a dresser.

Mitchell greeted Erin with a hug and kiss like they'd known each other for years. Jenny and I said "Hello" and "So we meet again," and those kinds of things. It wasn't awkward. Well, maybe it was.

"Can I get you guys something to drink?" Erin took the heavy juice bottle out of my hands and nearly buckled under its weight. Mitchell came to her aid.

"Why don't we make *this* a little lighter?" he said.

"I'm surprised you got in here with that."

"It's grape juice," I said. "It's only bottled to look like champagne."

The girls turned to collect four glasses, and Mitchell and I shared a brief knowing look—we knew we'd scored points, since neither Erin nor Jenny drank wine.

"Could one of you strong he-men open this thing?" Jenny asked.

I tore off the fancy foil wrapping and popped the cork like it was New Year's Eve. We cheered and filled the glasses with effervescent grape juice.

The four of us got along famously. Maybe it was because every twenty-year-old woman wants her birthday remembered and celebrated. Maybe it was because Mitchell had already told Erin he loved her, and she'd already realized she was falling in love with him. I was just a freshman from Overton who had been in the right place at the right time, landing a leading role in place of someone special not yet in Jenny's life. She didn't know me, but she appreciated the kindness, the regard Mitch and I showed her.

Jenny graciously donned the pointy paper hat we insisted she wear while blowing out her candles. Her expression went from ridiculous to delicate when she closed her eyes to make a wish. With one perfect exhale from two perfect lips, she extinguished the circle of blue candles on the chocolate-frosted cake.

The four of us talked, dined on cake and ice cream, and toasted with the mock champagne. We shared about our lives and revealed the most outrageous escapades, the kind only lifelong friends tell, confident that the stories wouldn't escape the safety of our friendship.

We talked about college, about the classes we were

taking, about what Erin and Jenny were going to do after college, a future just a year away. That night my affection for Jenny became hardwired in my brain. It was the way she looked when she talked about her family, the cadence and rhythm in her voice.

I watched Erin and Mitchell kiss each other good night as we were leaving. This was no high-school fling. I doubted Mitch would confide his feelings for Erin when we walked back to the apartment, but he didn't need to.

Jenny and I ended the evening awkwardly, shaking hands as if we'd just finished a job interview. I had feelings for Jenny, but clearly they were unrequited. We made no plans to see each other again.

Later that night, before I fell asleep, the wind picked up, blowing strong, portending harsher, colder days. The clouds closed our blue-sky Indian summer like heavy red velvet curtains at the end of a play. As I lay in bed before the last tick of conscious thought, I wondered if the time for Jenny and me had also been closed behind those curtains.

~ Twelve ~

Every day is Christmas, and every night is New Year's Eve.

—Sade
"The Sweetest Taboo"

Howard and Angela Cameron were already seated when I arrived at the Schneider Haus. I stood motionless inside the doorway, ensconced behind fluted columns and an oversize fern. They looked younger than I'd expected, considering it had been two decades since I'd last laid eyes on them. They were in their early fifties then.

Excitement and apprehension filled me. And guilt, too, over how I'd treated Jenny. Surely they'd heard how Jack Clayton had broken their daughter's heart. I shouldn't have worried; I was certain they would have long since forgiven me. But I did nonetheless. Why did they want to see me? Were they just passing through, their memories rekindled by a best-selling book? Maybe they were doing some creative fund-raising for missions work. I wouldn't be offended. I'd give whatever they asked.

When I stepped into the Schneider Haus, I stepped directly into Howard's gaze. He waved me over to their table, standing to shake my hand.

"How are you, Jack?" he asked, his grip firm and vigorous.

Angela rose and hugged me.

"I'm fine. It's good to see you two."

Howard's smile beamed. The six-foot-tall jolly man joggled my hand for a second time with warmth and energy as if twenty years ago were yesterday.

"Jack! It's good to see you. You've hardly changed a bit."

"Let's hope that's not the case," I said, returning an echo of his enthusiasm.

Howard's spirit hadn't dimmed, but the lines in his face had grown deeper. Angela was still slender, but her once jet black hair had turned white, and she wore it in a stately ponytail, more Audrey Hepburn than Earth Woman. The three of us sat.

"I can't tell you how good it is to see you both."

"Staying single all these years has kept you looking thin!" Howard laughed. "We've been looking forward to getting together with you, Jack. Angela and I read your book … uh … "—he looked at Angela—"a year ago, wasn't it?"

"Something like that," she said.

"We were in England at the time … So proud of you. Then just the other day, we got back from Christmas shopping with our good friends in Boston—well, Quincy, really—and who's on the cover of their issue of

Time magazine but Jack Clayton. It's remarkable, Jack, really remarkable what's happened with you."

"Praise God."

"Yes, praise God, indeed." Howard reached across the table and shook the back of my hand. "Until we read that book, we didn't know what had become of you. Of course, we hoped it was something good!" He laughed again, and I wondered what his secret was. Angela smiled, quiet and demure. Perhaps she had a better memory of the past.

"Thanks. So … you're both still serving as missionaries in England? It sounded like it from your messages."

"We've served in London for twenty-two years. This is our first trip back to the U.S. in three. We spent a week in Boston, and now we're headed to Indianapolis for good. We're staying stateside for a while."

"Really?" I said, the revelation flying across my mind like a "breaking news" ticker on CNN.

"Twenty-two years is a long time. We stayed just as long as the Lord wanted us there."

"That's an incredible accomplishment. You should be proud."

"Not proud," Howard said. "Satisfied. The Lord's given us a fulfilling and wonderful life. We wouldn't trade it for the world. He blessed us there, and now He's moving us on to a new phase." He sipped his ice water.

"We're going to be staying with Tessa and Mike over the next few months," Angela said. "You remember them, don't you, Jack?"

I did remember. It was right after I met Jenny, our first Christmas together. I went home to meet her parents; her sister, Tessa; and her brother-in-law, Mike.

"Of course. How are they doing?"

The waitress approached. Howard and Angela both ordered sauerbraten, and I asked for a bowl of chicken-noodle soup.

Angela removed her eyeglasses and set them on the table. "They're doing wonderfully. They have three children now—a fifteen-year-old, Virginia; a twelve-year-old son named Thomas; and a seven-year-old girl they adopted from China, Ming Chao. Mike's made partner at his law firm, and Tessa's working part-time from home, still in city law."

"Give them my best. I'm glad to hear they're well."

Howard put his hand on my shoulder. "Jack, we wanted to tell you how proud we are of you. The Lord has done wonderful things with your life."

"Well, He's been very gracious." I hoped my words conveyed a contrite spirit.

"Think of all the people who've been blessed by your work, not only here in Providence, but all over the world." When Angela spoke, she looked remarkably like Jenny. There'd always been a great deal of natural family resemblance, but when she encouraged me with that rapt expression in her eyes, she *was* Jenny.

"How is Jenny?" I could avoid the question no longer.

"Oh, she's doing fine," Angela continued. "You know she's still in London. Two beautiful boys. Andrew is ten, Nate's seven."

"That's great, really great," I said. But then I was stumped. I didn't know what to say next. "How did she and her husband meet?" Maybe not the smoothest segue in the world. But it kept the conversation going.

"You know about Murphy?" Angela asked.

"Yes," I said. I'd been in London too once.

"They met just weeks after she arrived in London. He put her on such a pedestal, loved to introduce her to his friends. Took her out on the town most every night. It was a good match."

"He was working for the Arthur Tidwell Insurance Company when they met," Howard said, picking up the story.

"English?"

"American. Transferred to London when the company expanded their offices. It was a fortunate break. He'd been struggling as a salesman in Connecticut, but over there he thrived. Murphy became one of their top people in the London bureau, and eventually the branch manager."

"That's impressive," I said. "So … they met in London?"

"Yes, a charity auction in Regent's Park," Angela said. "We'd organized the event; it's a great way for Christian missionaries to pool their resources and raise funds. There were lots of odds and ends at the auction—furniture, soccer memorabilia—only over there, you know they call it football."

"Yes," I said.

"It was so funny." Angela chuckled. "Jenny was on the organizing committee, and one of her jobs was to take the items to the auctioneer's block. Well, you know Jenny …"

I did once …

"… some of the bigger pieces—like these wooden shelves and this huge steamer trunk—were *too* heavy, and she couldn't get them onto the stage. Well, the crowd found this to be quite humorous, watching this petite girl determined to move those heavy objects. Murphy was at the auction, and it wasn't long before he was pitching in, muscling things around."

"So they met at an auction …"

"That was the start of it all," she said, satisfied by the memory. "They spent Christmas together, and it wasn't long after that Murphy proposed. They were married on March 2. Erin was there."

"Wow. And they had boys?"

"Yes. We're biased, but they're adorable."

"Well, we're grandparents," Howard said. "That's our right!"

"Would you like to see pictures?" Angela took out her billfold.

Lord, don't let it be a family photo. I'm not ready for that … Thank you, Lord. School photos.

"You're right, Angela, they're beautiful."

Holding the pictures in my hand, I was happy for Jenny. I really was. And perhaps a bit ashamed of my lingering longing for her. No one wants to hear that someone they love—or perhaps *once* loved—is unhappy. She was the mother of two glorious sons, the wife of a successful husband, a missionary in London alongside her parents. Hers was a wonderful life.

"I suspect lunch will be here in a moment," Angela said. "If you gentlemen will excuse me, I'd better go and freshen up before it arrives."

Howard and I stood, and then I saw how frail Angela was. I wondered if health issues had brought them back to the States. Howard helped Angela out of her chair, and she walked slowly toward the restrooms.

"Is Angela well?" I asked. It was none of my business, but I let concern get the best of me.

"It's called old age, Jack. She's fine. Years have their way of slowing the pace. You may still be in high gear, but we're downshifting to a lower speed."

Through a small window, I could see into the kitchen. The chef had just placed one of the sauerbraten orders on a high counter, which meant the other wasn't far behind.

"While Angela's away, I want to ask you something that's been on my mind since I first got your message." The question had been on my mind a whole lot longer than that, but until this moment, there'd been no way to ask it.

"Howard, I've been writing a new book—one that's got me looking rather closely at the past. And, well, I'm sorry for some of the things I did long ago. Do you know if Jenny ever forgave me for …" I couldn't find the words.

Howard picked up the discarded paper from his straw and began fidgeting with it, tying it into knots. My stomach could relate.

"You hurt her. There's no way around it, but Murphy healed those wounds, and she's gotten on with her life. She has an incredibly strong relationship with the Lord, so if you're worried if she's got a good life, don't be. She's doing fabulously."

"I'm happy for her," I said. My voice sounded

hoarse, my words coming out like a confession spoken to a priest. Underneath the table my hands were as cold as a cadaver. It was as if I'd pulled a cork to let out the words, and what poured out with them shivered and stirred me.

"It means a great deal to know she's all right. Has she ever said anything about me?" I knew the moment I let out the words, I should have kept them in.

Howard looked up. "About you? That was a long time ago, Jack."

"I've just wondered." *Can I sound any more selfish?*

"I'm sure she's come to terms with your memory. I imagine if she were asked, she would say she hopes you're well. I'm sure she does. I don't think there are any ill feelings anymore."

Angela returned to the table as the waitress delivered lunch. "Just in time!"

"I'll say grace," Howard said.

We asked the Lord for His blessing and began eating.

"Angela, Jack and I were just talking. He was asking if Jenny ever said—"

"Oh, Jack, that reminds me. Jenny thought your book was extraordinary."

I gazed up from my soup bowl. "She did?"

"She doesn't have a lot of time to read, so she bought tapes for the car and listened to them whenever she had an errand to run. I think she'd have wanted you to know how much she loved it."

I did want to know. I hadn't heard a word from her in years. Our last rendezvous had taken place in a restaurant far from Providence.

"She was surprised you'd never married. Always thought you'd wind up with a real looker!" She smiled.

"No, I never married." I blushed. So she *had* thought about me. "Got close once, but the girl was already engaged."

Lunch was over before we knew it. The food was delicious, the company superb. I motioned for the waitress to bring the check.

"Oh no you don't, Jack. This one's on me," Howard said.

"I think you got the last one twenty years ago, Howard. It's my turn."

The waitress dropped the check in the middle of the table, and Howard scooped it up. "Gotcha!"

"This has been a wonderful lunch. I'm happy we got together," Angela placed her hand on mine.

"So you'll be stateside for a while?" I asked.

"We're semiretired," Howard said, counting money from his wallet. "We're planning to buy or build around Indianapolis near the kids."

"Semiretired … That hardly seems possible."

"Time goes by quickly, Jack," Angela said. "Howard and I have been missionaries for forty-five years."

"I guess you could use a break."

"We still hope to be involved in some kind of ministry." Howard dropped bills on the table.

I loved Howard and Angela, even though they didn't know it and probably never would. They'd had a tremendous impact on my life.

"If you need any seed money, just—"

"Jack, we didn't come here for a donation." Howard

helped Angela up from the table. "We just wanted to see you."

"The offer stands should something come up."

I escorted the two of them to their car, a rental parked close to the front door. "You have my number here in Providence. I hope it won't be another twenty years before we see each other again." I threw out my hand. Howard took it.

"It was a pleasure, Jack." Angela leaned toward me. We embraced, and she kissed my cheek. "Take good care of yourself. Be well."

I watched as they pulled away from the curb, stopped for a red light, and turned out of view.

The past, which surfaced for a few moments into the present, had submerged again. I headed back to my hotel, imagining what might have been. Back at the Hyatt, I concentrated on the flowing black ink coming from the tip of the felt pen. The first week of marathon writing had produced nearly sixty pages. A respectable start.

Sparked by my lunch with the Camerons, memories were coming hard and fast. I wrote down whatever came to mind, one thought triggering another. A flash of something important, a small fragment dug from the sands of the subconscious. The memories were like broken pottery from an archaeologist's dig. It was my job to excavate them with care and fit the puzzle back together again.

~ THIRTEEN ~

I hear your name in certain circles,
And it always makes me smile.

—JOHN WAITE
"Missing You"

As our first college term unfolded, Erin quickly became a fixture in Mitchell's life, and my own. I liked Erin, which helped ease any potential tension, since she dominated most of Mitchell's time. I'd adjusted with grace to Mitchell's absence (due to work or class) and to Erin's presence in the apartment most evenings. The two of them wanted ample space to watch TV and to talk. Erin was friendly, a genuinely warm person who possessed many of the same qualities I'd seen in Jenny. Both women were straightforward people who cared about others. They were gracious and giving. They were modest—which only made them more attractive. And … they were smart.

One night while Mitch was busy getting ready for their date, I got a rare chance to talk to Erin alone. I asked about the one topic that had become foremost on my mind.

"What's the latest on Jenny these days?" I asked, opening a Yoo-hoo and leaning against the kitchen door.

"She's good. Busy. Jenny's writing some monster paper that's due at the end of the term, so she's basically moved into the library. She says they ought to have cots in there." Erin laughed. "Last weekend Jenny nodded off in a cubicle, and one of the janitors had to wake her up when the library was closing!"

"Is her paper on the sleep-ability of hard surfaces?"

"That must be it. She's field-testing."

I stepped into the living room and sat on the arm of Mitch's chair, the one where he always sat to do his homework.

"Is she still in the research program?"

"Yeah, that's the other thing. The department's been sending teams into impoverished neighborhoods to canvass and talk with the families. They're working to identify the most significant needs. I think there are about a half dozen students working on the project."

"I'm surprised she's got time for a social life."

"She doesn't. Dan's always asking for more time. He's lucky to get every other Friday."

"Dan? I assume he's her boyfriend?"

"Um … I wouldn't say boyfriend … More like someone she's dating. Dan's a frat guy, very into Providence football."

"A player?"

"Hardly. He and his frat buddies party Friday nights before game day and tailgate on Saturday at the stadium. Then they party even more when we win. It's a guy thing, I guess."

Erin dismissed the activities like they weren't her scene. I wondered if they were Jenny's.

"Dan's invited her to some of the parties, but she hasn't been able to go."

Darn.

Mitch stepped out from the back bedroom, and when he did, Erin's interest in our conversation vanished like a vapor. I thought Erin and I had been having a conversation; in reality, she'd only been waiting for Mitchell.

"You ready, honey?" Erin got up from the sofa with her coat and purse.

Honey? Oh, you've got to be kidding.

"Ready as ever … and Jack, don't wait up for us. We'll be out having a life."

"Mitchell!" Erin chastened him in good humor.

"You do that, Mitch. I'll be here eating your mom's Thanksgiving pie."

A few days later, I heard a polite knock on the apartment door. Thinking it was just one of the guys from upstairs, I put the apple I'd been eating on a bookshelf and opened the door. It wasn't anyone from upstairs, or even the beautiful Jennifer Carswell from across the hall. It was Jenny Cameron. She wore a yellow ski jacket with matching gloves and earmuffs. She looked as cute as … well … as Jenny.

We stood there in the doorway without saying a word. Then the tiniest smile appeared at the corners of her mouth, and she gave a wave with her glove. I couldn't imagine what she might have come by to say—her confession of undying love topping my fantasy list.

"Hi, Jack," she said. "Remember me?"

"I think so. Are you selling cookies?"

Her smile grew. "Not today. I'm here to pick up Erin's book bag. She said she left it here the other day."

Mitch mentioned that Erin had forgotten her book bag, but he'd neglected to say Jenny would be picking it up. I made a mental note to thank him later.

"Sure," I said. "Come on in. Mitchell's out, but I think I can help."

She came in, rubbing her gloved hands together inside the toasty apartment.

"Thanks. This is no time of year to be without study notes."

"I agree," I said, retreating out of sight, looking for the book bag. "What have you been doing since turning twenty?"

"Working mostly. I'm wrapping up a social-science paper and applying for a summer internship."

"Working, as in the sociology department?" I called out from Mitch's desk where Erin's book bag was in plain view on the chair.

"Yes, we're collecting data. It's a lot of research and polling. The team's writing a grant proposal to assist single moms."

I picked up the book bag and flung it over my shoulder. "I remember you mentioned something about that at the party." I walked back into the living room. "How likely is the internship?"

"Well, it's a long shot. It's in New York, which is

very expensive, particularly during the summer. They provide limited housing, so we'll see."

Silence filled the room. We stood several feet apart, both aware the object that had brought Jenny to the apartment was hanging over my shoulder.

She didn't reach for the bag, and I didn't offer it. The occasion for small talk had expired. I could either give her the bag and let her go, or say something.

"I'm fascinated with your work, Jenny. Do you think we could talk about it sometime?"

"There's a lot of material in the sociology building on the second floor." She politely gestured for the bag, and I gave it to her. Shifting its weight onto her shoulder, she said, "Do you know where—"

"I know where the sociology building is. I was more interested in finding out if *we* could spend some time together. To talk about the program, I mean."

I shaped my words into balanced tones, mimicking the verbal patterns Jenny used when she spoke. I'd thought about her ever since the night of the party. Now standing face-to-face with her in my apartment, I needed to find out if she'd thought at all about me—if she'd felt anything that night.

"I'm not sure that's such a good idea." She looked directly at me. "I'm very busy with work and school, and I'm in a semiserious relationship."

Just then the door opened, and Mitchell stepped in, nearly tripping over us with his awful, bad timing. "Oh! Sorry! Didn't mean to interrupt."

"You're not interrupting, Mitchell," Jenny said. "I was just leaving." And with that, Jenny stepped backward out the open door. Her eyes locked on mine.

"Thanks for your help, Jack. Oh, and Mitchell … Erin said you can call her at work after five."

"Right," Mitch pulled off his coat, oblivious to the strange tension that floated in the air.

Jenny glanced back at me. "Thanks," she said before disappearing down the stairs.

I shut the door and turned to Mitch. "Are you completely stupid?" I asked.

"What did I do? What are you so ticked about?"

"I'm ticked about …" My voice rose. I pulled the apple off the bookshelf. It had turned brown and dark. "That was Jenny, you may have noticed."

"Yeah, I see her ten times a week."

"Well, I *don't* see her ten times a week." I pointed the brown apple toward the door. "But I sure would like to. And you just interrupted the first conversation we've had in a month."

The more time passed, the more silly it was to still have feelings about a girl I barely knew. "I don't know if you've picked up on any of this, but she's … she's … " I stumbled.

"Jack!" I heard Mitchell laugh. He had the expression he wore when he thought I was being a moron. "It's all right to like somebody."

I rolled my eyes, sneering and mouthing his words with silent sarcasm. I grunted, grabbed my coat, and stormed out. When I got to the bottom of the stairs, I saw a familiar yellow coat. *Jenny*. I slowed my gait.

"Our meetings always seem to come in pairs," I said.

"So it seems. I was coming back up to see you." Jenny stepped closer. A fragile snow tumbled from the silent heavens. "I know I've said something like this before, but I think I keep coming off as abrupt and impolite, which I don't mean to do, and I want to apologize."

"I'll let you make it up to me," I said.

"I seem to always run into you when I'm involved or in a hurry. The worst times. I wanted to say I'm sorry if I seem aloof or unfriendly."

"I don't know you well," I said, "but I've already decided that aloof and unfriendly from you is better than friendly and warm from anyone else."

She looked genuinely flattered. "You're sweet," she said, still giving cues that she wasn't interested. One doesn't have to understand love to understand rejection.

"Why won't you go out with me?" I asked, opting for the direct approach.

"It's true this is a busy time of life," she said, her words soft and measured. "And I *have* been seeing someone, although I think that's probably not the case anymore. But the reason I won't go out with you is …" She paused. Delicate specks of snow fell onto her hair. "I'm sorry … This really isn't the best time or place to have this conversation."

"And when might that time be?" I asked.

"Are you free tonight to come by Lillian Hall? If you can't make it, I'll understand. It's just I'm in a rush now, and all the words I'd like to use aren't lining up like I want them to. If you could come by tonight, that would give me time to collect my thoughts."

"I can be free tonight," I said.

Large, heavy snowflakes landed on her eyelashes and melted on her cheeks. She nodded.

"Good. I need to get back on my way, but I'll see you tonight. All right?"

"All right."

I watched her walk up Burrows Avenue, yellow parka fading into the white-dotted blizzard.

"Jenny," I yelled when she reached the corner,

She turned around to look back.

"Don't get too tired of apologizing. These have been the best conversations."

She smiled and waved, her light piercing through the muddle of the snowstorm. I wondered what it would be like to kiss her.

~ FOURTEEN ~

I am the eye in the sky
Looking at you
I can read your mind.

—ALAN PARSONS PROJECT
"Eye in the Sky"

I rode the hotel elevator down from the seventh floor and stepped into the grand lobby, looking particularly sharp in my new tailored clothing. On Friday night the atrium had reverberated with the sounds of conference attendees and their business associates mingling in the cocktail lounge. On Saturday evening one lone attendant stood behind the desk, happily engaged in a phone conversation with someone whom I presumed was his girlfriend. Except for some Muzak version of a Kool and the Gang song dripping through hidden speakers, the lobby was dead quiet.

Outside I asked the doorman to hail a cab for me. He blew once on his whistle, and the only taxi at the stand switched on its low beams and rolled toward us.

"Where to?" the doorman asked.

"I'm not sure. Dinner somewhere," I said and climbed into the backseat of the taxi.

"You like Italian?"

"Love it."

The doorman spoke to the taxi driver "Take this gentleman to Antonio's." He tapped twice on the roof of the cab, and we were off.

A few minutes later the taxi pulled up in front of a small Italian restaurant—the only establishment open on the block. "Antonio's" was written in green neon script above a large plate-glass window. I paid the cab driver and went inside.

The restaurant was smoky and loud. It was packed with patrons, but not the college crowd I was most familiar with. The ceiling was low, multiplying the noise, making twenty tables sound like forty. It was like walking inside radio static.

Waiters in white shirts hustled from kitchen to dining room, delivering food like obedient drones. A skinny, vacant-faced man of about thirty-five peered through the kitchen's double doors and called out to me.

"How many?"

"One."

His eyes ran the length of the room looking for an open spot. He flagged down a striking black-haired woman holding a full bar tray.

"Vivian, you got a table for one?"

She shook her head like he had to be joking.

Then he called back to me, "'Bout twenty minutes. Have a seat at the bar."

I nodded my head the way you're supposed to when accepting orders. The deadpan man disappeared back through the kitchen doors, and I took a seat on a red swivel barstool. I ordered a glass of red wine, though I'm not much of a drinker. Well, I'd be no drinker at all except that I was trying to abide by my doctor's recommendation of a glass of red wine now and then. He said it would do me good. This would be my fourth glass in about six months.

I looked at the other men and women at the bar and wondered how long it'd been since I'd sat in a place like this. The unavoidable smoke, the free-flowing alcohol and equally free-flowing conversation. I looked to see if I knew anyone but didn't recognize a face.

Most of the guys at the bar were engrossed in the Providence football game on the small color TV mounted high behind the bar. We were ahead by ten points against Ohio. I learned early on in Providence that we're required to hate Ohio. At least when it comes to sports.

Conversation tumbled out with ease among the TV watchers. "Do not fumble! Two minutes on the clock. If they don't give up a touchdown here, it's the best second half we've played."

Derek Smith, a Providence student who had volunteered in Norwood, was the Badger's starting tight end. With two minutes on the clock, Derek caught a missile off the arm of quarterback Amos Bantley at the thirty and sliced through three defenders into the end zone. It was poetry.

"YES! YES! YES!" Antonio's was suddenly transformed into a sports bar filled with the sounds of boys being boys. Diners who hadn't been paying attention to the game looked over at the TV.

"Hey, turn up the sound. Turn up the sound!"

The bartender lifted the remote and boosted the sound of raucous cheers from Providence stadium, not five miles east of us. After a long kickoff and a strong defensive stand, we took possession and skillfully ran out the clock. The Badgers left the field victors, 27–10.

The screen went to a commercial, and the sound was muted. Those of us at the bar began our analysis of the brilliance we'd just witnessed. Joe, the man farthest away from me, got a funny cockeyed look on his face.

"Hey . . . " he said, pointing his finger in my direction. "Hey, aren't you the guy who wrote that book?"

Suddenly I felt like an outsider. I was glad he didn't say "the guy from *Time* magazine."

"Depends on which book you're talking about."

Joe smiled. "You know the one I'm talking about . . . The book about poor people here in Providence? The one that sold all those copies, number one and all that?"

"Laborers of the Orchard."

"Yeeeeeah! I thought it was you." Joe said, "You're on the cover of *Time* magazine!"

I nodded, not sure what to say. I hoped Joe's excitement would fade quickly, taking the sound of his voice with it. I wished the bartender could mute Joe like he'd muted the TV. But Joe spun his chair to the nine-o'clock position and stared straight at me. "What are you doing down here?"

"Just getting a bite to eat," I said, trying to make it

sound as normal as it was. Joe spun his chair around the other way and yelled back to the kitchen.

"Hey, Antonio! Lookie here."

Antonio stepped out of the kitchen to see what was causing the commotion.

"It's that writer guy! The one that sold all them books!" Joe turned back to me. "Hey, what's your name?"

Antonio looked at me. The waitress looked at me. Everyone in the now-quiet room looked at me.

"Jack Clayton," I said to him in a near whisper, pretending ours was still a private conversation. "You can call me Jack."

"Jack Clayton!" he shouted, his volume doubled by the drinks he'd already consumed. "You are awesome, man! What you did for those people! Hey, and don't worry about the wine, okay, pastor? Nobody's gonna say nothing."

"I'm not a pastor, Joe, and it's okay for me to have a glass of wine."

The buzz in the restaurant ground to a halt, the brake cord pulled by one of its patrons. The dark-haired man with the mustache turned out to be *an* Antonio, but not *the* Antonio. Just then, *the* Antonio stood up from his table in the back and spoke to me from across the room.

"Are you Jack Clayton?" The beefy sixty-year-old man asked, closing the last of the open mouths in the room, including Joe's.

"Yes," I said from my seat at the bar.

Big Antonio pointed his index finger at me, then dotted it around the room. "Anything you want tonight," he said with authority, "is on the house. Whatever you want." Then to the other Antonio, "You take care of him."

The silent, serious-faced Antonio gave the owner an exaggerated nod of compliance and snapped his fingers at a busboy now speeding up the clearing of an open table.

"Yeah!" Joe shouted, tossing his fist in the air the same way he'd done when Derek Smith had scored that touchdown. A few other customers cheered from their booths. These people wanted to celebrate. Antonio continued talking.

"What's brings you down here by yourself tonight?"

"Someone wanted me to have the best Italian food in the city, so he sent me here."

With that, the room exploded in applause, patrons celebrating not only the good food but also that they were at the right place at the right time.

Antonio smiled, pleased with my answer. He raised his hands, soaking in the applause, a confirmation of what he'd been telling his customers for years.

Before the clapping died down, Antonio walked around the curve of the bar to shake my hand. I stood. He placed his hand on my shoulder and turned us to face the diners, addressing the room like the village mayor speaking to his townspeople.

"For those of you who don't know who this guy is, this is Jack Clayton, the man who wrote the best-selling book to come out of Providence, ever." The restaurant hollered again.

"His book, my wife, Louise, bought for me, and I read it, loved it, recommend it." He looked at me. "Not that you need any more sales, right, Jack?"

Laughter erupted, and I looked across the room at the welcoming crowd, then laughed just a little bit myself. By the time Antonio pulled me from my seat, each heartbeat brought with it a flashbulb explosion of white. I heard low humming in my ears and could feel perspiration rolling past my collar.

One hundred eyes looked up at me, smiling. I concentrated on breathing—and prayed he wouldn't ask me to speak.

"Why don't you say something to the people 'cause I know they'd love to hear you speak."

Antonio and I stood together in the center of the dining room, his arm wrapped over my shoulder like I was his son. The first thing to pop into my head was "Like what?" Thankfully I stifled that inane response. I looked into the faces, surprised to see something I couldn't have predicted: These people seemed happy for the interruption. The room blurred and slowed in the racket of applause. I sensed God's presence in the room. I silently reframed their cheering—it wasn't for me, it was for what God had done in their town. It was for the expression of sacrifice and the infusion of hope. I prayed for words—wisdom and words.

"I'm sure you all came here tonight hoping an author would stand up and give a speech." This got a laugh. "I want to thank Antonio for his warm hospitality and his gracious introduction." I'd spoken at enough fund-raisers and faculty and alumni dinners to know the importance of thanking everyone for attending. But that was all I had. There was nothing but a flash of prayer, and I opened my mouth to speak.

"I've had … a pretty amazing couple of years. I can't

begin to tell you what it means having so many people read a book and care about the things you really care about. A lot of folks here in Providence got to have their stories told, and you know how much it means when someone listens. I'm not a pastor; I'm just a regular guy, your neighbor, someone who happens to live in Providence. I work at the college each day teaching students to remember those in need."

I had started to ramble, but I knew where I was going. I read it on their faces. They weren't excited because an author stood before them. They were excited that someone who knew God would step into their smoky world and watch a football game with them on their TV. They didn't want to hear from me. They wanted to hear from God. I spoke the words God gave me as if they had been written out on a teleprompter.

"Everyone wants to know if there's a God. They want to know if He loves them. I'm here tonight to tell you He lives, and that He died for all. And that He wants you to come home, to Him."

I paused, waiting to see if there was more, but no more came. "Thanks, thanks for listening."

I turned to go back to the bar, but Antonio grabbed my arm and escorted me to his personal table. The silence and reverence of the moment reverted to normal conversation, and Antonio sat down with me. He gave my order to the waiter.

"Jake, San Marino, portobello mushrooms … and bring another glass of wine."

Jake was gone in an instant, and Antonio fixed his friendly, day-worn eyes on me.

"Mr. Clayton, it's wonderful having you here, and while you're here, I want you to enjoy yourself. I'll keep people from bothering you."

"They won't bother me."

"No, no, let you eat your dinner in peace."

"You're very kind, Antonio."

He leaned back in his seat and smiled like a proud father. "This means a lot to me that you'd come down here. I want you to know that."

"You've got a great place here."

"I want to tell you … Your book, it did something for me." He pointed up toward the bar. "You see that picture over there behind the bar?"

I turned to look. High on the back wall was an eight-by-ten color photograph of a Little League baseball team in blue jerseys and white pants. All the players on the team were black. Antonio and two other men stood behind them.

"That's a team up in Indianapolis called the Blue Jays. We sponsor the team … You know, pay for their uniforms, equipment expenses. At the end of each season, win or lose, we invite all the players and their families into Antonio's to have a pizza party."

"I'm sure they love it."

"How could they not; it's Antonio's?" He grinned. Then he got quiet and leaned into the table, extending his arm across the white tablecloth. "Your book, Mr. Clayton, made me see the boys up there differently. Those boys …"—Antonio pointed up at the photo—"they formed that baseball team at the Boys Club."

"That's a good thing you're doing."

Antonio leaned in closer and spoke softly, so softly I

had to read his lips through the noise of the restaurant. "Mr. Clayton, I don't like black people."

He waited for my reaction, but I didn't give him any.

"I'm sixty-two years old, and I've never liked black people. But you know … those boys come from broken homes … *I* come from a broken home. I saw myself in that book of yours, Mr. Clayton. And then I saw these kids and realized they needed some help. That's when we started sponsoring teams. We got three up there now. Do you think you could help us start something like that here?"

"I'd love to."

After dinner I thanked Antonio and left what I thought was a reasonable tip, considering they'd fed me the best meal in the house for free. Another taxi took me back to the hotel.

Back in my suite, I took off my jacket and hung it carefully on a wooden hanger. I relaxed into a soft leather chair and grabbed the yellow legal pad to jot down the thought fragments that had come to me during the taxi ride. The pages were starting to pile up.

I knew as I wrote that this was going to be my last book. After writing it I would leave the literary world to real writers. If *Laborers* was the hit song, this would be my encore. The last installment in my brief four-book career.

As I sat there, I realized that remembering Jenny,

Mitch, and Erin—the way we all were then—was worth the trip. It was worth the tears when the memories appeared thick and powerful. I would write this book to remember—and for all the other young, untested college students who would walk alongside the four of us as we were then, forever young, filled with dreams and innocence and love.

Writing in longhand this weekend had made the story more intimate, like the letters I used to write to Jenny.

I shut off a multitude of lights and climbed into bed. The sheets were crisp and fresh. I clicked off the bedside lamp and rolled over to face the Providence moon shining brightly through my window. A thought occurred to me, a daydream that had me wishing the book could be finished by morning: I would check out in my new clothes, drop the manuscript in an anonymous FedEx box, then disappear forever.

~ Fifteen ~

And when we hear the voices sing
The book of love will open up and let us in.

—Mr. Mister
"Broken Wings"

It was a conversation, not a date. I knew that. Still, I showered and carefully groomed myself in the bathroom mirror, glad I'd washed my best pair of khakis. I borrowed a striped maize and blue polo from Mitchell's closet, sprinkled on Drakkar Cologne, and set out on foot for my third visit to Lillian Hall. This time would be different. I was going because Jenny Cameron asked me. I wondered why she wanted to talk with me. A few possibilities crossed my mind: I'd said something that offended her; or she was involved with someone else and didn't want to hurt my feelings; or I was a freshman, and she was only a year and a half from graduation, and spending any time with me now would undoubtedly lead to heartbreak in … a year and a half.

The reason didn't matter. I was elated at the thought of spending time with her. But still … whatever she had to say must be important. Anything inconsequential she could have told me on the street.

"Your name?" The brown-haired student covering the reception desk barely looked at me.

"Jack Clayton."

"Go ahead and sign in."

I scribbled my name on a clipboard while she dialed Jenny's room.

"Jenny, there's someone here for you."

"Be right there."

No sooner had I finished giving back the pen, Jenny was in the room with us. Her chestnut hair was pulled back in a black band, and she wore a simple gold cross, visible above the top button of her white blouse.

"Hi, there," she said, as if we did this sort of thing all the time. "Wanna come up?"

She took the two of us to a small recreation room on the second floor. It was little more than a couple of stuffed reading chairs, a fake-leather couch and TV, and a coffee table covered with magazines like *Seventeen* and *People*. The room was empty, but I doubted it would stay empty for long.

I took a seat on the faux-leather sofa. Jenny sat in one of the chairs. She wasted no time getting down to business.

"Jack, I've been thinking about what it is I want to say to you. And I haven't got it exactly right, but I think it's important I just come right out and say it."

In time I would learn this was trademark verbal cadence for Jenny. Her careful selection of words was like a chef selecting the finest ingredients, then measuring them in the right amounts before combining them into a gourmet feast.

"This afternoon you asked if we could spend some time together, and I said no. You wanted to know why, and I think you have every right … but …" Jenny paused for a moment, then continued. "Here's the tricky part to put into words," she said, clasping her hands together, entwining her fingers. "The part I wasn't prepared to tell you this afternoon, and the reason I said no to you is … I've found myself thinking about you since the night of the party." She stopped speaking to see how much of this I was getting.

"I've been thinking about you quite a lot … which isn't a bad thing, unless of course you're dating another man, supposed to be focusing your attention on an important paper, applying for an internship, and investing yourself completely in work you believe in. Then it's not so good. Do you see what I mean?"

"I see … Do you want to go on, or should I say something?"

"Actually, I'd like to go on. You can say something in a minute."

I kept a straight face, but just barely. As she spoke, a candle was lit inside me.

"Even though that's not so good, having you in my mind, I haven't been able to *stop* having you be there." She wrapped up in an awkward finish and sat silent, eyebrows arched, waiting for my reaction.

"Well, if you're saying this to get me off your mind, then I must warn you, your plan may backfire." I smiled at her.

Jenny smiled too, and I saw how beautiful she looked when happy, when everything was right. We sat there long enough to process what had been said, not the long-term implications, but the substance.

"Where are my manners? Do you want something to drink? Coke, tea, water?"

"Coke, water, sure, whatever."

Two girls entered the room talking. They stopped abruptly when they saw us. One asked if it would be all right if they watched TV, and it dawned on me how difficult it would be finding privacy in a house like this.

"That's fine," Jenny told them. She motioned for me to follow, and we exited down the back stairs that led to the kitchen. We made hot chocolate with water from the coffee tap and took it back upstairs to the rec room.

The room was filled with girls congregating around the TV to watch *Moonlighting*. We all sat around on the floor and laughed together. That's when I learned how watching TV in a group could be an absolute blast. The girls ogled David Addison, and Jenny and I drank our hot chocolate. Sometimes we made eye contact, our first private language. When the show ended, the room emptied as quickly as it had filled. By then it seemed late, the way long days get heavy around 10:00 p.m.

"This was a nice way to end the day," Jenny said, standing and then leaning against the doorframe in a sleepy, languid pose.

I stepped close enough to touch both of her hands. My heart was thumping so loudly inside my chest, I thought my teeth might begin to click.

"Better than nice," I said. "Thanks for the invitation."

Jenny softened, and I moved my hand to touch her face and pull her mouth close to mine. Her arms wrapped around my waist, and she met me with her kiss. I was immediately drawn into her, into a deep, rich, secret place behind her eyes. A bond was being formed that felt infinite and mighty. Our lips pressed together and formed a new world, a place of comfort and familiarity … and possibility.

I opened my eyes. Jenny had been sleepy before, soft and lithesome, but now her green eyes looked fully alert.

"I've wanted to kiss you since the moment I saw you," I whispered, her hands in mine. "You're the most beautiful woman I've ever seen," I went on, saying too much, going too fast.

I let my words trail off, letting go of her hands before she had a chance to respond. I turned to retrieve my coat still hanging on the back of a chair. I felt as if I'd been hit with a stun gun. Was this what Mitch and Erin felt when they were together?

I put on my coat, hoping that when I turned around, Jenny would have slipped away into the hallway. But her eyes still stared at me with the same unblinking tenderness.

"I didn't anticipate this happening tonight," she said in a voice of calm surrender.

"I didn't anticipate this could even exist," I said. Every word I said seemed bigger than life. But I didn't want to say too much. I didn't want to ruin what words couldn't define. I moved closer to her. We were somehow alone again in the busy dorm.

"I need to get going," I said, moving past Jenny in the doorway, cautious of more contact.

She placed her hand on my shoulder. "Jack, I don't know what's happened here tonight," her voice a mere whisper, "but it was … I'm not even sure what word to use. Let's not leave this like before, not knowing when we'll see each other again."

"I'm going to go home," I said, toppled by new emotions. "We can talk tomorrow."

I took one step, and her hand slipped off my shoulder. As it slid gently down my arm, a chill went up my spine. I heard a profound message in her touch. A message too big for words.

"I've found you."

~ Sixteen ~

When I was young I thought of growing old
Of what my life would mean to me
Would I have followed down my chosen road
Or only wished what I could be?

—Mr. Mister
"Kyrie"

The hotel phone rang early on Sunday morning. I answered and was whiplashed from a deep state of unconsciousness by a shrill voice on the other end. It belonged to Arthur Reed.

"Jack, what on earth are you doing at the Hyatt?" He sounded like an irate parent whose kid has stayed out too late.

I wondered how Arthur had known where to find me. If I'd been more alert, I would have figured out that he'd called Peter, who, thanks to caller ID, would have known where I was all along.

"Why are you calling me, Arthur?" The digital clock on the nightstand read 7:34.

"I've been calling all over creation trying to track you down. Have you seen this morning's paper?" His voice blistered.

"No. I've been sleeping, Arthur. What's going on? Has someone died?"

"Just your reputation. Do you know a journalist named Bud Abbott?"

I pulled away the sheets and blanket and sat upright on the edge of the bed, rubbing my burning eyes. "He called on Friday and asked me some questions about a story he was going to write."

"Yeah, well, he's written his story. Do you have today's paper?"

"What? What are you saying?" I tossed on the hotel robe and shuffled to the door, remembering the complimentary *Indy Star* that had been left outside the morning before. There it was, the Sunday-morning edition. I picked it up, walked back into the room, opened the sections, and let them fall across the glass dining table.

"Check the Lifestyle section, Jack."

Bud's story wasn't page one, but I didn't have to look very far. Next to a piece on Hollywood actors performing Christmas charity work in Los Angeles ran this story:

> *RECLUSIVE AUTHOR FOR THE POOR LIVES IN GRANDEUR —Bud Abbott,* Chicago Tribune
>
> *Providence, IN—This Christmas, as the homeless in America struggle to keep warm during one of the coldest winters on record, Jack Clayton,* Time

magazine's PERSON OF THE YEAR *and author of the mega-best seller* Laborers of the Orchard, *stays in luxury hotel rooms, wears tailormade suits, and employs a private maid. The extravagant lifestyle of this self-described "advocate for the poor" is well beyond the means of average Americans, let alone the poor.*

Laborers *has sold in excess of 18 million copies in the United States. The book details the work of the Campus Missions Office in Providence's poorer neighborhoods and has become an international sensation, earning Clayton an estimated 20 million dollars in royalties.*

Now high-lifestyle questions are being raised about Clayton's fortunes and his possible misuse of moneys earned from the poor he purports to serve. The reclusive Clayton, forty, has never granted an interview about his work or his finances. Other questions journalists are eager to ask Clayton stem from several run-ins with the law, including two mysterious shootings, one in Chicago and another near Clovis, New Mexico. These questions, like the repeated phone calls to his office, go unanswered.

"Can you believe it?" Arthur fumed. "He's twisted everything. If I wasn't concerned about creating more bad press, I'd sue."

There was indignation in Arthur's voice, but he didn't ask me for an explanation or a denial. Wasn't he wondering about the accusations? Didn't he want to know if any of the statements were true?

Two shootings …

"People don't believe everything they read."

"Jack, wake up. Your reputation has just been assassinated. Do you understand that? Not to mention your good standing. Someone has done this to you. Something has to be done. The college will suffer, the program will suffer, and you've got to be thinking about your memoir!" Arthur was as mad as a hornet's nest swatted by a Chicago newspaper.

"I'm sure it will die down soon. How far can this go, anyway?"

"How far can this thing go? Think California wildfire during a long summer drought. The story's already running all over the wire services this morning, the same week your face is on the cover of *Time*. Papers will absolutely run it, and by this time tomorrow, you'll be all over the TV, too."

I stood over the table rereading the story that opened my life like a can of sardines. Why was this happening? Bud Abbott was wrong about my commitment to Norwood and my normally spartan lifestyle. Surely everyone would understand this.

"We'll have to do a press conference. You'll need to be there, Jack. We can't let this stand. We'll take every accusation this hit-and-run jockey has made and stick them back down his throat."

"I'm not doing a press conference."

"I don't see any other way around it."

"One story isn't enough to make me dash for the nearest microphone to start defending myself."

"Jack, you don't have a clue how juicy this stuff is. It's blood in the water to sharks. This is just the lightning before the storm. The thunder won't even get here until tomorrow. If they find out more, Jack, your name will be in the paper for weeks, months."

I wanted to pack Mr. Duroth's hand-tailored suits and flee the scene of the crime. In my old life, I'd still be sleeping. The old Brookstone alarm wasn't set to ring for another hour. But fame had found me. Hiding from conspicuousness only inflated voyeuristic interest. As much as I had enjoyed the taste of the good life in my hotel room, I preferred the simple life. Waking up to brew a pot of coffee. Drinking orange juice straight from the carton dressed only in my pajamas. Looking forward to the connection I'd feel at church with God and people. These were the things I cared about. There was never anything scheduled on Sunday. Just plans to heat up a chicken dinner left by Mrs. Hernandez and watch football. I wanted that life back but knew instinctively that was going to be difficult if not impossible to find in light of Bud Abbott's little story.

"It's almost eight o'clock," I told Arthur. "I'm going to church. We can continue this conversation later this afternoon, or tonight if needed."

"If needed? You have to skip church and get up here to Indy as quickly as possible for some serious strategizing. We have more work to hack through today than we have time to hew."

I closed my eyes, overwrought with the immensity

of this developing circumstance. It was one thing having my name scandalized in the paper, but I could see visions of the fallout. The effect it could have on the college, the program, the people in Norwood. An enemy was attempting to pull me off course. I blew out my breath and fought the first small battle, the one for my will.

"No," I said. "I'll call you after church."

"Jack, listen—"

I said good-bye to Arthur and hung up the phone. He was out of control … So was Bud Abbott. Arthur's motivation was the preservation of his income stream—my next book. But what had provoked Bud Abbott?

I showered and dressed in a flurry, folding the clothes Mr. Duroth had given to me and placing them in a plastic bag, the only makeshift luggage I could find. Within fifteen minutes I was putting on my sunglasses and walking toward the elevators, my oasis of relaxation over. I'd miss being so high above the noise I couldn't hear the questions, but not those coming from the poor. It was the questions from the media I wanted to escape.

I rode the elevator down seven stories alone, anxious to get to church, where I could experience God's presence washing over me like cool river water over smooth stones.

When the elevator doors opened, two local news crews ambushed me with shoulder-mounted video cameras and blinding lights. A mob of television reporters rushed toward me.

"Mr. Clayton, is it true you're living here at the Providence Hyatt? Are you thinking of buying it?"

"Mr. Clayton, how do you respond to allegations that you're taking advantage of the poor here in Providence?"

"Mr. Clayton, is it true you've been recently fired from your job?"

I cut a path through the center of the crowd, and predictably they followed me step by step into the parking garage. I was never happier in my life to not own a Cadillac. My 2000 Jeep with the broken side mirror and missing radio was parked near the door, and I climbed up into it. I started the engine and backed out, causing the cluster of reporters to break into smaller scurrying groups.

I entered back into the shelterless *real* world through news vans plastered with photos of their smiling six o'clock news teams. I turned the Jeep up Ames Road, glancing in the rearview mirror to see if I was being followed. I chose not to drive home, expecting to find more reporters there. Peter's house was four miles out of town. I hoped he was still home.

I pulled around back and cut the engine. Through the kitchen window, I could see Peter looking out at me, amusement on his face. I failed to see the humor. The past week had been a long walk down the sterile corridors of the Green Mile for me. Peter saw it differently, as though these were merely the steps Jesus *wanted* me to take.

"You know, for a guy who doesn't like attention, you sure attract a lot of it." Peter met me at the back door.

"This is no time for jokes, Peter. First the book, then Arthur's deceptions, then a phone call from this reporter in Chicago. And this morning I was ambushed by reporters. I can't think of one thing in all this that is in the least bit funny."

"I'm not laughing at you. This morning you have my sympathy. How about some coffee?"

"What time is it? Are you going to church?"

"Relax, there's plenty of time. Sit down, chill."

Peter lifted a coffee mug from a peg and poured coffee into it.

I let out a long breath. "If Arthur's right about scandals spreading like wildfire," I said, "it's doubly true when it comes to religious figures. They're even more combustible."

"That's probably true, but why don't you stop worrying about it?" Peter handed me the coffee and sat at the table.

"It doesn't matter how far-fetched these accusations are," I said. "What if they torpedo the program? The people in Norwood could lose their trust. That would be tragic."

"Don't let a few flies buzzing around your head give you grief. When people do good, other people always want to spoil it. You know better than anyone how many obstacles we faced in Norwood. Then there was the flack that came out with the book, and the reporters, the break-in. You're starting something new, something good, so more static is being thrown at you."

"Is that what you think this is?" I asked. "Spiritual warfare?"

"Does it matter? Spiritual attack, the thoughtlessness of people. Maybe it's just envy, and when someone's balloon gets too big, someone comes along with a pin.

Anyway, your response shouldn't be any different. Pray, then move forward. Don't let barking dogs spook you."

"I was bitten by a dog once."

"Bite 'em back. I'd hate to see this annoyance interfere with your spa schedule at the Hyatt," he teased.

"Very funny. I'd only gone there to write, Peter. Because it was snowing, because I had the blues. You're the one who told me to take a vacation. How am I getting busted over this?"

"Jack, deep breaths. It's too early to dig into the really deep questions. Let's try a simpler one: Are you coming to church?"

"Only if I don't disrupt the service and cause a scene."

"That's the spirit. You're certainly dressed for it."

Peter drove, and I rode shotgun, the same way I'd always done with Mitchell. The sun was hot, and it warmed the back of my neck as I prayed quietly that there'd be no camera crews lying in wait outside the church. Thankfully, except for a few extra smiles and waves of support as Peter and I made our way to our usual seats, it was as if the story hadn't been written.

It was an inspiring service. We worshipped Christ in the music, and Pastor Lawrence's message on perseverance was timely. This was an hour of focus solely on God, and His peace, "which passeth all understanding," entered my soul. I counted every blessing on every face, every stranger and friend sitting around me.

After the service we waited until all the other worshippers had departed. A few stopped to share words of encouragement.

"What's your plan?" Peter asked, bringing back the reality of the outside world.

"I don't know. I'm not ready to go back and face the surreal life yet. I need to get to my place, but I have a nagging suspicion I won't be alone there."

"You can't run from this."

"Not going to." I rose to my feet, gazing up at the cedar-hewn ceiling forty feet above us. Sunlight beamed through the high windows. Specks of dust reflected light as they floated through the beams. "I'll need to speak with Aaron, see what the college needs from me. Arthur mentioned writing a statement of some kind."

Pastor Lawrence walked toward us down the long center aisle. His strides were quick and powerful, his white robe swinging. "Good morning, Jack … Peter."

"Morning," we each said.

I held my breath, hoping Pastor Lawrence had faith in me, that I wasn't a fraud. His initial trust had been influential in opening up Norwood to our ministry.

"Jack, I read the article. I wanted to let you know I'm here if you need a statement from me."

"A statement?"

"Yes, a statement. I assume you're going to fight this. Someone has taken your good name and smeared it. If I were you, I'd go get it back. If you need me to write something down for you, I will. As your pastor, someone who's walked with you all these years, and as someone who's familiar with the Norwood community, I believe in you."

Pastor Lawrence's sermon had renewed me. Now his words gave me the confidence to go to battle.

His confidence in me loomed like a battalion of reinforcements.

“Thank you, Pastor.”

“You call me when you need to, Jack.”

Pastor Lawrence walked back toward the pulpit. He was strong and muscular, the strength of his spirit manifested in his physique. Once a poor black kid from Alabama who had sweated on a football field until he'd earned a scholarship to play at Auburn, he'd worked his way through seminary and had become the senior pastor at one of Providence's largest white churches. Pastor Lawrence knew about adversity, and he knew how to stand up and fight.

And so did I.

~ Seventeen ~

Why don't they
Do what they say, say what they mean?

—The Fixx
"One Thing Leads to Another"

Twenty minutes later I pulled into my drive. An unfamiliar white Chevy Blazer with black tinted windows was parked half a block up the street. Otherwise, all was quiet. Upstairs the message machine was flashing the number 46 in red. A lot of messages for a single guy with an unlisted number.

I hung my new sports coat in the upstairs closet and went down to the kitchen to make a sandwich. Somewhere between the top of the stairs and the first-floor landing a strange thought struck me. It was so bizarre that somehow I knew it had to be true. I grabbed the remote and switched on CNN. There I was emerging from my residence at the Hyatt, dressed in a new tailor-made suit and wearing five-dollar sunglasses. The shades gave me the detached look of a Hollywood actor avoiding the paparazzi. Conspicuously missing was video of me peeling away in my crappy $5,000 Jeep. I turned up the volume to hear the reporter retelling the basic newspaper story, only with a new sinister twist:

> *Little is known about Clayton, who burst onto the best-seller list three years ago. His book* Laborers of the Orchard *became one of the best-selling nonfiction books of all time. He has vigorously avoided news reporters and ducked interviews for years, leading many in the media to speculate about what he might be hiding.*

Hiding. They say I'm hiding. I muted the sound. The phone rang. I saw from caller ID it was Arthur.

"Good, you're finally home. What are you doing?" He didn't give me time to answer. "We've got to get a handle on this, Jack. The Bud Abbott piece is already on television."

"Yes, I know. I've seen it."

"So has everyone else in the United States and probably the world. It's the hot chat topic of the day. By tomorrow night all the cable networks will carve space for it in their prime-time shows. This is *not* good for what we're trying to do with the new book."

I wished Arthur would have said it wasn't good for CMO, or for the college, or the Norwood program, or even for my reputation. I wished it weren't so blatantly obvious what Arthur cared most about.

"I thought any publicity was good publicity."

"After the book's in stores maybe, but not at this stage. We'll have buyers canceling orders come Tuesday morning. Shoppers won't reserve their advance copies. Bad press will turn people against you, Jack, and they'll probably question the reliability of anything you write."

I pictured cracks fracturing the walls of a dam; a trickle of water running out from the crevices, concrete being snapped off little by little until the current became a flood. My wall of privacy was coming down around me.

"Jack, I've got a plan to repair this, but I'll need your full cooperation."

"I agree we need to issue some kind of a response."

"Well, good," Arthur said, surprised by an agreement coming without a lot of arm wrestling. "It's about time. We're going to need a team effort here to beat this thing."

The white Chevy rolled to a silent stop in front of my house. The tinted driver's side window scrolled down and a long, black telescopic barrel emerged, pointed directly at me.

"You won't believe this, but I'm being photographed by paparazzi."

"Get away from the window." I stepped out of the view from the camera lens and watched the Blazer roll slowly around the corner and up the hill, parking on a side street.

"Are they gone?"

"For the moment."

Across the bottom of TV I saw my name crawl

by in the news ticker: AUTHOR TO THE POOR DUCKS QUESTIONS ABOUT LIVING LARGE • *LABORERS OF THE ORCHARD* AUTHOR JACK CLAYTON REFUSES TO ANSWER QUESTIONS ABOUT FINANCES, EXTRAVAGANT LIFESTYLE

"This just underscores the urgency we need to address this scandal."

Scandal. I was involved in a scandal. Arthur was right. This story needed to be stopped.

"Right now your story has more questions than answers. Reporters are going to dig things up, unless we give them their answers first."

"Why haven't you asked me about the details in the story?" I asked. I wandered the house, looking out windows for other unmarked vehicles.

"Because I don't care. My job is to publish your books, and to protect my investment. I'm your defense attorney in this respect. Your guilt or innocence doesn't change my job one iota. The only thing that matters to me is clearing your name and getting things back to where they should be."

"It matters to me that we protect the program, and the college, and my reputation—in that order. I'm willing to make some kind of statement, or a press release. Write whatever you like, but I'll need to see it first."

"I think it's going to require a lot more than that, Jack."

"What do you suggest?"

"A press release, a televised press conference, TV appearances, talk shows—the works. We've got to get your face out there. I know a PR firm up here in Indianapolis—McKinney & Company. Susan

McKinney runs it. She's fabulous. I've already been in contact with her, and she's agreed to work with us. Her specialty is restoring clients with … tarnished reputations."

"Is that what I have, a tarnished reputation? It's more like they've got the facts wrong." This was spinning well out of my control.

"Yes, they've got the facts wrong, but putting them all back in the right place takes more than a press release. You might find this hard to believe, Jack, but people lie all the time in press statements. The public isn't swayed by them. That's why we need to bring Susan on board. She'll have more than a few good ideas."

"When can we meet?"

"Today. And Jack, listen to Susan's advice. She knows what she's doing. A lot of innocent people will be unnecessarily hurt if we don't do something now."

We made plans to meet at my house at four.

Susan McKinney introduced herself by presenting a list of clients she'd worked with: professional athletes whose public ordeals had soured their reputations and corporate CEO's who wanted to "freshen up" their public personas. She'd even worked with the governor's office.

"Jack, Arthur filled me in on your situation. I spent some time this morning researching news sites and downloading what's running in papers around the country. I've also seen what's happening on cable news. I'm sorry for this situation; it doesn't sound fair. However, I don't believe it's as devastating as you and Arthur perceive it to be. It actually should be reasonably easy to clear up, if you're willing to do some things we haven't seen before."

"Like what?"

"Answer their accusations straight on. The first charge you face is that you dodge interviews. You can refute this by agreeing to sit down to one."

"Jack," Arthur interjected. "Susan and I were discussing this in the car and she thinks there's any number of national platforms where we can get a booking. *Larry King, Good Morning America, Fox News.*"

"We'll seek easy interviews, not hard hitters," Susan threw in. "They'll ask you to tell your story, then toss you softball versions of the questions raised by the press. Very straightforward. An easy fix. If we move fast enough, we can get your version out there right away so people can decide for themselves."

"I don't do interviews."

Arthur and Susan exchanged worried looks.

"I know, Jack," said Arthur. "You've made that perfectly clear. But don't you want your reputation cleared up? It doesn't matter how you got here. What matters is how you leave this."

"We'll send a statement to all television and print media addressing each of the so-called accusations," Susan continued. "We can include any information you feel comfortable releasing."

She reached into her large leather carry bag and produced a small, spiral notepad. She flipped through pages of preliminary notes until she reached a blank page.

"Okay, the first issue we need to address is the question of where your money goes—lifestyle questions, such as how extravagantly you spend. I can see by your house—is this the only one you own?—that the press certainly didn't do very good research before running the story. Arthur told me you're frugal on yourself, but generous with others. I think we can spin that in such a way that speaks to your generosity without making you sound like a saint. Then there's the maid-slash-housekeeper. I suggest presenting her as someone who helps you because you're a bachelor and you're busy. She only works part-time, right? Hope I'm not going too fast here. I just want to lay all the points on the table where we can strategize a response you're comfortable with."

I could tell Arthur was struggling to restrain himself from interrupting Susan.

"If you do end up making appearances on television," she went on, "you'll be asked about the circumstances by which this money was earned." Susan rested her writing tablet across her lap and let out a relaxed breath. "To be completely frank, some people are going to question how a white man goes into a poor black neighborhood, writes a book about their stories, and walks out with twenty million dollars. I know your program has done wonders, but these people are still living in basically the same socioeconomic environment." She held up the pen as if to halt my response. "To some it will look like the same old race story: White takes advantage of black."

Susan flipped to a new page in her notebook. It looked like she went through a lot of them. "The last important issue is the allegations of, here wait a minute …" She pulled a manilla folder from her leather satchel. Inside was a newspaper clipping and several printouts from the internet. She held a sheet of paper in front of her and studied it like incriminating evidence.

"Allegations of … several run-ins with law enforcement including two shootings: one in Chicago, and another near Clovis, New Mexico." She lowered the newspaper clipping and stared at me.

"Go on," I said, not taking the cue. She ran her tongue over her upper lip.

"Jack, problems with the law are a different matter. People aren't as forgiving of … certain things. It makes a *big difference* to our PR strategy if more facts are going to start surfacing about these events. Are there more details to this story that we should know about?"

All eyes and ears awaited my response. I pushed aside for the moment that none of this was anyone's business, and tried to forget how labeling the private lives of public people "news" gave the media license to wear their serious, sober faces while delivering nothing more than gossip.

"You're asking if there's other shoe waiting to drop?" She nodded. "Susan, I appreciate that you've come down here on a Sunday afternoon on my behalf. I'm going to be candid because I owe you that much. Each day I sit for eight hours looking at a computer screen and pulling out fragments from my past with a pair of pliers. It's like extracting shrapnel from underneath the skin." Arthur bristled at the comment. I suspect he'd never thought that writing could be a painful process. I continued, "Are there issues in your personal life, things you find particularly challenging that you scarcely have strength to face privately? Things you might speak about with a counselor or a clergyman?" Susan nodded again. "Picture working through your issues in front of the whole world, Susan, surrounded by journalists and cameramen."

Susan was silent.

"I can't go on national television. Not because I'm a stubborn person, but because I'm a private person. I will not sacrifice myself to the altar of the twenty-four-hour news cycle."

There were a few seconds of silence, an impasse.

"Can I say something?" Susan's assistant, Mary Young, spoke up. I turned to her.

"Yes."

"Mr. Clayton, it must be hard being asked to talk so much about your private life, but a lot of young people really look up to you. Think about how those people will feel if you *don't* respond to these allegations. They might lose hope in what they've seen at Norwood. They might wonder if it's all a big lie. I've read all three of your books, and I have to admit when I first heard the news story, I was crushed. Meeting you and listening to you, I'm embarrassed I believed it even for a second. But not everyone has the chance to come spend an hour with you."

"Thank you, Mary. Believe me, stealing hope from the people who need it most is the last thing I want to do."

I swiveled to face the rest of the group. "Upstairs on

my answering machine are dozens of messages—mostly from the twilight zone. There's a hostile board member who—though he's known me for twelve years—is demanding I meet with a special assembly this week to answer their questions. There are crank calls, and threats from reporters demanding I call them back and spill everything, or else they'll report how I'm dodging them." I stood up, the anger creeping back in. "I'm really fed up with this whole thing." I looked to Arthur. "I didn't want to write a memoir. I didn't ask to sell eighteen million books! I've only asked to follow God ..." *I've only asked to follow God, even if life gets crazy. That's been my prayer all along. God's giving me what I asked for.*

"I'm guilty of sidestepping interviews because I won't play their game, giving out my financial data, my medical records, sitting on their TV shows and answering all their questions about my past and present life."

I stood behind a chair and gripped the back to regain my composure. "So here's what I will and won't do. Susan, send out a response to the story our friend Bud Abbott has written. I'm sure you have enough to answer most of the allegations. I won't be conducting interviews or giving out financial information."

"You *have* to, Jack," Arthur was adamant.

"No, I don't have to. My book will be out by summer. I'll cover any of the financial stuff there, but in a dignified manner." I worked to shake off the straight jacket so many strangers were trying to fit me with. "There's one more thing I think I can do, but I'll have to get back to you on it."

Susan's eyebrows shot up and down, her wise counsel rejected. "Jack, you should at least consider some sort of two-way communication."

"Such as?"

"Maybe a Web conference. People could email their questions. Or we … you could talk to someone you trust in the news media like the writer of that *Time* magazine article …"

"No. You'll have to trust me. I think I know how to fix this."

"Well, would you mind sharing your plan with us?" Arthur asked.

"Not yet, Arthur. But soon."

By six o'clock the trio was back on their way to Indianapolis. Susan probably thought I was in need of psychiatric help. Arthur probably would have severed our increasingly contentious relationship right then and there were it not for a little book I was still writing. He needed me to find a screw I'd lost, and how do you talk someone into that?

Only a week ago I'd started writing my life story. Now I was writing a plan to extricate myself from this quagmire. I felt confident my plan would take me off defense and give me back the ball. I would be like tailback Derek Smith, heading to the end zone. There was enough time on the clock. I just needed to keep the chains moving along the sidelines.

Back in my office I switched on the iMac. In the wake of my plan, I could almost smell the grass of college football fields. I thought of chilly October days and the end of that first football season at Providence. The summer-warm day in November, and the snowy weeks that followed, all of which led to a tender hand on a shoulder and the unspoken words sent through an electric current of touch.

I've found you.

Part of me longed for a way to go back in time. I didn't have a time machine, but at least I had this computer to send me. I headed back to Providence. This town, this same place, familiar landmarks all still here. But a different time, different people. I couldn't reach them in the physical world, but I would be with them soon.

I pressed Return.

~ Eighteen ~

Some walk by night
Some fly by day …
Moonlighting strangers
Who just met on the way.

—Al Jarreau
"Moonlighting"

After that night in Lillian Hall, Jenny Cameron stepped completely into my world. Whatever magic comes with the onset of young love, I had it. I had what I'd seen in Erin's eyes for Mitchell and in his eyes for her, the enchanting emotion that casts its soft shadows in private moments. During those months of discovery, I experienced the intensity of first love. Maybe it's this way for everyone who falls in love, or maybe love's so unique that what's created between two people is only theirs, never repeated.

Life changed after Bruce Willis chased Cybill Shepherd in *Moonlighting* that night. It was the little things at first. Like Jenny calling me out of the blue to see how I was, or leaving little "forget-me-nots" tucked in the top drawer of my desk, or hiding scribbled love notes inside my coat pockets.

In December, two weeks before the end of fall term, a Christmas formal was held in the newly renovated student-union building. Jenny wore a pretty red and black dress. Her hair was cut shoulder length, tucked behind her ears, showing off a pair of silver earrings shaped like miniature Christmas trees. That night we danced to a little big band set up in the cavernlike Morton Room. Jenny clasped her hands loosely around my neck, swaying with the music. We talked about our Christmas plans. I told her Marianne was hinting that she'd like me to come back to Overton, but I'd yet to commit.

"I think you should go. You can't spend Christmas alone in your apartment, Jack."

"It's not that simple. Overton holds too many memories … It's complicated."

"How complicated?"

"Do you remember me telling you about my sister, Ruthie? There's just a lot of sadness to an empty house at Christmas."

"I empathize with your mother's situation. While you've lost two important people in your family, she's lost three."

"When Thomas Wolfe said you can't go home again, I think he may have been giving good advice."

"A lot has changed since last summer, Jack. You've got your first semester of college under your belt, you've got a job, your own apartment, and an enchanting and beautiful girlfriend." She smiled, pulling me closer.

"Yes, I do have that."

"And you can't stay here in Providence all alone—that's just too depressing to think about. Would you consider coming home with me for part of the break?" she asked.

"I thought your parents were still out of the country?"

"Didn't I tell you? They're coming in on the twenty-second. Then they start a new assignment in London after the first of the year."

"London? Where do I sign up to be a missionary?"

"No kidding. Actually, we spent two years in Suffolk when I was twelve. My parents are only going to be here a short time. I'd like them to meet you."

"Possible. When are you and Erin going?"

"You mean Erin, Mitchell, and me." It was the first I'd heard of this.

"They're going to spend Christmas with Erin's family, then go to Mitchell's for New Year's. We're carpooling, the first stint of the trip, anyway."

"I had no idea you were all such good planners."

"It's come together quickly. I can't think of a reason to slow down the spontaneity."

"And it's all right with your parents for me to visit?"

"I think so. I sort of brought it up to my sister over the phone, and she didn't think it was a problem. They have plenty of room. I'll talk to my mom this weekend. What about *your* mom? What will you do?"

"Send a nice gift?"

"Jack!" Jenny slapped my arm.

"What do you think I should do?" I asked.

"I think we should all go to Indianapolis for

Christmas. Then, before New Year's, we can all drive to Overton and see what this mythical town is all about."

"You'd stay at my mom's house?"

"If you asked me nicely." Jenny looked up. Her body softened as she pressed up against me on the dance floor. "Does that surprise you?"

"Pleasantly so."

"Maybe it's time to breathe some life into the old place." We kissed to close the deal.

My last final exam ended on a Thursday. Erin and Jenny would wrap up their last test on Friday morning. By noon Mitch and I had loaded up the Cutlass for our Christmas road trip.

The skies opened, launching a heavy snowfall just before noon, making the scene at Lillian Hall a madhouse. Every student at Providence was heading home for the holidays. The line of cars waiting to get into Lillian's rear parking lot was staggering. Parents who'd dropped off their freshmen daughters in September returned (riding on snow tires) to collect them from a winter wonderland. Boyfriends picked up girlfriends. Groups of underclassmen loaded themselves into the backseats of huge Buicks and Oldsmobiles, their parents falsely comforted by the safety of all that metal.

Mitchell steered the Cutlass over the curb and onto the snowy lawn next to the lot. Jenny waved madly to us from the back door, propped open with someone's suitcase. We zigzagged through a tangle of cars, dodging suitcases and trunks and open car doors.

"Come rescue us!" Jenny cried.

Inside the dorm room, we collected two sets of matching luggage, a small Igloo cooler weighed down by an assortment of snacks, and two women ready to roll. Mitch and I pushed through the pandemonium, using the bags to shield us from bursts of arctic air that blew up the stairs whenever the back door was opened.

We stormed outside and threw the bags into the Cutlass's oversize trunk while Mitchell fired up the engine. With a toss of newly fallen snow from the back tires, Mitchell slipped and slid across the lawn, bypassing lines of bottlenecked traffic. We escaped the fracas of the last day of school in blizzardlike conditions.

In fifteen minutes we were on the highway, one hundred twenty miles from Indianapolis.

"You guys are awesome!" We exchanged high fives like a four-person bowling team after four perfect games.

"I am sooo glad to be getting out of there," Jenny said. "Between finishing my paper on Monday, then not sleeping for a week while Erin and I crammed every textbook fact into our heads, I thought this term would never end."

"I don't want to see another book for two weeks," added Erin. "I don't want to read a newspaper. I don't want to read the back of an aspirin bottle."

We laughed.

"Providence will be a ghost town by four o'clock," said Mitch.

The girls opened the cooler, grabbing snacks for Mitch and me.

"What about you, Jack? How did your final exams go?"

"I don't know what you guys are talking about. I could do it all over again. Piece of cake!"

"Shut up!!"

By four o'clock we were in North Indy after a nonstop fifty-five mile-per-hour flight and one time-zone change. When Jenny saw a rental car in the U-shaped driveway at her sister's house, she became noticeably excited. She hadn't seen her parents in more than a year.

"Hello, everybody!" Jenny's mom, Angela, opened the front door to greet us, ushering four college kids from the cold into the cozy warmth of the Midwest farmhouse.

Mitchell and I watched Erin and Jenny get hugged and loved on, Mike and Tessa awaiting their turn.

"You're all so cold," Angela said, holding Jenny's face in her hands.

"Howard Cameron." Howard extended his hand to me, and I shook it, trying hard to make a strong first impression. He was strong, fiftyish, with a brawny frame and a wide smile. He gave me one of the friendliest greetings I'd ever received.

"Mom and Dad, these are our boyfriends," Jenny said, and we all laughed at her bluntness. "This is Mitchell McDaniels; he's with Erin. And this is Jack … he's mine."

The atmosphere inside Mike and Tessa's house was like a Frank Capra film. Perry Como sang "chestnuts roasting on an open fire" as if he could somehow see the large open stone fireplace. An eight-foot Christmas tree in the corner of the room glistened with elegant white lights and expensive ornaments. It wasn't *my* home, but it felt like home.

"We're glad to meet you!" Angela said. She gave me a hug as if I were a long-lost son.

"Mom adopts young people, Jack. That's the first thing you have to know around here," Tessa said.

Mitch and Erin didn't stay long, but we made plans for Christmas shopping on Saturday morning at the mall.

After settling in and stowing my things in the rec-room basement, I cleaned up for a family dinner. There were six of us seated at the rustic table in the dining room. They'd prepared a smorgasbord that looked like a Thanksgiving meal, but with unusual additions like deli meats and cheeses, Manhattan clam chowder, and egg rolls. After giving thanks, dishes were passed and conversations began.

"Jack, Angela and I belong to a ministry that plants churches in different parts of the world, to reach out to others, teach English, and whenever possible, share the message of Christ."

"Where are you headed next?" I asked.

"After the first of the year, London. I have a feeling we'll be there a long time."

Jenny took on the role of table host, directing the flow of conversational traffic, asking everyone to share what they'd been up to lately.

"Mike is working in the state attorney general's office. This is apparently his crowning moment of glory, since he can't stop talking about it," Tessa said.

"Hey, it was my number-one law-school fantasy! What can I say?" Mike blushed.

"Meanwhile I'm still struggling away in private practice. I did however bring on a paralegal in October, and it's helped enormously." Tessa sipped from her glass. "What about you, sister?"

"My free time's been gobbled up by a pilot program Dr. Holland launched in Providence. We're researching the needs in the inner city. This semester we've mostly just been taking stock of the situation because there's so much that needs to be done. No one's sure how to approach the task. Every time we think we've seen everything there is, another layer appears."

"And what about you, Jack?" Angela turned her gaze from Jenny to me. "What's your first year of college been like?"

"It's been extraordinary, Mrs. Cameron. Sometimes it's hard to believe I was in high school eight months ago."

Tessa raised her eyebrows.

"I'm sure your parents are proud of you. Jenny's told us how focused you are on your work … and school."

"My mom is, I think."

"Jack's parents divorced when he was young," Jenny said.

I was sure she'd already told her mom about my situation.

"I'm sorry to hear that, Jack. Do both your parents still live in Iowa?"

"My dad's in California. We don't see him much anymore."

Tessa excused herself and went into the kitchen.

"Do you know what you'd like to do when you get out of school?" Howard asked.

Tessa returned carrying in a real New York–style cheesecake. "Okay, everybody. Here it is … the best cheesecake on the planet, FedExed in fresh this morning from Montell's in Lower Manhattan."

The five of us oohed and aahed. She set out dessert plates, and the smell of brewing coffee wafted in from the kitchen.

"You were saying, Jack?" Howard and Angela may have been scribbling notes in their mental personnel files, but it didn't feel that way. I would have been more nervous had I known Jenny had never brought a boy home before.

"After college? I know I should have this all figured out, but—"

"Nonsense," Angela said. "What young man's ever had his life course mapped out by his freshman year of college? I know Howard didn't." She touched his arm and smiled at him. "He knew his purpose and calling were to serve the Lord. That's what first brought him to Chicago, but that was it. Howard and I met in college when he was a freshman and I was a junior at school. My father and mother had been missionaries in India and the Philippines. I knew God was calling me, but Howard was just open and waiting."

"She told me we were going on a world cruise." Howard said, getting the night's first big laugh.

"Oh, I did not!" Angela said. They looked as if they'd fallen in love in October along with the rest of us.

"Jack, I believe the Lord has wonderful things in

store for your life, and if you'll watch for those things, follow His leading, He'll take care of the rest."

Angela's words proved true over the years, as true as refined gold. But at the time, I couldn't possibly comprehend their meaning.

"I haven't known you long, but you're a special person, I can tell. I'm thankful you're spending Christmas with us." With that Angela raised her glass to me, and I felt accepted.

"Thank you."

After dinner Jenny and I sat alone on the sofa in the rec room downstairs. Our long day of adventure was winding down, tempered by a good meal and the late hour. We rested. Jenny stretched out across the red plaid couch, strands of chestnut hair falling across her face.

"I think you were a hit with my family," she whispered, her eyes barely open.

"They're wonderful. You're lucky to have them."

"I don't see it as luck. I think of it as the Lord's blessing."

"Okay, then, you're blessed." Eyes closed, she smiled.

I'd seen Jenny's genuine faith at work in her daily life. Seen it in the title of a book she carried called *A Woman's Field Guide to Faith* by Allison Miller. The small devotional went everywhere with her, stuffed into her red book bag with the rest of her textbooks. I'd seen it at Dr. Holland's clinic when she kneeled to comfort a worried child, or patiently explained something to a mother who spoke only broken English. She was gracious in response to the frustrations of life or when facing disagreeable, unhappy people.

"Did you ever go to church?" Jenny asked. Her eyes opened in the soft glow of a lamp.

"My parents took us when we were little, but I don't remember much."

"We're going this Sunday. Will you come with us? There's also a Christmas Eve service we attend every year."

"Yes," I said, wondering if I could find there what the Camerons had discovered in the house of faith.

"You know God loves you, don't you, Jack? I mean, someone has explained this to you?"

"More or less."

"This visit could be good for you in a lot of ways," she said sitting up, more awake now. "Are you getting used to me in your life?"

"Too much so," I said, not thinking.

"What does that mean?"

"Sometimes I think we're getting too close, and that worries me."

Jenny turned on another lamp, brushing the shade tassels with the back of her hand.

"Why would that worry you?" she asked.

"Worry's not the right word," I said. "I mean to say I get confused sometimes. You're graduating from college next year. I'm just getting started. I don't know what's going to happen then. Don't you ever think about it?"

We'd rarely talked about the future, but as all young people in love know, it's an issue, whether spoken or not. Our romance was intrinsically tied to who we were as students. A hedge of immaturity blocked me from seeing what it could be after college.

"Jack, honey, what I think about us is that I love you." Jenny parsed each word. "When I think about the future, I think about *us*. What *we* could be like." Her voice was calm and confident. "I think we could be good together, really good."

She crossed her legs Indian-style and held both my hands. "Jack, do you remember me telling you I grew up part of the time in England?"

"Yeah."

"When I was a teenager, I used to sit up at night and look out my bedroom window, asking God if He had chosen a special man to be my husband someday. I didn't think he'd be English, but I believed God had someone special, somewhere. He could be anyone in the world, even someone on the other side of town."

She stared into space, the golden lamplight painting a halo around her hair. "If it's the Lord's will for me to have a husband"—Jenny wrapped her fingers around my hand and squeezed them—"I'd so love that future to be with you."

At forty the phrase "I'd love that future to be with you" demands a response. Hearing that as a teenager, the proclamation was enough in itself. The discussion needed go no further.

I realize the phrase "This was all so new" doesn't delve very deep. But I'd never held a woman so long that hours and even days later I could still feel the texture of the fabric she wore against my fingertips, or the soft touch of her face resting on my shoulder. I'd never known the responsibility that comes with the realization that there's nowhere else on earth she'd rather be than with me. I was old enough to be in love, just not old enough to know what a rare thing it is.

Jenny reached for a thin tangerine blanket resting on the back of the sofa and draped it over both of us. She found her place cuddled against me where her body fit perfectly with mine. I moved my lips toward hers, and we kissed. In the world we see with our eyes shut—she was making a pledge, securing a bond. She was giving me her heart and saying a promise to stay in love forever.

The basement door opened with a scrape, and we heard Angela's voice at the top of the stairs. "Jenny, it's nearly midnight. You need to let Jack get some sleep."

"Okay."

I have fond memories of the days when Jenny and I, though legally adults, were still under the watchful eye of her protective parents.

"I'll be right there," she said, and we heard the door upstairs close again.

Quietly, and without fully understanding, I surrendered myself to her that night, clueless that twenty years later I would still be thinking about that moment. That I would write about it until the hands of an antique clock ticked 2:37 a.m.

On that night twenty years ago, I didn't think about the next day or the day after that. We were together, and there was nowhere on earth I'd rather have been.

~ NINETEEN ~

Motoring
What's your price for flight?

—NIGHT RANGER
"Sister Christian"

"We've finished our response to the Abbott piece. We're releasing it to the press this morning." Arthur Reed was ready for a fight. "Susan and I worked on it last night during the drive back to Indy. I think you should know, we're not going easy on him."

"Can you read it to me over the phone? I need to know exactly what you mean by 'not going easy.'"

"Ah, not just yet," Arthur said. "I'll fax you an approval copy later this morning."

It was Monday morning. D-day for the defensive press blitz Arthur was eager to launch.

"Susan wants to get this thing serviced as widely as possible before journalists leave their desks for lunch. She'll send it to newspapers, wire services, print media, television and radio stations, Web bloggers, and gossip columnists. Everywhere McKinney and Company has contacts. She'll send out over fourteen hundred e-mails and faxes by day's end."

"Impressive," I said.

"I want you to consider letting Susan set up something on cable. We could definitely do O'Reilly. That guy hates your guts. His senior producer has already called my office twice this morning. They're planning to rip into you on tonight's program. I guess he has strong feelings on nonprofits that abuse their privileged status."

"Sounds like a lot of fun, but I'm working on another plan."

For all his protests, deep down I suspected Arthur liked what was happening. Some of it had to do with book sales, but mostly I think he just liked being involved in big-league play. His premier author was a sudden celebrity immersed in a big scandal that required a bigger response. Arthur enjoyed life supersized.

"I want you to reconsider. They would give you twenty minutes. We could fly to New York this afternoon, and you could tell your story to the world—clear this all up before you go to bed tonight."

I picked up the remote that was sitting next to a candy dish filled with red and green M&M's and clicked the TV back to life. The same incomplete story cycled at the bottom of the screen. "I'll pass."

"So what is this other idea of yours?"

"I'll tell you soon enough, but no TV appearances, okay?" I said.

"What we're doing here requires a team effort.

We need to all be on the same page. If you have a plan that's—"

"Don't push me, Art." The abrupt interruption shut Arthur off like a spigot. "You and Susan have your work to do, and when it comes time to tell you what I'm working on, I will. That should happen soon enough."

"How are you coming with the book?" Arthur shifted into his other topic of personal interest.

"Don't ask me about the book again either. You'll have it on time," I said.

There was silence on Arthur's end of the line. For three years he'd gotten everything he wanted, but an arrow shot into the sky climbs only for a while before returning to earth. Arthur's arrow had peaked. I owed him a book, not my life. In spite of the day's deafening chaos, there would come a day when all the frenzy and fireworks would be over. For now, our friendship would continue walking on broken glass.

"Whatever you say, Jack."

An hour later I drove north up I-65 toward Chicago on my first manhunt. I planned to ferret out an ace journalist who fit the description of a coward and a liar. I was working from a loosely fitted plan, one having to do with an up-close-and-personal confrontation. It was something I doubted Bud Abbott had ever seen as a reporter inside the walled city of the *Chicago Tribune*.

I'd lived in the windy city for a short while, so I knew to exit at Lake Shore Drive and work my way over to the Tribune building on Michigan Avenue. Even with the fresh lakefront snowfall, I was downtown by midday and parked in a structure adjacent to the building. I crossed Michigan and entered the revolving doors.

My honest and famous face worked like a charm, a dual set of keys opening the gates from the ground floor up to the receptionist on the Tribune floor. I wound my way through an enormous room filled with small brown cubicles and found Bud Abbott eating lunch in his. I stood in his doorway, immediately grabbing his attention.

"Clayton?" A nervous thirtyish boy of a reporter looked up at me. His expression froze. He was probably wondering if I'd managed to sneak an Uzi into the building.

"It's me, Bud," I said, sounding more like Dirty Harry than Jack Clayton, benevolent, best-selling author.

He reached for the phone but stopped short, his hand suspended in midair at the end of a long, thin arm, a slight tremor visible at his narrow wrist. I'm not a big guy, but the surprise of showing up, an arm's length away, inside a claustrophobic cubicle stopped Bud Abbott dead in his tracks. Raw emotions read like newsprint on his face.

"What do you want?" he asked.

"That's right, Bud. I want something. You're going to give me exactly what I came in here for."

I could see dozens of story lines playing out in his eyes. Could a reclusive writer snap under the pressure of a newspaper story? Could bad press make a narcissistic hermit leave his shanty for the big city with vengeance on his mind? Would tomorrow's headline read: TRIB WRITER SLAIN AFTER CRITICAL STORY?

"What do you want?" he asked again, the words coming out so dry, they almost snapped off in his mouth.

"I want you, Bud. I want the next month of your life. I'm going to come live in your house, eat in your kitchen, and watch your TV. And you're going to let me do that, because the story you wrote was a lie. You don't know me, Bud, but you're going to get to know me, and after you do, you're going to set the record straight."

Jesus commands us to love our enemies. When someone strikes your cheek, turn and give the other. If they demand you carry their pack for a mile, carry it two. I had caught Bud's flaming arrow and was now returning it to his door in singed fingers.

Bud Abbott didn't know whom he was dealing with. No one knew the real Jack Clayton or why he avoided the public. Perhaps Bud wondered if there really were dark and sinister reasons. Dumbfounded, he sat in silence, open-mouthed and squinty-eyed behind wire-framed glasses.

"What do you *really* want, Clayton? If you've come here to play mind games, forget it; I don't play. If you're mad about the story, write a letter to the editor. Other than that, get out of my office, or I'll call security," he said and stood to the fullness of his six-foot-two frame.

Now I wondered if I'd be the one taking it on the chops.

"You called me for an interview, Bud. You're not

going to throw me out for coming all the way to Chicago for it, are you?"

His eyes rolled upward. We both knew he hadn't expected an interview that day. He'd just wanted to shake me up, to cause me to say something foolish in anger. For all the highbrow acceptance-speech pronouncements journalists make about the power and salience of the press, to some it was merely a game.

Abbott's weekend piece had run all across the nation, flying off newspaper stands and onto cable TV. Even his editor had called him at home. It was more sensational than Bud had dreamed.

"Let me get this straight. You're agreeing to an interview with me?" he asked, a prosecuting attorney questioning a witness on the verge of self-incrimination.

"Under certain circumstances, yes."

"What circumstances?" He sat back in his chair.

"It's not a traditional interview, Bud," I said, making sure he was locking in on my words. "I'm giving you a once-in-a-lifetime opportunity to ask me any questions you want through a *series* of interviews—exclusive interviews. And then you'll finish writing my last book."

Blitzed, Bud shook his head in disbelief.

"Fame, fortune, and unprecedented access to the country's most notoriously sought-after interview. Only a fool would say no, Bud. What say you?"

"You're not serious."

"I *am* serious. I need a finished draft in eight weeks. Are you going to turn down my offer for an interview?"

This wasn't a ruse. I was making a real offer, and

a doggone good one. When Bud's head cleared, he'd soon see the sales possibilities, the boost to his career, the cable-news interviews, even if I did turn out to be a total loon.

He bit on the end of a yellow pencil, then clicked it across his teeth.

"You think it's a trick," I said, "but it's not. You'll get what you want, and I'll get what I want."

"And what is it you want, Clayton?"

"I think I already expressed that," I said.

"Suppose I said yes, Clayton. What are you proposing? Some kind of an interview for your book?"

"It wouldn't be an interview, Bud. You would write the book *with* me. It's my life story, Bud. You can ask any questions you want. And your name will appear on the cover with mine."

"What's the catch?"

"There isn't a catch, Bud," I lied, because there was one. The biggest catch of all.

"Right," he said, not believing any of it.

"I'm offering you the opportunity of a lifetime, to write the follow-up to a best-selling book. But, of course, it's up to you, Bud. You can always say no. Do you think there's even *one* reporter in this building who wouldn't quit his job to start this afternoon?"

The game I was playing wasn't only out of Bud Abbott's league; it was out of his universe. His eyes darted around the cluttered room, searching for something to bring the situation back to his understanding of normalcy.

"Where would these interviews take place? How many?"

"It'll require your complete attention for the next eight weeks."

"You want me to quit my job?" he roared, shaking his head.

"Or take a leave of absence."

"I can't get two months off. Are you trying to get me fired? Is that your game?"

"If you can't do it, I understand. Of course, my publisher would pay you an advance for your half of the work."

This got his attention. "How much?"

"Twenty-five thousand dollars."

That put a hook in him. He hated the idea, and every time his face blinked serious consideration, it was tinted with sourness. I imagined him wrestling with my offer, wondering if, like Fortunato in "The Cask of Amontillado," he was being lured into the cellar for a taste of the amontillado, only to be sealed up in there forever.

"Sorry, Clayton, I don't see myself driving to Providence, Indiana, anytime soon. That's going to be a kil—"

"Actually, Bud, I'm staying in Chicago for a while," I said. "I think I'd like to move into your place."

The blood drained from his face, followed by violent shaking of his head. "No way! There is *no way* you're going to come live in my house!" He spat out my suggestion like spoiled milk. "Do you honestly think you can come in here to my office, entice me with your twisted game, and then ask to live in my house? You're out of your mind. Do you know that? There's no way I would work with you."

I stepped out of his small cubicle and noticed we were no longer alone. Half a dozen journalists and staffers poked their heads above cubicle walls, eavesdropping.

"This is a serious offer, Bud. I need your full-time involvement. I can't write the book in the evenings and on weekends. But if you can't muster writing something more challenging than the potshots you took in your sophomoric piece, then I understand."

I buttoned the front of my coat. "I'm staying at the Westin here in town. You can reach me there if you're interested."

I turned to leave, not meaning for my exit to be so dramatic, but how could it not be? Pockets of *Tribune* employees ducked back behind their cubicles as the "reclusive author" walked past them to the elevators. Perhaps they were disappointed by the lack of violence. Maybe their journalist souls secretly wished I had punched one of their own, only to be tackled in dramatic fashion by security guards. That would have made front-page news for sure.

I exited the building and walked up Michigan Avenue. The windy city lived up to its nickname; Chicago's unforgiving cold whipped at my uncovered face. I didn't mind. I had just experienced red-zone chutzpah. It felt fantastic.

A few blocks down Michigan, I stepped into a restaurant called Melvin's Underground and ordered a hamburger. It came to the table still steaming hot, and I ate it in minutes.

I was doing what I needed to do, but doing it blindly. I know I'd confused Bud Abbott, and I wasn't sure about it all either. I only knew this is what God *wanted* me to do. Maybe He would have wanted me to be a little less brash, but still, I'd been obedient, the only thing that's ever really asked of us.

A classic neon jukebox spun records at the back of the room. "Almost Paradise" was playing. One of Erin's favorites, a song from the *Footloose* movie. Jenny liked it too. I saw myself on Frank Willis's tractor the summer before I left Overton, mirroring the farm scenes from the movie. Was life simpler then? I hadn't known then what life would be like when Mitch and I moved to Providence. But I was certain it would be good.

Sitting in a small booth in the back room of Melvin's Underground, I felt anything but certain. The uneasiness was as thick as the smell of burger grease and stale beer. I reached for the only thing sharp enough to cut through it all: hope that things would work out for good.

~ Twenty ~

I swear that I can see forever in your eyes.

—Mike Reno and Ann Wilson
"Almost Paradise"

During the six days with the Camerons, we played eight games of chess, five rounds of cribbage, and one marathon night of high-dollar Monopoly. We talked nonstop, got to know one another well. There were last-minute shopping trips to Fairfield Mall, long, spontaneous afternoon naps, and two occasions when Jenny and I spent time with Mitch and Erin in Indy.

On December 27, we said our good-byes to Howard, Angela, Tessa, and Mike. Jenny and I hugged everyone, and I thanked the Camerons for giving me the warmest Christmas in memory. We must have looked like the steady couple, staying together a week at Mike and Tessa's, then leaving for our next stop on our holiday tour of parents' homes.

Jenny was excited about meeting Marianne. I wondered what kind of greeting we'd receive, considering the scene when I'd left, but Marianne was hospitable and warm.

"Welcome home." Marianne gave me the first hug, the second to Jenny. "You must be Jenny," she said, squeezing her as if something was owed, a debt of gratitude perhaps. The third embrace went to Erin, who'd come inside to check out my home before abandoning her best friend.

"Mitchell's in the car," said Erin, "and we still have one more stop to make. Jenny, call us tomorrow. Maybe we can all get together."

Erin left. We heard the heavy door of the Cutlass open and slam, then the same chugging muffler I'd waited to hear the day of my exodus, sounding louder in the frost of winter.

I carried Jenny's bags up to Ruthie's room. I'd be sleeping in my old bedroom again, only this night would be different from other nights. Jenny would be sleeping in a room where no one had stayed for the past three years. Seeing a girl in Ruthie's room brought back a powerful flood of memories.

Jenny unpacked her suitcase on top of the bed. Around her were all the things that made it Ruthie's room. A collection of ceramic figurines—a bashful bassett hound, a devoted farm collie. Souvenirs Marianne brought her from Davenport and Des Moines. A mahogany jewelry box with yellow hand-painted daffodils across the lid, a pink satin bed pillow embroidered with the words "Everybody Footloose!" Ruthie's clothes still hung on their hangers in her closet, and underneath them on the floor was her high-school band clarinet in its case. My room looked no different than when I'd left it either. Nothing had changed; our rooms were portraits of the two of us brushed in another era when we were other people.

The days spent in Overton were remarkable. My mom and Aunt Nancy felt instantly at ease in Jenny's presence. Jenny seemed ready even then to step into the family, perfectly happy watching *Jeopardy* in the evenings with my mom, the two of them chatting away in the den.

We spent New Year's Eve at the Pizza Hut in Davenport. Jenny and I met up with Erin and Mitch afterward at his place, and the four of us played cards with his parents until midnight. Then we kissed our girls and sang "Auld Lang Syne," accompanied by music from an antique Victrola.

On New Year's afternoon, the four of us left Overton for Providence, feeling like rock stars coming off a ten-day concert tour. Jenny and I talked quietly in the backseat of the Cutlass as the late-afternoon sun gave way to evening.

"Did you have a nice Christmas?" I asked.

"I got everything I wanted. Time with my parents, time with you."

"Do you know how happy seeing you happy makes me?" The words sounded like nonsense, but she sighed her approval anyway. "Could you tell how much my mom likes you?"

"I like her. She's a strong woman."

"Did you notice how everyone treated Mitchell and me as if we were grown up?"

"You are grown up, Jack. Your mother and Mitch's family see you both differently because you've moved away, been successful at school, and brought home two smart chicks who don't take any crap from you." She chuckled, and I gave her a playful jab in the ribs.

The falling darkness chased away the last of the sun's light. Erin leaned her head on Mitch's shoulder. A few frozen, solitary cars passed us on the frozen highway. The warm hum of the engine and the coziness of the backseat turned our conversation deeper.

"So what do you think about Mitch and Erin? Do you think they're getting close?"

"Well, he's asked her to marry him. I'd say that's pretty close."

"You're kidding?" I said, surprised. "When?"

"He asked her while they were staying at Erin's house. Don't say anything to him because he doesn't want anyone to know, especially you."

"Especially me. Why?"

"Because he doesn't want to get ribbed over someone he cares deeply about."

"Is that what I do?"

Jenny drew nearer to me, her voice inches from my ear. "Jack, Mitchell's found someone he's in love with. I don't think he likes it very much when you tease him about all his high-school girlfriends. Mitchell's changing. Did you know he met with one of the pastors at our church?"

"What about?"

"His faith. He's accepted the Lord and wanted to talk about being baptized. I think he's getting serious about a lot of things in his life, the kinds of things he doesn't want you to joke about."

"I'm not that insensitive, am I?"

"No, Jack, you're not insensitive. But you and Mitchell grew up together playing football and listening to John Cougar and making each other laugh. What he's doing now doesn't have anything to do with those things."

"I'm hurt."

"Don't be. He loves you very much. He's just … different. I'm sure he'll talk to you when he feels comfortable with that. Now, do you want to hear more about the engagement?"

"Yeah."

"I don't know when or even if they plan to make it official, but he's definitely serious about it. They both are."

"How serious can they be?" I asked, sounding like the parent of a lovesick teenager. "He's only just gotten out of high school."

"People get married just out of high school all the time. Plus, she's not just out of school."

"So they could conceivably be married in a year or two?" I said, still feeling stung that Mitch would consider such a major decision without talking to me.

"Jack, conceivably they could be married next week."

I sat in silence. I'd wanted change when we'd left Overton months earlier, but exactly what had been left unchanged?

"Let him tell you in his own time." She reached through the darkness, feeling for my arm, then worked her way down to my hand and held it. "Jack, do you think we're serious?"

"I know how I feel about you. That's serious."

"I don't just mean in our feelings for each other. Do you ever think of us in any kind of future sense?"

"I don't think that far ahead. I know you think about these things. But … well … isn't it enough to have the here and now?"

That should have been a warning sign for Jenny, a flashing yellow light signaling her to slow down. We had every needed piece for building the perfect relationship, except one: my long-term commitment. These emotionally clumsy moments were small intimate reminders that something foreboding was looming just ahead. For entirely different reasons, we each invented our own rationale that allowed us to shrug it off.

"I'm not trying to rush you, Jack," she said, sensing my uneasiness.

She was utterly unaware, as was I, of private beliefs held in the vault of the subconscious, which I doubt I could have expressed then had either of us even known what they were. We continued to talk as we traveled the last stretch of highway to Providence, but what about, I don't remember. What I do recall is an awareness of a shadow. A sickening feeling that while my love for Jenny would grow every day, something else was growing too. She was in love and committed. I was only in love.

~ Twenty-One ~

Your kiss is on my list of the best things in life.

—Hall and Oates
"Kiss on My List"

A bitterly cold wind blew through all thirty-one days of January 1986. It carved furrows in the frozen snow, cutting abstract ice sculptures across the four corners of campus. It blasted against the sides of the buildings, launching clusters of snowflakes high into the colorless night, and it compelled students to sequester themselves voluntarily inside their warm apartments, braving the frozen outerworld only for classes or emergencies.

We kept our apartment at a snug seventy-two degrees, thanks to two hearty ancient cast-iron heaters we worked like a team of rented mules. Through the large windows in the living room, I watched the chapped and bundled faces of the Providence student body returning from late classes, wrapped in layers of thick clothing. My day had ended by two thirty. After an arctic trek home, I eagerly embraced the warmth and shelter of the apartment. I'd worked the night before and was grateful not to have to go out and wait tables at City Club. Mitchell and Erin were in Ontario, Canada, on a short-term mission trip and wouldn't be back until Sunday. Jenny had spent her morning in classes, and afternoon in a work-study lab. An hour earlier she'd called to talk.

"Hello, is this the man who used to jog around campus in those cute little running shorts?" she teased.

"Speaking."

"I want to file a complaint."

"What about?"

"I want to complain about this scandalous weather that's kept me from seeing you in them."

I grinned at her flirtation.

"Sorry, I've been banned from public streets. But I still do private shows."

She laughed. "What are you doing right now?"

"I'm cleaning this disgusting pig sty I call home. But I have cabin fever. Are you thinking of coming by for a surprise visit?"

"Only if I can tempt you away from housecleaning."

"I thought you had a full day of school and work-study?"

"I did have a full day. It's four thirty. I've been here since eight."

"Oh, I see. You've had a hard day at the office, and now you want to come home to someone who will cook your dinner and fetch you your pipe and slippers."

"And my newspaper," she added without missing a beat. "And while you're at it, cancel all my appointments for tomorrow. I could use a break."

"Well, I'm no secretary, but I think I can manage dinner. The apartment's clean; that's reason enough to come over."

"What are we having?"

The cupboards were bare except for Mitchell's last can of tomato soup. "Let's just say it's a surprise."

"Sounds delicious," she played along. "Give me another twenty minutes, then I'll be on my way."

I slogged to the corner grocery, picked up Diet Coke, angel-hair pasta, and a jar of spaghetti sauce. I spotted a raspberry coffee cake, thick with white icing, one of Jenny's comfort foods, and bought that, too, then brought it home.

A few frozen Eskimos, numbed by the cold, made their way past my window in the dark. Then I caught sight of Jenny coming up the sidewalk. I darted across the room and opened the door before she reached the top of the stairs, bitterly cold air biting at my arms and stocking feet.

"Get in here!" I said.

Jenny rushed in. I shut the door and held her mittened hands, rubbing the cold away.

"I'm only going to say this once, and then I'll stop complaining, but man is it freezing out there!"

I sat her down on the sofa, fussing over her, and helped her take off her coat and icy mittens. Then I held her close, warming her chilled body.

"This is the kind of reception I was hoping for," she said.

I pushed my face into the chilled nape of her neck.

She giggled and squirmed. "Jack, you'd better stop that!"

I pulled back to arm's length and looked at her. We hadn't seen each other in twenty-four hours. Too long to be apart. She put her arms around my neck.

"I've missed you, Jack Clayton."

"I'm never letting you go."

"Promise?"

I smiled, not knowing the answer.

Jenny didn't see a college freshman in her arms, or a small-town boy from the corn-row world of Iowa. She saw her best friend and suitor, a man and a rose growing beautifully in her generous heart. She was wise enough to know all roses have thorns, but inexperience convinced her they could all be pruned away. What she wanted more than anything was to be my wife, my best friend, and my lover. We were both aware of the intensity she brought to our relationship.

"Are you hungry?" I asked.

"Only starved."

"How's spaghetti sound?"

"Mmm," Jenny reluctantly pulled herself away, and we moved into the kitchen. She rummaged through the refrigerator, pulling out a bottle of Diet Coke.

"There's coffee cake on the table. Why don't you start with that? How long can you stay?"

"A little while," she said, tearing at the cardboard-and-cellophane box. "I've got to call my mom tonight when she gets home from work, and I've got to get a message to Anne in my study group. Otherwise, I'm all yours."

"Have you heard anything from Erin?" I poured spaghetti sauce into a pan and set it on the stove. "Mitch doesn't know how to operate a telephone."

"She called last night. Everything's fine. They're both fine."

"And she's getting college credit for the trip to boot."

"Right. I've never seen two people so magnetically attracted to each other."

"Have they said anything more about marriage?"

"It's just a guess, but I think they'll wait until after she graduates. She's taken classes every summer, so fall is Erin's last semester."

Jenny waltzed into the kitchen and stuffed a thin piece of the sweet cake into my mouth. After we kissed, a brief unceremonious peck, she rested her head against my chest, and we rocked gently to and fro, a private dance in our candlelit kitchen dance hall. I realized then just how romantic and out of time everything felt. A silent snowfall had painted Providence quiet and empty, but inside the apartment I felt full, complete, everything I loved safely closed in my arms.

"Do you know you're a much-loved man, Jack Clayton?" Jenny's body was a perfect fit against mine. "There will never be anyone who will love you as much as I do."

"How do you know?" I asked.

She looked up at me, holding my hands loosely in her own. "Jack, when I was sixteen, my dad took me camping one weekend at a cabin on a lake, just the two of us. He told me the story of how he and my mom met and fell in love. I wasn't allowed to date then, not until eighteen, but my dad gave me a journal to write in, to record my thoughts and dreams about the man I would someday love with all my heart. That journal … It turns out I've been writing about you, Jack."

"Jenny, there's nothing I wouldn't do for you. Sometimes I can't believe you feel this way." I thought back to the day we'd met in front of Lillian Hall.

Jenny laughed. "I'm not perfect."

"I can still be in awe of you, can't I?"

Jenny let go of my hands and walked backward to the other side of the kitchen. "Promise me something, Jack? Promise you'll never leave me, okay," she asked. "Will you do that?"

Her face had become suddenly serious. Her tender, unguarded heart exposed and made vulnerable by love. This was no trifling question. Inexperience with the opposite sex didn't hinder my recognition of the importance of these emotions, some of which came leaping out like a jack-in-the-box.

Her question sounded like a contract—maybe it was. A promise to be written in eternity. I closed the distance between us, my words pouring out in the serious tone one uses when taking an oath.

"Jenny, I will never leave you. I will always, always love you."

She closed her eyes, speeding two tears down her face, and we embraced again.

After dinner we sat on the carpet next to the kitchen. The living room was dark except for the glow from a candle and a small lamp by the door. I leaned against the wall, holding her. I would never leave her. How could I? She fell asleep in my embrace, confident we were one. I drifted off soon after.

It was after midnight when I awoke, Jenny still sound asleep.

"Jenny," I whispered.

She opened her eyes in an instant, incoherent and childlike.

"Come on," I instructed.

I helped her to her feet, led her through the dark apartment to my room. She sat on the edge of the bed, and I knelt down to slip off her shoes. Jenny, barely conscious, sat quietly, drifting back to sleep. She didn't question the situation or my intent. She trusted me as I rolled down her socks. I tried to guide her toward the pillow, but she stopped me with hand gestures, got up, and disappeared into the bathroom.

A moment later she stepped out of the bathroom. I was blinded by the bright flash of light piercing through the doorway. She shut out the light, but then I was night blind. The only thing visible, a photographic negative–like imprint of Jenny developing on the inside of my eyelids. Before I opened my eyes, I felt Jenny's lips on mine, then heard her gentle voice. "As much as I'd enjoy spending the rest of the night with you, I've got to go home."

"I know," I said. "I can walk you back or call a cab."

Her desire to stay was powerful. Jenny sat next to me on the bed, and I could read her thoughts as she laid her head on my shoulder.

"I wish I could just stay here," she said, dreaming.

"Maybe someday."

Ten minutes later I closed the door of a Providence city taxi and handed the driver a five-dollar bill. Jenny was merely a shape in the backseat of the dark car, but I knew her eyes were wide and staring at me, into me. Her thoughts projected through the glass like a flare.

"Someday."

~ Twenty-two ~

You look at me once, you look at me twice
Look at me again and there's gonna be a fight.

—Stray Cats
"Rock This Town"

Bud Abbott telephoned at nine o'clock the next morning, exhibiting more of the unsavory traits I'd already seen in him: distrust, suspicion. He'd been up half the night mulling over my offer. They say you're supposed to start your day with the most difficult phone call. Kick the day off with it. His call came while I was sitting at the desk in another plush hotel room, lifting a coffee cup to drink the last tepid sip from a pot I'd brewed an hour earlier. The morning paper lay across the desk, thankfully absent of stories about me.

"G'morning, Bud."

"Good morning," he said. "I wanted to call and ask a few questions about … this writing thing." Bud was all business.

"Ask away." I heard what sounded like the shuffle of papers. Perhaps he was reading from notes.

"I need to know if you're serious about this. If it's a game, just tell me."

"It's not a game."

Bud was silent. I let him do some thinking. "All right, so if I decided to do this—which I'm not sure is a great idea—where would you expect me to show up to work?"

"Two choices. I can set up shop somewhere near my hotel …"—I carefully considered how to say the next part—"or I could bunk in your guest room, and we could work out of your home. Oh, and in case this helps with your decision, I like poached eggs for breakfast. You do know how to make poached eggs, don't you?"

"I hate poached eggs. But there's *no way* you're going to live in my house, Clayton," he said. "If I decide to do this, I don't see it lasting for weeks, or going on until all hours of the night. And I'm going to need a bigger advance. Fifty thousand dollars before I write a word."

Writing a newspaper story to annihilate me was one thing, working in the same room was something else—something that made Bud uncomfortable at best, disgusted at worst. But there was a price for everything, and I could sense in Bud's demeanor that he'd been carefully calculating just what that price ought to be. This plumb assignment was a career maker most writers would take on spec, but Bud wanted some kind of insurance policy, or maybe just compensation to make working with a rich religious hypocrite like me less distasteful. Bud didn't appreciate that day what surely must have gone through his mind the day before—I didn't need him to write this book. I could write books without his secretarial assistance. Yet he was acting as if his talents were necessary, using his unique position as its own sort of bargaining chip.

"I'll set up an office here in Chicago. The work will go on until I'm satisfied with it. I'll ask my publisher to send you twenty-five thousand dollars now and another twenty-five when the project's completed."

Bud's end of the line was silent once more. It was like a bizarre game show. Which door would he pick? What was the real prize waiting behind it?

"All right," he said. "When do we get started?"

Bud Abbott, the only man in the country I could begin to think of as my enemy, had just signed up to assist me with the most personal and private writing I'd ever attempt. It's not exactly what you'd call normal, and yes, it flipped Arthur out.

"You hired that *#$@ to work for you?" he shouted.

"Yes, that's the plan I was telling you about. Bud Abbott will sit down in a chair across a coffee table from me for the next six weeks and write down every memory I can dig up."

Arthur gave up without a fight. "As long as this doesn't keep you from turning in the book on time, I couldn't care less."

"I'm glad to hear you say that because I need you to send him twenty-five thousand dollars."

"Twenty-five thousand dollars! You've got to

be kidding! I didn't pay *you* twenty-five thousand dollars!"

"Just write the check and send it to him. I'll e-mail Shirley his address."

"You've lost your mind, Jack. This is going to blow up in your face. I don't know what you think is going to happen, but Abbott isn't about to warm up to you like a character in some syrupy TV drama. He's going to listen and type and listen and type, and quietly plot against you."

"By the time we're done with the book, there won't be anything left to expose, Art."

This changed Arthur's tune. "You're going to tell ... *everything?*"

"Yes."

"Ooh, I like, I like," he said, salivating with greed. "Just don't let this interfere with the deadline. I don't want to have to step in—"

"Art, I love you for the trust you showed in my writing years ago and the role you played with *Laborers,* but you won't interfere with this. What I write and how I get it written is not your concern."

"You don't have to bark so loudly, Jack. My job is to keep the train running on time, that's all. If I see wolves on the tracks, I sound the warning whistle, but I don't pull the brake. The train must keep moving. We've got a schedule to keep, and the train must make the station, Jack. Even if an unwanted predator foolishly wanders in front of it."

"Who's the predator—Bud Abbott or me?"

"Neither. It's this whole situation. You moving to Chicago, putting your faith in an enemy, placing your most important work in his hands. My company is riding on this."

"Just write the check, Art. My faith isn't in Bud Abbott, or in your deftness as a train conductor. God will bring the train in on time, according to His schedule. And only He knows the station."

"Jack, you know I don't follow when you bring God into the conversation."

"Do you not see God's blueprints? He's building something wonderful, so wonderful that just watching it come together satisfies. You can have your plans, Art, but they're nowhere near as spectacular as what God's doing."

"We'll have to sit down and talk about this sometime. For now, just write."

My next call was to Maureen Mallei, a commercial real-estate agent I picked at random from the yellow pages. I asked about short-term office space available for lease on Michigan Avenue within walking distance of Melvin's. An hour later she showed me a nine-hundred-square-foot space two blocks from the diner. It was furnished with everything I needed: an inspiring view from the twenty-second floor, living space with a desk, a kitchen, and one bedroom for me to crash in at the end of each long day.

"You'll love being in this building, Mr. Clayton," Maureen said. "You'll be among screenwriters, advertising executives, commercial artists. I think you'll fit right in."

I paid the deposit and two months rent in full. The next day Office Depot delivered and stocked supplies, including a new iMac and printer for me. With twenty-five thousand dollars coming his way, Bud Abbott could supply his own computer.

I printed what I'd written so far and sent the pages by courier to Bud's home. I knew inviting Bud into the writing process would be a challenge, but I had done what I'd made a career out of: followed the intangible Spirit.

I looked out at the Chicago night skyline, at checkered windows lit up in buildings all over the city, finished the leftovers from Melvin's, and went to bed early. Tomorrow would be the start of a new chapter, both in my life and in the book. I wanted to be well rested.

Five percussive knocks rattled the door the next morning at 9:15. I opened it for a tardy, shadow-faced Bud Abbott bearing gifts—two venti cups of coffee from Starbucks and a box of Dunkin' Donuts. Over his shoulder he carried a soft-leather pouch, and folded under his arm, the morning edition of the *Tribune*. There was a donut in his mouth.

"Sorry I'm late," he said, pulling out the pastry and walking past me into the kitchen.

I watched him move in, my new part-time roommate, dropping the donuts on the counter and making himself comfortable at the end of the leather sofa.

"Hope traffic wasn't too bad."

"I'm used to it." He peeled off his jacket and set up his PowerBook, not yet making eye contact with me.

Behind his silhouette, skyscrapers pierced a clouded, heavy sky. I felt profoundly uncomfortable and suspected he felt the same, like college dorm mates meeting for the first time.

"Thanks for the coffee," I said. I thought of adding, "At least there's one thing we agree on," but didn't.

"No problem."

"I want to get started right away. I'll explain how I think this situation can best work. Did you get the manuscript?"

"Yeah, I got it, but I haven't had a chance to look at it."

He sounded like a school kid giving an excuse for missing homework. I ignored the feeling that Bud might prove to be no help whatsoever.

Bud pulled the pages, rolled up like a tube, from his backpack.

"I want to give you a chance to get up to speed," I said.

I reiterated what I'd already told him—that he'd been caught telling a fib and now had to spend the next six weeks in detention with the guy he'd fibbed on.

"I'll tell you my story, and you'll write it down. I'm used to finishing six or seven pages a day. I'll still write some parts I either don't want to share with you or I prefer to write alone. We'll e-mail our work at the end of each day to my editor."

"Whatever you say."

This was going nowhere fast. Bud wasn't remotely engaged in this project. I prayed silently.

"Bud, you called me once for an interview. Do you still want to do that?"

"Do you mean something I can use in the paper?"

"No, I mean for here, for right now. You have doubts about my character, my integrity, my faith, my finances. Why don't you conduct that interview with me right now?"

"You'd let me ask *any* questions, and you'll answer them?"

"That's what I'm saying, Bud."

"How do I know you'll tell me the truth?"

"I guess you'll just have to trust me."

"I don't do trust without verification. And just for the record, I particularly don't trust wealthy religious hypocrites professing solidarity with the poor. I believe you're hiding a checkered past and probably a lot more than that. And if you think you're going to buy me off to get your reputation back, you're really a whack job. So, no, I don't believe I'm gonna just trust you."

"Clearly you've got it all worked out, but can you stand hearing my side of your story? Or have you gotten too comfortable with the lie? Some people would rather believe lies because hearing the truth requires actual thinking. That doesn't seem like how a journalist would think. Is that you?"

"I can hear the truth. I just don't think you have any to tell."

"If we're going to get anything done today, we have to get past this." I sat at one of the tall swivel stools in the kitchen. "So, go ahead … ask away."

"Just to let you know … When I'm not here, I'll be researching your answers, and if they don't add up, I'll tell the whole world." Bud stood, grabbed his book bag, and strode to the door. He clutched my manuscript in his left hand.

"I'll read this and get my questions together. Be back later." The door shut behind him.

Bud returned an hour later. He'd eaten breakfast at one of the restaurants downstairs while reading through my pages. Thunder and lightning appeared to have left him, and he seemed grounded now by either the story or the pancakes.

He sat on a bar stool at the counter and flipped open his yellow legal pad. It was filled with questions, written in large letters and in a barely legible combination of script and printing. He'd obviously prepped during breakfast.

"Let's talk finance. You own one home in Providence. What can you tell me about your other properties, condos, or castles?"

"There aren't any, Bud."

"None?" His eyes flashed over the top of his notepad, reminding me of a lawyer cross-examining his witness.

"That's what I said."

"Zero?"

"Right."

"I don't know if I buy that, but let's move on. You drive a 2001 Jeep Wrangler. List all the other vehicles you own."

I ignored his irritating deposition-style interrogation and answered, "Just the Jeep, Bud. And it's a 2000."

"Why just a Jeep?"

"I like the Jeep."

He tried helping me jog my memory. "C'mon … any sports cars, SUVs, Hummers, maybe …"

"Nope, nope, and no."

"What's your net worth? How much money do you actually have?"

I let out a sigh. "Oh, I don't know, Bud. My accountant, Richard Hines, would know better than I do"

"You wouldn't mind if I set up an interview with him, would you?"

I'd dreaded this sort of encounter ever since my flag of notoriety shot up the flagpole. "I've got a couple thousand dollars in my checking account, about six thousand in a savings account, a few hundred in my wallet, a few dollars in change on my dresser at home."

"What else?" He sounded like a butcher who's learned the secret of suggestive selling.

"That's about it."

He looked up again. "You've earned over twenty million dollars. Where'd it all go?"

"I gave it away, Bud."

"You gave it all away."

I pulled myself from the leather sofa and stood on the thick Oriental rug in the middle of the floor.

"People wonder what they'd do if they came into that kind of money. Here's what I did. For Christmas that first year, I gave everyone at CMO a check for ten thousand dollars. That was a big hit with the staff. I tried giving a friend of mine, Raymond Mac, the same amount. I thought he might use some of it to visit his sister in Baltimore. He said, 'What am I gonna do with this?' and refused it.

"Millions went to CMO. Every project Aaron had ever dreamed of was funded, green-lighted, and switched on. He built a neighborhood medical center. Do you know how many people in Norwood didn't have prescription glasses? The clinic has twenty-four-hour emergency care within walking distance for people who hadn't seen a doctor in years.

"We founded Norwood Academy. Nothing has affected the community like that school, Bud. It's used to teach children during the day and adults in the evenings. President Bush visited our school during his 2004 reelection campaign and recognized its impact on the community. CMO also built Norwood Community Church."

"Did anyone suggest you were giving too much to the community? I mean you can do too much for people, right?" Bud asked.

"We offer assistance to those who prove themselves by acting responsibly, but I don't think even you would expect people to earn the right to things like medical care, education, and a place to go to church. And about that school ... Parents overwhelmingly voted for school uniforms. Students are expected to maintain a high grade-point average. Parents are expected to volunteer time as part of their tuition grant. There's also a zero-tolerance drug and gun policy."

"And the results?"

"Drug arrests are down 65 percent. Violent crime has fallen to its lowest levels since 1981. Compare those statistics to the Providence student-housing communities, where levels have increased every year since 1998. This is where my money went, Bud. Because of *Laborers,* illiterate adults are learning to read, men and women are moving up the economic ladder, and test scores are climbing higher each year."

"Okay, so some good has come from your success, but—"

"Bud, I don't take advantage of poor black people, or of anyone. I was staying in the hotel—something I *never* do—because … I needed a vacation. Yes, I've made millions, but most of it went to CMO."

"I know," he said.

I wasn't sure I'd heard him right.

"I'm sorry … What did you say?"

"I know. I investigated your tax records, public since you work for a nonprofit. I've seen your credit-card statements for the past three years too. You're cheap, Clayton. You don't spend any money."

"You knew all this and *still* wrote that story?"

"Yeah, I did. I'm a bad boy." He looked slightly cocky, slightly contrite. "I didn't know about the spending *before* the story, but I did by the time it hit the newsstands. I had a gut feeling you were dirty, and you probably still are. I think you're still hiding something. But the hotel thing and driving that crap Jeep—that I can clear you of."

I was infuriated. "There is nothing I've done that's underhanded or illegal. Your own investigation made that clear, but you still wrote your misleading article."

"That's the way the game's played. If someone's clean, the truth eventually comes out."

"Months later, after lives are destroyed. Why don't you reprint what you know to be true now and end the misery you've put me, and others, through?"

"Can't do it. I'm not done asking questions."

I walked into the kitchenette and ran cold water into the sink. It was ice cold instantly, and I tossed it up in handfuls onto my face, trying to lower my swelling rage. I shut off the water, my face dripping wet.

"Fine," I said. You're going to investigate me until your eyes are bloodshot. You're going to learn more about me than you ever thought was possible, and then you're going to clear my name," I shouted at him, cutting the distance between us in half. "And you're going to write it well, Bud. Because that's what you're being paid to do!"

I yanked my coat from the back of a chair and opened the door to leave. Bud shouted back at me from the writing lounge.

"You're going to *tell* me everything I need to know. Are you prepared to do that? And if I find out you've lied, I'm going to write another book, an unauthorized biography. One filled with the truth."

I turned around in the hallway and headed back inside. I refused to be pushed around. "All I have to tell is the truth. You'll have to judge whether or not you're satisfied with it."

There was no official documentation of our agreed-upon terms, but we went to work anyway. Bud asked his questions, typed on his PowerBook, and filled microcassettes with the details of my life. Part interview, part deposition.

We worked on working together. It was a job both of us hated.

~ Twenty-three ~

Vacation
All I ever wanted
Vacation
Had to get away
Vacation
Meant to be spent alone.

—The Go-Go's
"Vacation"

Winter term ended on May 26, exactly a year to the day after our high-school graduation. Mitch and I planned to stay in our apartment through the summer. The girls resigned from dorm living and leased their own apartment. The first Saturday in June, with help from Howard and Angela Cameron, Mitch, and me, they moved into their new living space.

"I asked Erin to marry me," Mitchell said as we lifted Erin's heavy hope chest and waddled it into the girls' apartment in Meadowbrook.

"I'd heard something about it," I said. "Have you set a date?"

"Next June, we think. I declared my major, too—business management. I'll either get my degree in accounting or general business. Thanks to summer school, by fall next year, I'll be a senior."

All the changes I'd undergone in my first year at Providence paled in comparison to what was going on with Mitch.

Erin would finish school in December. Jenny had decided not to pursue the internship, instead taking a paid student-director position in Dr. Holland's program.

And then there was me.

I was restless but didn't know it yet. My summer plans were simple. I doubled my shifts at City Club, since my savings had dwindled to less than eleven thousand dollars. My summer of '86 proved to be about Jenny, City Club, and hanging out with Brian Aspen and Reggie Mohler watching the Cincinnati Reds. There was just enough "good" in my life for everything to seem perfect. What I didn't see—what none of us saw—were the icebergs floating off in the distance, hiding beneath the surface.

Jenny didn't come to Providence to fall in love, or to find her future husband. But I knew she thought about that. And what it would be like to raise a family. I'd seen the fear in her eyes when she thought of us not being together. I wondered what she saw in mine when I told her at times that I needed space. That I needed time to be alone. She viewed Mitchell's pairing with Erin as a model of what would naturally come together for us.

In August Brian dropped out of college and went back to Chicago. He got a job tending bar in a trendy downtown dance club. I enrolled for fall semester, cutting my savings in half. But a few weeks into the semester, something didn't feel right. I started to be less satisfied with school. The classes didn't interest me. My depleted savings unnerved me. Then I discovered that if I dropped out of the semester less than six weeks in, half of my tuition would be refunded.

I made a fateful decision to quit school. This came as a shock to Jenny.

"You're kidding! Jack, that's the stupidest thing I've ever heard! You've barely gotten started here!" Her voice was unusually shrill.

"It's not what I want to do right now. My grades are down, my money's half gone. The three of you know what you want, but I know less about my future than I did when I got here."

I had no idea how much I was hurting Jenny. Her face reddened, and she began to tremble.

"Brian Aspen's in Chicago now. He's working in a club there making two hundred dollars a night."

Jenny looked at me in disbelief. "Please don't tell me you're going to leave ..." This jolt had scrambled her brain, and she struggled to formulate a persuasive point of view capable of stopping my plan.

We were only halfway through the pain of pulling off a Band-Aid, so I forged ahead. "I need to take some time off and figure out what I'm supposed to be doing with my life."

Tears swelled up in Jenny's eyes until they poured out in long streaks down her face. She rallied quickly.

"*I'm* what you're supposed to be doing with your life, Jack! What are you thinking?" she asked. "What were you thinking about doing with us? Don't you care about me?"

"Of course I care about you!"

"Then how can you do this?"

I wanted to run. I wanted to escape the things that scared me most about life. I knew it wasn't logical, but I would rather have given up the love I'd found in Jenny than give up the mad hunt for inner peace.

"Jenny, haven't you ever felt like there was something you were supposed to do? Someone you were supposed to be, and you couldn't get comfortable with yourself until you figured out who it was?"

Jenny nodded in absolute agreement. "Yes, Jack, and when you find it, *you keep it*. You hold on to it. You don't throw it away." She paused for a moment, collecting herself. "Honey, you say you want to find out who you're supposed to be. I understand this and want it for you." She grabbed the front of my jacket, pulled me toward her gently, to focus my attention on her words. "But, Jack, honey, listen; this is it. Don't you see how rare what we've got is? Don't you see how what we're doing is special?"

I knew it was special. What I didn't know was how it could all unravel, how hearts are broken. "Yes, I know. But I'm … I'm not like Mitch or Erin. Or you. I'm not sure I'm ready for grown-up life."

"You sound *afraid* to grow up."

"I have to do things for me!" I shouted, a poor attempt to compensate for her emotional astuteness.

"Jack," Jenny said, "don't you think about how your

decisions affect others? When the man I love announces he's moving two hundred miles away, don't you think my life might be affected?"

Jenny continued to sob as we sat, holding each other's hands. All I wanted to do was get out of there. I spoke as slowly and softly as I could.

"I don't want to hurt you, but I have to go."

Jenny closed her eyes tightly as if trying to block out the pain. "Jack …" She struggled to regain her composure. "Don't go."

She knelt down on the floor and laid her head on my knees. I stroked her hair, watching her cry, her body heaving in jerky motions.

I stood. "You'll get over this. It's not the end of us; we'll still see each other when I come back."

"When you come back? And when will that be?"

I turned the door handle.

"So that's it, Jack? You're just going to leave? What's happened to you? Where's the Jack I once knew?"

I didn't answer. I didn't have an answer.

"Jack …" Jenny opened her mouth to speak calmer words, but they came out like a pained scream, "DON'T LEAVE!"

Fear lifted the hair on my neck.

"I have to go."

~ Twenty-four ~

I never meant to be so bad to you
One thing I said that I would never do.

—Asia
"Heat of the Moment"

"So you left Providence and came to Chicago?" Bud asked, refilling his coffee mug in the white tile kitchen, where it always seemed cold.

"Right. It was mid-October 1986."

"You left the woman who loved you?" he added.

My silence was all the answer he needed to that question.

Bud ferried the hot mug back into our work area, setting it down on a cork coaster and returning to his notepad. He set the small Panasonic tape recorder on the coffee table between us.

I'll hire someone to come in and ghostwrite for you. All you have to do is remember and talk. You can do that, right?

"You got yourself to Chicago and … what?"

"Moved in with Brian. He was working at a club called XN-tricity and said he could get me a job there."

"I remember that place," Bud said with a fondness in his voice. "It closed down about ten years ago, but I was there." He whistled. "Very hot."

"Anyway, I moved into Brian's crummy apartment on his invitation to come up and have a good time, and at the beginning it was fun. Within a few days I was working at the club and making exactly the kind of money Brian had described."

"What was it like working there?"

Bud kept his eyes on his notes as he asked his questions, typing notations on his PowerBook and sometimes writing on his yellow pad. I ignored the intense feelings of paranoia generated by the slow-turning spindles on the recorder, trying not to think about where the tapes might someday end up. Bud wasn't my shrink, although by all appearances, it looked like he was. He wasn't bound by client confidentiality, either. I didn't trust him, but I trusted God, and so I recounted my story as clearly as I could.

"The first night was frantic and exhilarating. It was hard work because it was busy and we were in constant motion, but the money was great. Two hundred dollars a night minimum—cash. Some nights I left with as much as three hundred dollars. Of course, quitting time was three in the morning. We'd all roll out of the club half starving, too wired to go to bed."

"You're no stranger to money, are you, Jack?"

"I worked hard for it from 5:00 p.m. until 3:00 in the morning, on my feet, with no breaks."

"Yeah, yeah, I know, and you used to walk five miles to school in ten feet of snow."

"Why is it you don't like me, Bud? Is it something I've done to you? I'd really like to know."

"I retract the comment." Bud held up his right hand with his black felt pen in it. "Let's keep it moving."

Bud was playing chicken with me, but he'd flinched. It was true he didn't like me, but he either didn't know why or he didn't *want* to know why.

"What did you do with your little fortune?"

"You'll be happy to learn that I blew it all on myself. I bought new clothes to fit my new lifestyle. Bought a car. Paid my rent a month in advance. I ate whatever I wanted, whenever I wanted, wherever I wanted. No restaurant was too exclusive.

"Sounds very wholesome. And what were Mitchell, Erin, and Jenny doing all this time?"

"They stayed at school. Mitch kept the apartment, and Brian's old roommate, Reggie Mohler, moved in. I kept in touch with Mitchell, but not often."

"How often?"

"I don't know. Every month, I guess. He kept me informed about what Jenny was doing. By Christmas I was missing her and wanted to call, but—"

"You hadn't talked to her in all that time?"

"No. I didn't think it was right to remind her I wasn't around. I thought she needed space."

"I thought it was you who needed space."

"Ah … good catch. Right. I guess I thought it would be easier just to break contact for a while."

"So, had you broken up?"

"I don't know. I didn't feel like it. It was more like a

break, an indefinite break, but I think I was still hoping there'd be another chapter together."

"Did you two ever talk again?"

"Yeah, that next Christmas. I called her parents' house and spoke with her mom. By then she was convinced I'd been bad news in her daughter's life."

"She was right." I didn't appreciate Bud's caustic ad-libs, especially when they were true.

"A lot had changed in the year since I'd come home with Jenny for Christmas."

"What happened?"

I stood up, placing my hands on top of my head, and walked away from the interview.

Bud looked up. "What's the problem, Jack?"

"Stupid, stupid …"

I pulled a bottle of water from out of the icebox, a sickening feeling intensifying inside me. "The problem is locked up twenty years in the past, Bud. I have the key now, but it's twenty years too late. That's the problem."

"You … you still have feelings for the girl." Bud laughed. "So, you made the wrong move at the wrong time, and she hung you out to dry. Ouch, that hurts pal. Isn't it about time to get over her, Clayton?"

As difficult as it was remembering these times alone in the privacy of my own home, it was galling going through them alongside a hostile collaborator.

"Let's take a break."

Fifteen minutes later I rejoined Bud, and we picked it up again.

"Sorry about the laughter, there, Jack. Won't happen again."

"You may not realize it, but you're doing something good by me. You're tearing out the last traces of pride from my character. For the past twenty years, I've felt like I was being squeezed in a vise. I believe you're here to help beat out the last bits of me."

Bud stared. "You're not exactly what you might call easygoing, are you, Jack."

I laughed; we both laughed.

"So did you get to talk to Jenny or what?"

"Yes. Angela put down the phone, and when I heard Jenny's footsteps approaching, I braced myself for rejection."

"What'd she say?"

"'Hello.'"

We both laughed again, punchy from the long hours of work.

"Hey, don't laugh; this is serious stuff!"

"Jack, you're better when you're not so serious. Anyone ever told you that?"

"Not anyone I like." I smiled.

"Can I say something here? You're too down on yourself, Jack. I mean, you were in love during college, and you didn't commit for life. So what? Every other guy who's gone to college has that story. I dated a girl named Bethany Carson at Illinois, and we talked about marriage all the time. But it didn't happen. I'm sure she's as happy about it as I am. My wife, Katie, is happy it didn't happen too."

"For you, there was a Katie. For me, there wasn't. That's not the only reason I think about Jenny … And let me say for the record, my life hasn't been all about years of lonely pining. I've more than made peace with the things I can't change. Still, she's someone who never acted against me, never said an evil word, even when I acted my worst." I leaned forward; I wanted Bud to hear the weight of my words. "Yet I treated her so commonly, acting like her kind were a nickel for nine. But the truth is, we were together even when we were separate. Different towns, different places, but still always connected. There's hardly been a day I haven't thought of her."

"You got fixated. Nobody's worth that much mind play."

"It was obviously more complex than that."

"All right, no argument. What'd you say when she picked up the phone?"

"I apologized for the way I'd treated her. Asked if she'd be able to forgive me. I expected she couldn't, but she was light-years from *un*forgiveness. She was delighted to hear from me. Time apart was irrelevant. She just repeated what she'd said before—that she knew we were meant to be together."

"Were you seeing other women in Chicago?"

"No. Sometimes a group of us went out on the town, but life was pretty superficial."

"Then what happened?"

"We talked for an hour. I told her I was doing well and invited her to Chicago and told her I'd show her the town. She said, 'You shouldn't say that unless you mean it. I might just take you up on it.'"

"She forgave you?"

"Yes. I'd sent her something in the mail a few days earlier."

"What?"

"A coffee-table book of London gardens—something I knew she'd love—and a pair of sapphire earrings I hoped would help heal the wounds."

"Nice touch."

"She told me there was nothing that would ever break her love for me."

"Did she come to Chicago?"

"No. We hung up and didn't speak again for months. She was in her last semester at school by then, and I wasn't coming back. We went on with our lives, a kind of suspended animation. I ran wild, and she waited for meaningful commitment."

The telephone rang. I glanced over at the caller ID. "Arthur Reed Pub" appeared in the letter box, and I put the call on speakerphone.

"Hello, Arthur."

Bud went into the kitchen to make a sandwich.

"Jack, Jack, Jack. My rainmaker friend." Arthur's voice came through giddy and greedy.

"What's going on?"

"I'm calling you with news, Jack. Thought you could use a little break from the writing. You've heard of the Hollywood director Adi Seffe, right?"

"No."

"Well, you should get to know him, because this morning he bought the film rights to *Laborers*." Arthur let out with a burst.

"You're kidding."

I looked at Bud spreading mayo on a slice of bread. He rolled his eyes, disgusted by the freight train of blessing pulling once again into my town.

"I never kid about money. He's developing a full-length feature film based on your book. It's a natural when you think about how successful it's been as a vehicle."

"But it's nonfiction."

"Doesn't matter. It's a great story. I spoke with him and his agent this morning. It was the *Time* cover that sealed the deal. He said they're considering Nate Hillman and Rachel LoMack for the leads."

"Playing who?"

"You and your love interest, of course!"

"I don't have a love interest."

"That's Hollywood."

Bud and I exchanged grimaces.

"They *are* going to keep the faith content though, right?" I asked. "You wouldn't make a deal with them without a guarantee …"

"Adi Seffe is an Oscar-nominated director. It's my understanding he's a Christian. He said he wants to explore the 'spiritual story inside the human story.' He talks a lot like you."

Arthur waxed on about the movie. After interpreting Bud's hand signals, I reminded Arthur to send him a check.

The two of us worked the rest of the afternoon, taking a three-hour dinner break so he could go home and see his family. I called Bud at home and told him to just stay put. We could get back to it after Christmas.

Bud's wife, Katie, had picked up the phone. She told me she'd read *Laborers* and loved it. Imagine that. Bud Abbott living with a Jack Clayton fan. I still didn't trust Bud, but I had hopes.

That night under the twin shadows of doubt and fear, the writing continued. The next stop on the journey would be the most difficult of all.

~ Twenty-five ~

This is the sound of my soul,
this is the sound.

—Spandau Ballet
"True"

Had I known that in five short hours, my best friend would be dead, I would have sobered up enough to jettison my Chicago life, or simply have given up my own life. As a hot iron leaves its scalding brand on leather, so that day left its brand on me. The world forever changed the moment Mitchell's life forever ended. I carry the guilt and the grief inside me like a tumor, and not a day goes by that I don't think of a death I was responsible for. I'm sorry, Mitch. I've said these words to you thousands of times before, but not enough.

"When I get done in here, I want to be out of this apartment in like two seconds," Brian called from the bathroom, where he stood shaving at the sink.

He had the attention span of a spastic gnat.

Over his right shoulder, I could see my reflection in the medicine-cabinet mirror. A thin black belt held his pants to his one-hundred-thirty-pound frame.

Mitchell sat with me in the living room. It was early June. Jenny had just graduated. She sent me an announcement card with a pretty graduation photo and a two-page letter. Erin and Jenny went back to Indianapolis after the ceremony, and I had asked Mitchell to come up to Chicago for a visit.

Mitch was working hard to catch up with Erin. He'd sold the Cutlass to pay his tuition and put his Harley-Davidson up for sale in Overton to help pay for an August wedding. He rode the bus from Providence that afternoon, and I was planning to drive him back on Sunday, a quick five-hour trip.

"What do you think of Chicago?"

"It's cool. I'll like it even better when we get that pizza you promised."

"We will … tomorrow. Tonight I'm taking you to a party that's going to knock you out."

"I didn't come here to party; I came here to spend time with Jack Clayton. No one's really sure what's become of him."

"Take a look." I extended my arms, showing off the new me.

He wasn't impressed. "I don't understand why you left Providence for this. You didn't talk it over with anyone, not even me."

"I traded bad grades and going broke for less stress and a lot of money. All in all, I'd say it's worked out rather well."

"Not so much for Jenny—"

"Now don't start …"

"What about school? Are you dropping out?"

"No … But what's the rush? I'm happy *you* found Erin. Why can't you be happy for me?"

I went to the kitchen.

"Hey, as long as you're in there, grab me a beer," Brian shouted from the bathroom. After every cutting stroke of the razor, he would swish the blade in the dirty water in a way that reminded me of a pendulum swinging inside a clock.

I tossed an unopened can of beer at Brian and sat next to Mitch.

"You surprised me when you left. You surprised all of us. I didn't think you had it in you. Don't you remember how you dragged me to Providence in the first place?"

"Seems to have worked out."

"A year later you disappear, ripping a hole in Jenny's heart."

"Look, we've worked it out, okay? Why don't you understand that? I talked to her on the phone not long ago—"

"That was Christmas, Jack. Six months ago. You did everything you could to make her fall in love with you, then you crushed her, then called her to make up, sent her some guilt-induced gift, then you disappeared again."

"I didn't know you were so up on the details of my life."

"Yeah, I know about it all," Mitch said. "Every time Jenny cries over you, Erin's there to listen. Don't you know what you've done to her? I know we used to be best friends, but I wouldn't be here if Erin didn't think someone ought to make an effort to reel you back in."

Used to be best friends?

Brian stepped out from the bathroom. "We're supposed to meet up with Jason and Terry at eight over at the Fire Yard. This is going to be the night of your lives, gentlemen. I *promise* you. Mitchell, I hope you like having a good time 'cause that's what's going to happen to you, my friend."

I smiled, checking to see if the bravado was boosting Mitchell's spirits. It wasn't.

"Before we party tonight, there's something we gotta do," Brian said, his tone was casual and calm. "I've got to see a friend on business."

"What kind of business?" Mitch asked.

Brian rolled his eyes and stepped back into the bathroom. Mitch wanted me to say we weren't going to the party, that we were going out for pizza instead, but I wanted to show him the Chicago I'd been running around in. Maybe then he would see the logic of my choices. I wanted him to be the Mitchell who'd gone to Providence with me.

"I'm different than I was," he told me. "I'm a Christian now. I was baptized at Erin and Jenny's church. I don't want to go to this party. Why don't *we* do something else, just the two of us, and let Brian go his own way?"

"Look, let's go for an hour. If you aren't having the *best* time, we'll get a cab and do whatever you want. Deal?"

Brian picked his keys up from the table. "You ladies ready for the ball? Let's go."

Brian's black BMW flew through the city streets until we entered areas I no longer recognized. Climbing a steep hill in the darkness, we crossed some invisible line between "good neighborhood" and a neighborhood where the streetlights had all been burnt or shot out. I looked at Mitchell in the dark of the backseat slouched low in the shadow.

"You okay, buddy?" I asked.

Mitchell nodded in silent misery.

Sometimes when I dream of that night, it's all different. We don't go to the party. We go downtown to Pizzeria Uno and sit at a table. We talk and laugh until it's late, and he tells me he understands why I had to go but that it's time to come home. That I have to go back to Providence. And in that dream, I just know he's right. We drive through the night and surprise the girls the next morning in Indianapolis. We take them to breakfast at the Waffle House, and everything is put back together.

"How much farther?" I asked. The streets began to look like war zones. There were abandoned cars, buildings with boarded-over windows.

"Half a mile," Brian said, but there was fear in his voice. His bony hands were gripping the wheel too tightly, his Ichabod Crane face so close he could have hung his nose on it.

He'd been cocky back at the apartment, but not here. I felt the adrenaline rush of blue anger race up the back of my spine. He'd said it was safe, but it wasn't. We weren't just his passengers, we were his protection.

"Brian!" I said in a voice that startled him. "Turn the car back."

"Shut up! We're almost there."

"Turn the car around. You're about to pee in your pants. You know something you're not telling us."

"Don't be such a baby. We're here, and we're going to do this."

Brian turned the car into a drive, the last house on a deadened street, and shoved the shifter into park, leaving the motor running. A lone streetlight behind us beamed murky light on a row of slum houses.

"What are we doing here?" Mitchell asked.

"Relax," Brian instructed. "I'll be back in two minutes." He pushed open the glove box, revealing a handgun.

"What are you doing?"

He shushed me and slid out the door. "Use it if you need to."

Brian entered the gate of a chain-link fence. Through the shadows we saw his dark figure ascend the front-porch stairs, cross the plank-boarded porch, and knock on the front door. It opened, and he slipped inside.

Mitch and I sat in silence. We were no longer college goof-offs going to a party. We left that world six blocks earlier. This was a different, dangerous world.

"Well, this is interesting," said Mitchell.

Outside, the night was hot and humid. I could feel beads of perspiration roll underneath my shirt, and my skin itched as if ants were crawling up my back.

"It'll be all right," I said as much to myself as to Mitchell.

Five minutes passed, and no Brian. Then the silence

broke with the sound of a creaking screen door. Two men stood in the shadows on the porch next door, the orange glow from their cigarettes burning bright when they inhaled.

"This isn't what I had planned," I said.

"It's not what I had in mind either."

"I know I'm not doing everything the way I should, but—"

"Nothing about this is right." Mitchell was nervous *and* upset. "I've never thought of you as a loser, but that's what you've become."

"I'm not a loser. I told you, this isn't my scene. I don't do drugs. This is Brian's thing."

"Yeah, and look who lives with him. Look who goes to his parties and goes along with everything he does. You knew he was doing a drug deal tonight."

"I didn't know … Okay, I knew it was drugs, but I didn't know we would be here."

"Where did you think we'd go? Kmart? Face the facts. You left Providence, you moved in with a drug dealer, you work where he works, you go to his parties. It's not just his life, Jack; it's yours."

Brian emerged from the dark house, closing the door behind him. As he walked back through the yard, one of the smoking men said something to him, and Brian turned.

"Why don't you mind your own business?" he sneered, suddenly cocky again.

Instantly the shadowy figures leaped over the high wall and landed solidly in the front yard. In the thick, dreamless half dark, we could see their faces, both of them had shaved heads and muscular physiques. One of the men moved aggressively toward Brian, who turned on his heel and raised the palms of his hands defensively.

"Hey, man, it's cool. I'm just jerkin' ya! It's cool, it's cool!"

The man continued moving closer to Brian, his pace slowing.

Mitch said, "Looks like company."

Three more guys appeared in the street behind us, one tapping the barrel of a gun on Mitch's window.

Brian was talking to the first guy in tones that sounded like he was seeking terms for release, then bluffing and threatening. Finally he said, "Listen, why don't I just make this right?" He reached into his coat pocket, pulled out a small plastic bag, and laid it on the car. The man snatched the bag off the hood and opened it. He took it back to the porch.

We were on a razor's edge, ready at any second to leap from the car and fight for our lives.

The man returned, demanding Brian's money. My mouth felt dry, and I closed my eyes to pray. Brian was walking backward, toward the car.

"You want money?" he said.

Step.

"You want *my* money?"

Step.

"You're taking everything from me, man!" Brian reached for the door handle. "I've got a thousand dollars in the glove box. You can have it, but then we're out of here." He coolly opened the car door, his body language saying, "I'm not going anywhere. I'm going to give you a thousand dollars."

But the men came closer. It was a slow-motion race, but Brian had the lead. He put his knee on the driver's seat and reached inside the car for the glove box. The men glared at him.

Brian whispered, "When I say 'now,' duck." He pulled the gun from the glove box, along with road maps. "Five seconds."

In the gloomy streetlight, Brian held out the maps. "You want my stinkin' money? Here!" He threw the maps over the hood and into the yard.

As the man reached for his thousand dollars in the dark, Brian whispered, "Now" and jumped in, shoving the gears into reverse, hitting the gas hard, and knocking the window tapper to the ground with the back bumper.

We ducked for cover as the sound of gunshots shattered the eerie silence. Brian lowered his head, shifted into drive, and mashed the pedal into the floor. Tires squealed and screamed, the sickening smell of burning rubber filled the car.

Pang, pang, pang.

Small holes appeared in the windows. A second later we were out of there, two blocks away, going sixty miles an hour through dark streets.

The car was silent. I shook my head in disbelief and thought of how I would beat up Brian when we got home. I brushed pieces of broken glass off my shirt and jeans, then turned back to check on Mitchell. He was still on the floor, shaking with fear.

"Hey, buddy, it's all right. Come on. Get up."

But Mitchell didn't move. I grabbed his arm and pushed him up onto the backseat. There was blood on his face, in his hair, on his hands.

"Mitchell's been shot! Brian, get us to the hospital!"

Brian slowed down, weighing the consequences of bringing in a shooting victim and dealing with the police.

"Brian, now!" I screamed.

"All right!"

I climbed into the backseat to examine Mitchell. The streetlights high above us dispersed their light in rhythm, brighter as they approached, dimmer as they passed. Mitchell was covered in blood, too much blood.

"Mitchell, hang in there. We're going to get you to a hospital." I held his bloody hand and squeezed it. He didn't squeeze back.

"Mitchell!" I shouted, but his eyes were unresponsive. I prayed for the first time in years. *Oh, dear Lord, please don't let him die!*

I'm sorry. I'm sorry, Mitchell! Hang in there. Please don't die!

Mitchell turned his head toward me and spoke, his voice a mere rasp. "It's all right."

"Mitchell, I love you like a brother. I'm sorry, I'm so sorry about tonight." I cradled his head in my arms, whispering to him as the car neared the ER. "It's all right, Mitchell; we're almost home."

I was watching Mitchell's life passing before me, and you know what I thought of? Tossing a football back and forth with Mitchell when we were just kids. His dad had just bought it for me. An official-sized, officially licensed leather football.

"Do you remember that football, Mitch?"

His body was resting against mine, and I brushed the hair from his face. When we pulled into the bright ER bay, the black stains on his clothes and the seat turned crimson, and his eyes stared directly into mine. He spoke only one word.

"Time."

It was his last word.

~ Twenty-six ~

Coming up close
Everything sounds like welcome home
Come home.

—'Til Tuesday
"Coming Up Close"

I went back to Providence to untangle my wearied head. I'd missed sleeping in the wrought-iron-and-wood bed I bought a year before the book came out. I'd missed seeing Mrs. Hernandez, Providence all decorated with Christmas lights, and just being home. Since I'd given Bud a break, I figured I'd grant one to myself.

After dropping my luggage back at the house, I headed toward the Old Village district and parked the Jeep on the gas-lantern-lined streets of West Providence. There's a Christmas tradition here at Shafford's department store, one of a handful of downtown stand-alones that, like Duroth's, has survived the onslaught of suburban malls. The store does most of its business between October and December when customers are in the market for elegant gifts and treasured traditions. Here, people can touch the past, since Shafford's hasn't changed much in the past year, or in the past forty.

A small silver bell rang when I opened the door; the same checkered brown and white linoleum that's been there forever greeted me. I bought a bag of wrapped caramels at the candy counter. It had been years since I'd last been in Shafford's.

"Can I help you find something?"

I turned toward a beautiful dark-haired saleswoman in her early forties. She wore oval glasses with brown frames securely fastened on a silver chain.

"I'm looking for something special for Christmas," I told her.

"Something for your wife? Children?" She asked ordinary salesclerk questions, but at Christmas they just reminded me of my singleness.

"Coworkers," I said.

The woman stepped from behind a window display she'd been rearranging, brushing a wrinkle from her skirt where she'd been kneeling.

"I'm looking for one item I can give to a number of people, something memorable. A sort of keepsake."

"Do you have a price range in mind?"

"No, just something nice, appropriate for both men and women."

I followed her to a display case with a glass counter in the corner of the store. "You'll need more than one? That narrows choices a bit. How many are you looking for?"

I counted aloud. "Let's see … There's Arthur and Aaron, Peter, Nancy … Mrs. Hernandez and Raymond … Six I'd guess."

The woman removed her glasses, and they hung in front of her blue sweater.

So familiar. Have we met before?

"If you're looking for something distinctive, this may interest you." She pulled a box from the display case and set it on the counter. Opening it, she lifted out an exquisite clock—a crystal timepiece. She set it on a plum velvet display cloth as gently as you'd free a newborn kitten.

"This is a Swiss timepiece by Louis Demler. It's not antique, but it's very high quality. It's handcrafted, assembled in Boston and layered by hand. If you look, you'll see the many layers of enameling on the clock face."

I'm not getting the face; the voice … maybe.

"The works are Swiss quartz, guaranteed to last a hundred years."

"That's longer than I'll be around," I said, and she smiled.

The bell at the front door rang again, and I glanced over my shoulder to see two white-haired ladies shuffle in from the cold.

"It's very nice." I said. "If you have enough, I'll take them."

"We have two here, but I can check and see if more are available."

"Thanks."

She punched a number on the speed dial. "It's kind of uncommon, getting everyone on your Christmas list the same gift," she told me while waiting for the other line to pick up.

"I usually pick out something different for everyone, but this year—and maybe this sounds ironic—but it just seems more special this way."

Would you like to know what they cost?" she asked.

"Not really," I said, sounding garish, not as I'd intended. Her eyebrows raised, and I suspected I'd come across like a card-carrying member of the leisure class. I quickly added, "But you'd better tell me anyway."

"They're twelve hundred dollars apiece."

"That's fine," I said. I didn't care what they cost. I could imagine one in Arthur's study, next to his twenty-year-old bottles of scotch, Peter setting his in his curio at work, and Mrs. Hernandez gushing when she saw hers for the first time. "Do you still offer gift wrapping and delivery?"

"Yes, it's usually extra, but I'll wave the costs since this is such a large order … Hi, Jill; this is Jennifer at Shafford's in Providence. Can you check on an item to see if you have it in inventory? Yes, thanks." She paused again.

Jennifer.

"Yes, I'm trying to find four Louis Demler timepieces. I have an item number for you." She began to rewrap the clock, nodding to me that they did indeed have what I needed. I pulled out my Visa card and slid it across the glass countertop. "Can I call you back in ten minutes and give you the shipping information? Thanks, Jill."

She hung up the phone. "Well, this is your day. If

you'll write down the delivery addresses on this sheet, they'll be delivered directly from our store in Indy."

"Well, you've made shopping easy. Thank you."

"You're quite welcome, Mr. Clayton. Helping someone find what they're looking for is my favorite part of the job." She picked up my Visa card and swiped it through the reader.

"You know my name?"

"I read it on your card, but we've met before. Come to think of it, I've also read your book, so I'd know you any number of ways." She smiled, deepening the mystery. "I don't suppose you recognize me?"

"You look familiar, as cliché as that sounds. Where did we meet?"

She extended her hand to shake mine. "I'm Jennifer Shafford, but before I was married, my name was Jennifer Carswell. I used to live across the hall from you in an apartment on Alder Street and Thatcher."

"Oh my gosh!" I said, instinctively reaching across the counter to hug her. "I haven't seen you since freshman year."

"It's been awhile. I suppose you heard through the rumor mill, but I left school that year to have a baby. He's twenty-one now." We shook our heads in disbelief.

"Well, I feel old."

"And Roger and I have a daughter who's fifteen."

"That's amazing. I've thought of you over the years, wondered what had happened. Looks like you've done well for yourself."

"I came back after Jason was born, finished my degree. And while I was here, I met Roger and got married."

The register printed the sales receipt, and she tore it off but kept it in her hand. She seemed to be stepping back in time, back to 1985.

"It was a tough decision, you know, whether or not to keep the baby."

I listened, aware that no one else was in earshot.

"Now I can't even imagine the alternative. Jason's such a great kid, but at the time ..." Jennifer's voice quieted like a parishioner's in a confessional booth. "A girlfriend of mine walked with me through the entire pregnancy when my parents were confused and heartbroken ... and disappointed."

I reached out my hand and rested it on hers.

"She was so strong in her faith in Christ. I came to know the Lord too, like I guess you did."

Her dark eyes stared into mine, not romantically, but held by a thread of connection that links people who have shared a moment in time.

"Yes, I came to Him later too."

"I kind of figured that from your book. You're different from the person I remember in the old days. It's funny how the Lord changes everything for the good. New creation, the old things pass away."

"Yes," I agreed.

"I was in Delton for two years raising Jason, going to church, studying the Bible. I just trusted God and hoped He had a new life for me. He did," Jennifer said, then returned to her work, handing me the receipt. "Have you ever thought of where you'd be right now without the Lord?"

I had. There were half-opened boxes full of the person I used to be warehoused in the thinker's loft.

She laughed a happy, carefree laugh. "He brought me through the pregnancy, brought Roger into my life. Even my working here in this store is His miracle."

"How's that?"

She became exuberant. "My degree is in retail merchandising, and I'd always wanted to travel to Europe as a buyer. But with Jason, I didn't see any way that could happen. I'd thought about moving to New York and working for the big retailers." She shook her head. "Well, Roger goes to London every year to buy for the store …"

London …

"Every time the wheels touch down at Heathrow, I say a little prayer, thanking the Lord for how generous He's been. He put the broken pieces back together again." Her face glowed as she recounted the blessings the Lord had stored away in her heart.

I left Shafford's and headed for the Jeep, Jennifer's words still echoing in my mind. She was a flesh-and-blood reminder of Providence past. However brief our season had been that summer of 1985, seeing her again left a powerful wake of vivid memories.

I hit Big Bad Burger on the way home and got takeout. Back in my home office, I started up the iMac and opened a new document. I continued writing my tales of woe and wonder, transferring my memory into the computer's memory. Once again I traveled back to the land where the ghosts inside my head climbed out of their boxes, dusted themselves off, and remembered me back.

~ Twenty-seven ~

When you go you're gone forever.

—Culture Club
"Karma Chameleon"

The funeral was held on a Monday. It was at the graveside where I finally saw what Mitchell had been trying to tell me. If I live to be a thousand, I'll never forget Jenny and Erin wearing black mourner's dresses symbolizing not only the end of Mitch's life but the end of college, and the end of our innocence.

Afterward, at the reception, I sat on the back porch listening to the muted, humorless voices of my mother, Marianne, and my uncle Carlton coming from the kitchen. Then Jenny's voice sweetened the bitterness like cream in a cup of black coffee. After working her soothing effect on the kitchen conversation, I heard the back-porch door creak open, then felt her gentle hands behind me.

"I am so sorry about Mitchell," she breathed, pouring out words to still my shattered heart.

She crouched down and put her arms around me. My head fell to her arm, but no words came. I felt a guilt that made me sick. I might as well have pulled the trigger that killed Mitchell. I reviewed the mental videotape of Mitchell's last day over and over again in my mind, looking for some supernatural portal I could reach through and pull him back to safety. This was not supposed to be.

"Do you need me to do anything for you?" she asked.

"I'm finished with Chicago," I said, the words falling out of my mouth like broken teeth. A cool breeze blew into the yard from the farmland, a short green crop waving beneath an unseen hand.

"I killed him, Jenny. I killed Mitchell. He should never have come to Chicago."

"No, you didn't, Jack. Don't blame yourself for this."

"I made him go! He didn't want to, but I made him. I'll never forgive myself for this. God will punish me."

Jenny shushed me like a child. With the strength of her character and her intimate knowledge of the Savior, she said, "God doesn't want to punish you, Jack. He loves you. And He loved Mitchell."

We sat together, alone on the back porch in the quiet of the day. "Jack, I want you to come back to Providence with me. I want us to be together. To be … a family to one another."

"Mitchell," I said, unaware. "Mitchell, where are you?"

"Jack, look at me."

"Mitchell. I'm sorry, Mitchell. I'm so sorry."

The digital clock read 7:35. It was dark, and I didn't know where I was. The cool breeze of a brewing storm blew in through an open window. It was all reminiscent of a night at the beginning, a thousand years before. The door cracked open, and a narrow sliver of light poured in. Jenny entered, crawling into bed with me in the dark.

"Are you all right?" she asked.

"Where am I? What's happening?"

"Your mother's downstairs cleaning up the house. You've been sleeping for a couple of hours."

"Sorry I'm such a wreck. Thank you for staying with me."

"Jack, I love you, and I promise, no matter what happens, I will always stay with you."

I wrapped my hands around her thin waist and pulled her on top of me. Her lips and mine met in the darkness. She pushed sweat off my forehead with the heel of her hand. Her heartbeat tapped against my chest.

"I remember the first day I saw you," I said. "You were walking up Augustine Hill to your dorm in those beige leggings, that tan skirt, and corduroy shoes."

Jenny laughed.

"I fell in love with your face. Did you know that?" I asked, seeing that moment clearly in my mind. "You had something I thought I could never reach from my world."

"Shh, Jack," she said, perfect words in perfect moments. "I don't want you to insult the man I love."

Downstairs the dishwasher rumbled and spit,

cleaning crumbs from the good china and chocolate frosting from rarely used dessert dishes.

"I'm sorry you can't sleep here all night."

"Me, too."

"I would do anything to be married to you right now," I said. And I meant it. "To be able to sleep with you until the sun comes up. We could watch it rise over the elm trees in the window."

Jenny laid her head on my chest and let out a contented sigh. "Do you know what you're going to do tomorrow?"

"I'm going to go over to Mitch's house. Did you know he had a Harley-Davidson motorcycle?"

"Yeah. He was going to sell it, right?"

"Mitch's parents want to give it to me."

"Why?"

"His dad said he thought Mitch would want me to have it. I said no, but they want to give it to me anyway."

"Do you think it's their way of saying they forgive you?" Jenny asked.

"I don't know. Mr. McDaniels spoke to me at the funeral, but his words were measured, like he was just going through the motions. He admitted they were still in shock, and still upset, but that they understood—whatever that means."

"They're just trying to work through this … We all are. I'm sure they'll forgive you in time—"

"How could they?" I said, interrupting her gentle ministering. "What's happened can never be undone. I don't deserve their forgiveness, and I don't want Mitch's motorcycle. But I guess I have no choice. I'm picking it up tomorrow."

"Do you want me to go with you?"

"No. I need to face them by myself."

"What else did you say to Mr. McDaniels?"

"I told him how sorry I was, not that those words mean anything when you've done what I've done, but I said them anyway."

"And what did he say to that?"

"Nothing. He tried to smile but failed. He just dropped his eyes and turned away."

At this Jenny was quiet. Her compassion may have prompted consolation, but she knew I had done something wrong and that Mitchell had died because of it. My best friend, Erin's fiancé.

None of us knew how we'd live with the loss, or the guilt, or the shame. But at that moment, I didn't want to live at all.

"What are you going to do with a motorcycle?" Jenny asked.

I felt like we'd had this conversation somewhere before.

~ Twenty-eight ~

You broke the bonds and you
Loosed the chains
Carried the cross
Of my shame
Of my shame.

—U2

"I Still Haven't Found What I'm Looking For"

The pages describing Mitchell's death inched out from the printer. I faxed them to our working office in Chicago so Bud would find them when he came in, and I wouldn't have to be there while he read them. I called Howard Cameron and asked if he would have time to meet with me before Christmas. Howard invited me up to Mike and Tessa's the next day.

On Christmas Eve morning, I left Providence for Indianapolis, the same route we'd all traveled that first Christmas after my first semester at college. I pulled into the drive next to a sporty Lexus, a minivan, and a pickup truck. Mike and Tessa's home was just as I remembered it, except the maple and birch trees had doubled in size, and the yard had been landscaped.

I parked the Jeep in the winding pebble driveway. This time I wasn't visiting as Jenny's new college boyfriend but as a forty-year-old ghost from the past.

I rang the doorbell and waited on the country porch, breathing in the crisp, cool winter air. Tessa opened the door.

"Well, well, well. Look who's here. Hi, Jack, come on in!"

I walked through the door, and Tessa gave me a kiss on the cheek and a welcoming embrace.

"It's good to see you after all these years."

"Yes, it's good to see you, too."

She hadn't changed much. Angela, Mike, and Howard came into the room when they heard the door, followed by three young children.

"Merry Christmas, Jack!" Howard patted me on the shoulder.

"Long time no see," Mike said, gripping my hand and shaking it. He was still strong, slightly heavier in the middle.

A young boy stood politely in front of Tessa. "We have some new additions since the last time you were here. This is Tom. He's twelve. Over here is our oldest, Virginia, and over there is our youngest, Ming Chao, who turned seven this month."

"Nice to meet you all. I hope I'm not interrupting Christmas."

"Of course not. Don't be silly." Angela put her arm through mine and escorted me into the den. A real wood fire burned in the fieldstone fireplace.

"Jack, Mom and I just put on a pot of coffee. Can I interest you in a cup?"

"Thanks, Tessa. That would be nice."

The kids were excited about having a stranger in the house. Curiosity brought Ming Chao as close to me as she dared, hiding safely behind her grandpa's leg.

"Still drinking it black?"

"Cream, if you've got it."

After we'd spent a little time catching up, Howard made an announcement to the family. "Everyone, I know Jack appreciates this attention. After all, it's been a whole week since he's been on the cover of *Time* magazine." Everybody laughed. "But I'm going to steal him away now for some one-on-one conversation."

Angela turned to the kids, "Why don't we go downstairs and get our skates on? This is a perfect day for skating!"

"Skating?" I asked.

Mike was refilling his coffee mug in the kitchen. "We have a pond out back that freezes up rather nicely. I cleared off the center this morning with a blade shovel. It should be smooth enough to skate on."

While everyone else scrambled downstairs to bundle up and pull on their skates, Howard and I sat at the kitchen table.

"Jack, I'm glad you called. What's going on?"

"Thanks for making time to see me, Howard. I've had something on my mind for a while, and I'd like to talk to you about it."

"You've got my ear. Go ahead."

"My publisher's asked me to write a memoir, and

I've been working on it this month. Working on it has brought up a lot of memories, many I'm not proud of."

"Jack, if you're here to seek forgiveness for something twenty years in the past, don't worry. You've already got it." Howard chuckled, swatting at my knee.

"Actually, there *are* some things I wish I had your forgiveness for—"

"Jack," Howard interrupted. "I don't know if anyone's told you this or not, but the past is over. Whatever happened long ago, we dealt with then, and it's finished. I don't think about it anymore."

"I know. I just regret how I treated Jenny."

"I don't think she has an ounce of ill will for you, Jack. Murphy gave her the marriage and the family she always wanted."

"I'm sorry things didn't work out another way. Being single all my life, perhaps you can understand that I've wondered what might have been ..."

"I do understand, but there's something you need to realize: You weren't ready. That's what made a commitment impossible. Don't play the what-if game. It's pointless. Given who you were at the time, there was no way you could have given Jenny something you didn't have."

I started to speak, then stopped. I sensed Howard had more wisdom yet to offer.

"It's not like you overslept a ringing alarm clock, and if only given a second chance, you'd wake up on time. It's more like you were a caterpillar, and Jenny was a butterfly. Now that you're older and wiser, you wish you could go back and be a butterfly too. But you *weren't* a butterfly then, Jack."

"You're right, of course. When I think about the past, I think of myself going back as I am now, not as who I was then."

"If we had a time machine, and I sent you back as you are now, things would likely be very different between the two of you. But if we sent you back exactly like the person you were then, do you think the outcome would be different?"

"No."

"I don't think so either." Howard's eyes showed infinite compassion and love. "There are many opportunities to do good, Jack, but the truth is, you're going to miss a few along the way. Want my advice?"

"I do, actually."

"Do something about today. It's the only day we truly have. And if you'll make this day matter for the things Christ taught us, you'll be doing what He wants you to do and living with purpose. You won't have regrets, especially when you learn to love others more than anything else … except for the love you have for God. Here, you can write this down for your next book: Pour out everything you can to others."

I smiled and Howard continued.

"Here's another way of looking at it. When you were twenty, you thought with your own mind, mostly about yourself and what you wanted, and look where it got you. But now you think with His mind, focusing on what He's interested in. And look at the result: God's blessed you, and others through your work."

Howard had a great gift of settling things. What he was saying wasn't completely new to me, but hearing it from him in his calm, confident voice, it finally made sense. He spoke to me with more than words.

"I could use a guy like you around, Howard. I don't know when someone has spoken so clearly to me."

"I'm a minister, Jack. That's a verb, not a noun."

Angela came in to check on us. "Are the two of you doing all right?"

"Jack seems to be doing just fine."

"You two want to see something adorable? Look outside." Angela pointed past us, and we turned to see three heavily wrapped bundles on ice skates displaying three radically different levels of skating ability. Mike was there with the shovel and the dogs.

"Looks like they're having fun." Howard pulled back the sheer drapes to get a better look.

"Makes me wish the boys were here too," Angela said.

"Yes," I said, getting up from the table. "I think I'm going to let you all get on with the rest of your Christmas."

"We're so glad you came. Everyone has enjoyed seeing you again, Jack. You know, now that we're all going to be back in Indiana, please don't be a stranger."

"I won't. I promise," I said. I grabbed my coat from the back of the couch and slid my arms through the sleeves.

"I don't know how you keep warm in that Jeep, Jack. I would freeze to death in that thing." Angela rubbed her arms.

"It's easier staying cool in the summer. Just pop the top." I smiled and made my way toward the front door. "Well, Merry Christmas. Thanks again for seeing me, Howard. And for your wise words."

Angela stepped closer and gave me a hug like one I remembered seeing her give Jenny. "Merry Christmas, Jack. God be with you." Her eyes beamed genuine warmth. I was finally at peace with my past.

"God be with you, too. And when you talk to Jenny again, please tell her I said hello and Merry Christmas."

"You can tell her yourself," Howard said.

"Come again?"

"She'll be here in six weeks."

"She'll be … Six weeks?" I stammered.

"We're all moving on from our work in London. Jenny stayed on to help bridge the transition to a new director, but she'll be here by mid-February."

"I … I can't believe it. You were all so far away a few weeks ago. I would never have imagined you'd all pick up and return to Indiana."

"Jack," Howard said slowly and clearly to help me grasp it once and for all. "We'd been there *twenty years*."

"What about Murphy? Will he be able to transfer to Indianapolis?" They both looked at me with blank expressions.

"Oh, Jack." Angela's face took on a pained, embarrassed look. "I'm sorry; you made it sound as if you knew. Murphy died two years ago."

"What?" I said, shock registering off the charts.

"I'm so sorry. When I asked if you knew about Murphy and you said yes, it just sounded like you knew."

"Heart attack," Howard said. "He was only forty-two."

~ Twenty-nine ~

I hear the secrets that you keep
When you're talking in your sleep.

—The Romantics
"Talking in Your Sleep"

I left Mike and Tessa's dumbfounded. Jenny was coming back to live in Indiana, a familiar two-hour drive from Providence. England was a faraway storybook place, unreachable; the Atlantic Ocean an uncrossable moat surrounding Jenny's castle.

There had been another barrier of course, Jenny's heart. We'd been out of contact all these many years because of mistakes, hurts that had closed the door to her heart. Of course, when I discovered that God gave Jenny the desires of her heart in a good man—in Murphy—I stopped trying to figure out how to repair the rift, how to win her back.

Angela's revelation spun my heart in a thousand directions. To hear of Murphy's death grieved me deeply. I felt a profound sadness for Jenny, as if he'd died just the day before. And then, layered on top of that sadness, or beneath it, or perhaps beside it, I felt a hint of hope, a hope that almost felt wrong to feel. But it *wasn't* wrong. This was a God-directed hope that I might see Jenny again, if only to say I was sorry and make amends.

I hadn't spoken to Jenny in almost twenty years, but I'd been in a one-way communication with her through words printed in a book. But she didn't read it; she'd listened to it on tape—*she'd heard my voice.* She'd heard me talk about Norwood, the place where I'd learned to practice love when there was no more Jenny to train with.

I used my cell phone to call Peter and ask if he planned on going to the Christmas Eve service. It was short notice, but with my nose stuck in a book, Christmas had snuck up on me. Peter was out. I left a message and continued on to Providence.

Mrs. Hernandez was making her rounds, having already rendered the place spotless and filled the refrigerator. The answering machine blinked. I lingered for a moment in a question: Would there ever be a message from Jenny on my machine?

I pushed the playback button. The first communiqué was from Peter wanting to know where I was. The second was from Bud. He'd read the pages on Mitchell. He offered what sounded like words of condolence. He also wanted to know if my faxes meant we were finished working in the same office. The last message was from Marianne. She'd called CMO and had the impression I wasn't working there anymore.

I shut off the machine and called her right away.

She asked if there was any chance I might come home to Iowa over the Christmas holiday.

"Would today be soon enough?"

I tossed fresh clothes in an overnight bag, retrieved my minicassette recorder from the supply closet, and grabbed one of Mrs. H's burritos from the fridge.

In the past few days, I'd made trips from Chicago to Providence, then Providence to Indianapolis, and now Providence to Overton. Constant traveling, just like after Mitchell's death. But there was a difference: These trips each had purpose, known destinations. I remember little of those months on Mitchell's bike, the last stop before the bottom fell out. Before the world grinded to a halt.

Born again. A man must be born again.

As I chased the setting sun, it was time to put on tape another memory. There were only a few left, but they were significant. The sun painted red streaks over the clouds, a gateway to the western world. The Jeep ran noisily in the winter wind, but it was quiet in comparison to, say, a Harley-Davidson.

~ Thirty ~

And I can tell you my love for you will still be strong
After the boys of summer have gone.

—Don Henley
"The Boys of Summer"

I'd asked Mitch's parents for forgiveness. They'd given me Mitch's bike. They offered their forgiveness, too. I'm sure they meant it, but it came across like something they knew they were *supposed* to do but didn't particularly feel like doing.

I rode the bike home and rolled it into the garage for a tune-up like I'd done with Mitch so many times.

"Your mom told me you're leaving." Jenny stood in the open doorway of our greasy fix-it-shop garage, waiting for my response.

"I gotta get away for a while," I said, my focus remaining on the disassembled bike.

Jenny stepped over the oily work rags and the open toolbox. Wrenches and other tools lay on the floor between us like a minefield.

"Jack, what are you running from?"

"Can't explain."

I took a socket wrench from the toolbox and yanked at a spark plug. What damage a year of neglect could do.

"Jack, you can't keep running."

"I'm messed up right now. Just go back to Providence."

She crossed the minefield and crouched down near me. She touched me with her hand, guiding my face to look at hers.

"Jack, listen to me. You don't have to do this. If you're not ready to come back to school, if you don't want to stay here with your mom, you don't have to. Come back to Providence with me. You aren't in any condition to get lost. You need time to mend. Time with people who care about you."

Like a corridor of heavy metal doors in a sci-fi movie, my mind was closing down, systematically shutting off reason and rationality. I was locking myself away from Jenny.

"Why can't I get through to you?" She raised her voice. "Nothing you do is going to bring Mitchell back, but if you leave here like this, *you* might not come back."

I rose to my feet. "You'd better go, Jenny."

"I don't want to go, Jack. I want you to come with me," she said, fighting for me when I didn't want to be fought for.

"Why don't you stay out of my life?" I said, turning my back.

"Why are you trying so hard to hurt me? I *care* about you."

"Maybe you're getting the picture of who I really

am. I don't want you. I don't want to marry you. I don't want to live with you. What I want is for you to get out of here!"

"You may think you're proving something here, but you're ..." Jenny gasped, sobbing uncontrollably. Something inside her clicked. "You *don't* care about me. Why can't I get that? You don't want me, and you don't care what happens to us." She said this epiphany to herself, not to me. "Why do I keep trying to make you love me when it's clear that's not what you want?"

Jenny wiped hot tears from her cheeks. It was my turn to say something if I wanted any chance of fixing things. But I stood there, stoic, a hardened soldier waging a battle on another front.

Jenny squeezed her eyes shut, as if trying to force the reality away, wringing down more tears. For all my lostness, I still didn't want to see her this low. I tried to hug her.

"Don't touch me!" she cried. "You had a chance to do something good with your life, with school, and with me. But instead, you're throwing it all away."

She wanted to make another point, then shook it off, going back into the house. A few minutes later, I looked up to see her walking away, suitcases in hand. She gave no last glance. She was done with me. Not over me—that would come later, but she was finished investing herself in me. Leaving would be one of the most difficult things Jenny would do, but she would do it because she was nobody's fool. She climbed into her car.

"Jenny, I'm sorry," I yelled to her.

She shifted the car into reverse and began backing down the driveway. I ran beside the car.

"Jenny!" I shouted, knocking on the window, "Jenny …"

She stopped the car.

"You may not know who I am to you, Jack. You may not know the tears I've cried over you, or the prayers I've prayed. But you are going to know the loss, because no one will *ever* love you as deeply as I've loved you." Sadness returned to her face, her eyes bleeding tears, her mouth quivering. "I'm sorry, but I have to go."

I opened my mouth to say something, but the wind stole my words. She turned the car around in the grass and was gone.

In the blink of an eye (or was it months later?), I was somewhere in New Mexico, lying under the stars, trying to sort out my life. Somewhere in Indiana slept a woman who had figured it all out in our first kiss. I wrote her a letter by the light of the campfire.

> *Dear Jenny,*
>
> *I'm deeply sorry for how I've hurt you. You're precious to me, and the thought of life without you is unfathomable. You deserve to be loved and cared for. I have been so stupid. So selfish.*
>
> *Jenny, I'm lost here where I am. I need you.*
>
> *Jack*

What would it mean if I had truly lost Jenny? I lost more of myself in each mile that passed. I was tired of riding, tired of being. I closed my eyes.

Lord, I wish you'd show me what's real.

I prayed for a moment of clarity, a vision in the desert. My burning bush would arrive in the person of Carlos Hernandez, a local I'd met in the Desert Rose Cantina. I made the mistake of telling him where I was camped. While I lay in the dark praying that God would change my life, Carlos Hernandez was drinking shots of tequila in town. As he sat there drinking, a plan was forming in his mind.

The next morning I awoke to the sound of a pistol's hammer clicking in my right ear. I opened my eyes to see Carlos Hernandez and another man standing over me with guns drawn. There wasn't a lot of talk like you see in the movies. The shadowy figure standing in front of the rising sun pointed his pistol into my chest and pulled the trigger. I felt like I'd been hit with a sledgehammer. My breath left me as adrenaline flooded panic into my brain.

The one without a name yelled, "What are you doing? You weren't supposed to kill him!"

"Shut up," Hernandez said, indifferent to both the living and the dead. He rifled through the pockets of my jean jacket and pulled out my keys.

"Someone's coming," the other man shouted. His eyes darted back and forth from the mesa to the highway.

"Not done yet."

I looked down at my shirt filling with red blood. Hernandez kicked sand on the fire pit, stuck the key in the Harley, and gave the starter a kick.

"You just gonna leave him here?"

Carlos Hernandez didn't say a word. He walked back to me, lowered his face over mine, burning it into my memory. His eyes were unflinching. He pressed the steel barrel of the gun to the center of my forehead, looked into my eyes, and for a second time that morning, pulled the trigger.

The next few hours or days were captured only in snapshots. Snippets of memories interrupted by blank spaces.

Being dragged by my feet.

An arm over my shoulder.

A thin woman, black hair. Bald man, older.

"It's all right, it's all right. Everything's going to be fine."

"Sorry." My voice, but it was unrecognizable.

Feeling sick. Immobilized.

Panic.

A woman peering back at me. *I'm in a car?*

"Jim, his eyes are open! Go faster!"

"You may not know who I am … You may not know the tears I've cried."

A white room. Bright lights.

"Or the prayers I've prayed."

"Can you hear me?"

Eyes closed.

ER commands … skilled responses … background questions.

"What's your name?"

"Who was driving the car?"

"He came in without identification. Single GSW to the chest …"

"No one will ever love you as much as I've loved you … "

"Two pints of O positive. Chest X-ray. Get him prepped for surgery."

"Do you remember that football, Mitch?"

"Page the OR. We're taking him up right now!"

"It's all right, Mitch. We're almost home."

"Code Red! Lost the pulse! Get him on the table, now!"

"Time."

~ Thirty-one ~

If you're lost you can look and you will find me
Time after time
If you fall I will catch you, I'll be waiting
Time after time.

—Cyndi Lauper
"Time after Time"

"Well, hello there. It's good to see those eyes open. Can you tell me how you're feeling today? You had us all worried for a while."

"Your heart is beating better, but I'm going to need you to start talking pretty soon, or I'm not going to know what to call you. Can you tell me your name?"

No talk. Tired.

"The doctor will be in to see you later this morning. I'm going to open this shade and let a little sunlight in. Maybe this will help."

"And here he is again. I told you his eyes opened this morning. How are you doing? We know you can get lots of sleep, but we need you to show us you can wake up and talk. Can you do that? You don't want us to have to make up your name, do ya?"

"Where am I?" I asked. My voice crackled.

"He speaks! You're in the Albuquerque Medical Center in New Mexico. I don't suppose you know how you got here, do you?" They waited for an answer, but I wasn't fast enough. "Can you tell us your name?"

"Jack. I'm Jack Clayton."

"Welcome to Albuquerque, Jack. We were hoping you'd join us. I'm going to sit you up in bed and let you talk to us a little bit."

Two nurses raised my bed and pulled me upright by my armpits. It felt like they were tearing muscles away from my bones. They ignored my cries, puffing pillows, propping me up.

"That's better."

"I was shot," I said.

"Yes, that's right. You were brought in a week ago. You were lucky the bullet missed your heart. You might not be here right now."

"How did I get here?"

"Somebody saw you lying on the side of the road. A couple on vacation. Apparently you crawled to the highway. You lost a lot of blood out there."

I raised my hand to touch my neck and felt a neck brace. "Your neck was sprained, but it's not broken. You're going to have to wear the brace for a while. Somebody must have been pretty upset with you."

The bullet missed my heart.

After two weeks I was released. In what some of the hospital staff referred to as a miraculous feat, I walked out the front door of the hospital on foot. The bus terminal was four blocks away. As I lowered myself slowly onto the vinyl bus seat, I started to think about what had happened. My bike was gone, my wallet was gone, a Timex watch I'd had since I was twelve was gone, and so was a gold cross necklace Jenny had given me for Christmas.

The Albuquerque police department had interviewed me in the hospital and asked for a description of the men, but I was of little help. I described a face, a name the police thought was fake, and where I'd been camping in the desert as near as I could recall. I told them about the gun being pressed against my head, how I'd heard the cylinder turn and click. The luck of an empty chamber.

Marianne wired money to the hospital, not for my medical bills, which were astronomical, but for a bus ticket back to Overton.

"Where ya going?" the Greyhound clerk asked from behind the ticket window.

"Des Moines," I told him, though if he'd meant in life, I was clueless.

"Eighty-one dollars and thirty-nine cents."

I had twenty hours to think things over, but it took only minutes to come to the conclusion that everything dear to me was gone.

~ Thirty-two ~

I thought that pain and truth were things that really mattered
But you can't stay here with every single hope you had shattered.

—Big Country
"In a Big Country"

As I pulled the Jeep into the long driveway, I could see Christmas lights shining silver and blue through the living-room window. I hoped she'd have a fire going. The Jeep's heater had conked out at the Iowa state line.

It was the first time I'd seen her in two years. When she opened the door, we both stood there, motionless.

"Come on in, Jack."

Marianne made way for her cold middle-aged son and his overnight bag, and I stepped into a warm and welcoming house. After a hug that was longer than expected, we decided to make it an early night and do our catching up in the morning. I climbed into my old bed and drifted off quickly to a long and dreamless sleep.

The next morning, before I came down to breakfast, I put on a sleeveless V-neck sweater over my Oxford, because it was a special morning.

"Merry Christmas, Mom."

"Merry Christmas, Jack."

I poured a cup of coffee and went into the living room to see how much the place had changed. New carpeting, furniture, no dog. My mother was still a thin, angular woman with a bold streak of silver in her hair.

"Things look different around here."

"Things are different around here, Jack. I had all the carpets replaced in August when I came back from vacation, had new linoleum installed in the kitchen, and I bought a Cadillac."

"I'm impressed."

I joined her at the kitchen table. "What else is going on? It sounds like there are more things happening around here than home improvements."

"There are a few things. For one, I'm retiring this summer." Her announcement caught me off guard.

"Really?"

"Well, I've been there almost thirty years, Jack. They've offered me early retirement, and I'm taking them up on it."

Thirty years …

"When is your last day?"

"May first. Then I'm taking a cruise to Cancun."

I laughed. "You're kidding."

"What's so funny about that?"

"Nothing. You just don't seem the cruise type."

"How would you know what type I am?"

I didn't know.

"I'm taking a cruise in June because I'm getting married. You can close your mouth now, Jack." She got up for the Mr. Coffee pot and refilled both our cups. "It's not going to be a huge deal. Frank and I—I'll tell you about him in a second—are getting married by the ship's captain in Miami, and then we'll cruise on to Cancun for the honeymoon."

"Congratulations," I said.

I'd never thought about my mother remarrying. She'd been divorced for thirty years. Single all that time. Marianne deserved more than what she'd gotten out of life. The loss of a daughter, abandonment from a husband, estrangement from a son. I was happy for her. "Tell me about Frank."

"He's good to me." She blew across her coffee. "We met bowling. I suppose that's another new thing around here. I've been in a bowling league for years."

"I didn't know."

She nodded and went on. "They started a company bowling league four years ago. At first I just went to cheer everybody on, but then I started playing too." She waved her hand like it wasn't worth making a big deal over. "It's a lot of fun. Anyway, Frank plays for Davenport Hardware. He's played all over the state. We met bowling and have pretty much been together ever since."

"I'm happy for you."

"My life hasn't been easy, Jack. But I've worked hard, and it's turned out okay. You're the last family I have, along with your Aunt Nancy. But then I'm all *you've* got too, and when I'm gone, you'll really be on your own."

Part of me wanted to tell her I'd been on my own since the tenth grade, but that wasn't exactly true, and this wasn't the time to bring it up. What was my role in all this living and dying and falling apart, and learning how to live again? God was working everything out in His own way, in His own timing. I didn't feel sorry for myself anymore, and not because Marianne had suffered too, but because the time had come to put everything right again. Every day, a new chapter in a book.

"After we're back from the honeymoon, I'm putting the house up for sale and moving to Davenport. I guess you can tell why I wanted to see you. I wanted you to know what's going on around here. I'd hate to have you show up out of the blue one day and find someone else sleeping in your room." She laughed. "So what's new with you?"

"I'm writing … again. A book my publisher wants me to write."

"Oh," she said. "Do you think it will do as well as the last one?"

"I hope not. Actually, I shouldn't say that. I don't care how it does. It's not up to me."

"Well, they can't all be best sellers Jack. You've got to take the good with the bad."

Eighteen million copies, Mom. There's no "bad" after that.

"I'm okay with whatever it does," I told her.

"What else? I mean, don't you ever get lonely? Don't you ever think about getting married?"

"Yes to both."

"So why don't you do something about it? You're young. And if I can do it, so can you."

"I just go where God tells me as fast as He allows. I'm right where I need to be."

"You don't have what it takes to be single for the rest of your life. You may think you've done pretty well on your own so far, but is that really true? I'll bet everybody can tell you're lonely. You lost that pretty little girl from college … What was her name again?"

"You tell me."

"Oh, you know. You lost her, and now you think you're better off alone. But time marches on. You'll be set in your ways before you know it and wish you had somebody."

"Maybe." I poured down the last sip of my coffee. "Why don't we go into Davenport and get breakfast somewhere?"

"If we can find something open on Christmas Day. Wait … There is a Chinese-food buffet open."

"Perfect."

We cleared up the kitchen and rolled the new white Cadillac out for a Christmas-morning drive and a Chinese brunch. Fresh snow had fallen overnight. There was smoke coming from farmhouse chimneys, and the only other automobile on the road was an old red truck loaded up with packages and driven by a beaming grandfather, his equally happy wife leaning into him with a look of contentment that seemed to underline what Marianne had been saying.

"When I called your office, they said you weren't there anymore."

"They gave me a leave of absence to write the book."

"Are they trying to give you early retirement?"

"No, that's not it. The book is about me, my life. Everyone thinks it's a good idea to take time off and reflect. Think over things … like marriage, I'm sure."

"Don't laugh. They probably see the same things I see. You're moody, always have been, I think. You were touchy in high school. Then you had all that trouble."

All that trouble. Was that what had happened to me? Had I just run into a bad patch of ice on the highway of life, slipped, and gone into the ditch?

"I'm sure they only want what's best for me."

"Maybe they want you to do something with your life. I mean something for *you*."

"I believe that expectation is reserved for mothers."

"But aren't you hiding, Jack? Hiding behind those good deeds of yours?"

"I'm doing exactly what I should be doing. I'm trying to follow God, His ways, His plan."

"And what will you do if He's planned happiness for you? Are you gonna be able to handle that?"

We pulled into the half-full parking lot of the Canton Buffet. The smiling owner greeted us wearing a red and white Santa Claus hat and shouting "Merry Christmas."

We filled our plates at the buffet, and after thanking the Lord for the food and Christmas Day, dug in.

"Do you ever hear from Dad?"

"No. He's still married to Clarice, which surprises me. I hate to say it, but it does. Have you heard from him?"

"He sent me a telegram, of all things, after *Laborers* became a best seller."

"That's George. What did he say?"

"Congratulations, mainly."

"I'm surprised he didn't ask you to invest in something."

"He did that, too."

"Doesn't surprise me."

I watched Marianne from the other side of the white-linen tablecloth, our plates full of unfamiliar foods. Our conversation full of unfamiliar words.

"You know, you've made a good life considering the cards you were dealt," I said to Marianne as she lifted her ice tea.

She tipped the glass to me on the way up, a sort of knock-on-wood gesture. "Jack, when your father said he was seeing someone else—"

"Wait a minute. What do you mean, 'seeing someone else'? I thought you never heard from him after he left."

"No, no. I mean before he left us. A long time ago."

This was new information for me. A broadside. "I didn't know he'd been seeing someone else. I thought—"

Marianne shook her head. "He was having an affair with a woman in Coldside. That's what crippled our marriage. It didn't go on for long, I guess, but after I found out about it, he wanted a divorce."

"And then he moved to California."

"Right. You were too young to know, but your dad hated being married to me, and he didn't like family life much either."

I thought it best to change the subject.

"Tell me more about Frank."

"He's nice, low key, friendly. He has a good sense of humor, which I really need at this time in my life. I'm not looking for someone to pool finances with or build a family with. I'm just looking for companionship. That's what he's looking for too."

"Any chance I'll get to meet him?"

"Depends on how long you're staying around."

"Not long."

"Jack, what's going on? Is there something you want to tell me?"

I put my knife and fork across my plate and looked up at her, wondering if she would see through my answer to the truth.

"There isn't. But if there were, I wouldn't know how to put it into words."

"Some writer you are."

After lunch we drove back home, and I made a couple of phone calls. One to the office telling Bud I would be sending him some cassette tapes to transcribe; another to Peter just to catch up.

"So, I take it you haven't moved to the Bahamas yet?" he asked.

"No, but it grows more tempting each day."

"When I told you to stop moping around CMO, I didn't mean we should never hear from you again."

"I've been in Chicago. You know the guy who wrote that article telling the world I was living off the poor in my own penthouse palace? I hired him to help me write my story."

"So I'd heard."

"From who? Arthur? I try to keep my worlds divided, Peter."

"I gave him a call to track you down. I've never heard anyone so full of energy. What's his secret?"

"Enslave best-selling authors. Make them write against their will."

"You're not still singing the 'Woe is me; I have to write my auto bio' song, are you? There are thousands of writers who'd shave off their eyebrows to get published, and I'm just talking about the guys."

"No, I'm past that."

"Good. Because Arthur wanted me to tell you he hopes you're writing over Christmas while he's off enjoying the holiday!" Peter laughed.

The morning after Christmas, as I prepared to head back to Providence, I told Marianne I was sorry I hadn't gotten to meet Frank but hoped I would soon. This departure was dramatically different from the one twenty years earlier. I told her I loved her. We hugged and kissed at the doorway.

"I love you, too, Jack."

I tossed my clothes in the passenger seat. The sky was brilliantly blue, the clouds chased off by the cold. I climbed up into the Jeep, my mom standing in the sun just inside her front door. She was smiling and waving, perhaps imagining how things could have been years earlier. I thought about Howard's words. Perhaps things couldn't have been any different. Maybe we both had to be pulled for twenty years through a too-narrow passage to shape our hearts into the people we were now.

I wanted Marianne to be happy. I wasn't a jerk anymore, fleeing to faraway places, but a son who'd come home for a visit and to tell his mother he loved her.

I waved back and pulled out of the driveway. Once on the road, I popped a fresh cassette into my portable tape recorder and settled back into my story.

~ Thirty-three ~

Every time you go away you take a piece of me with you.

—Paul Young

"Every Time You Go Away"

I'd been drifting for more than a year, looking for myself and for meaning. I wasn't sure I'd found either, but I knew one thing for sure: I wanted Jenny. I needed her.

Lisa Corothers, the nurse practitioner in Dr. Holland's office back at the college, remembered me and told me how I could find Jenny. She'd gone to work with her parents after graduation at a place called Heart of the Savior Mission. I ignored my massive hospital bills, took the last two grand from my college account, and bought a ticket to London, England.

My plane landed at Heathrow late in the afternoon. By the time I'd picked up my luggage, I was becoming acutely aware of how late in the day it was. If the Heart of the Savior Mission stayed open until six, I was all right. But if it closed by five, I might miss Jenny. I thought about calling to let her know I was coming, but

I thought a surprise visit would speak more eloquently of my change of heart, of my desire to be with her after all.

I boarded the shuttle for London. Two double-decker buses later, I was traveling on foot, blocks from the Heart of the Savior Mission.

"Fantastic! I hoped you'd still be open," I told a young woman greeting the men entering the shelter.

"Yes, you're in luck. The mission takes men until six."

"Oh, I'm not looking for shelter. I'm looking for an old friend of mine, Jenny Cameron. Is she here?"

"I think she is." The woman lifted up a telephone from a small wooden desk and held it against her ear. "Is she expecting you?"

"No. I just flew in from the United States. It's kind of a surprise."

The woman squinted, tilting her head sideways as if that might shed more light on my trustworthiness. After a full day of international travel, I looked rather scruffy.

"I see. Who can I tell her is calling?"

"If you could ask her to come to the reception area. I think it would be best."

"I don't know if I should do that," she said. "Why don't you just tell me your name first?"

"Please, it really is a surprise. We went to college together."

She squinted again, then dialed Jenny's extension.

"Hi, Jen. There's a man out here in the lobby who says he's a friend of yours from the United States. Can you pop out for a moment?"

There was a long pause while she listened to

Jenny's response. "Right. I'll tell him." She returned the phone to its mount. "Please have a seat. She'll be out momentarily."

I took a seat in one of the plain wooden chairs along the wall in the lobby. Less than a minute later, Jenny entered the room. The look on her face was one of utter shock.

"Jack! What are you doing here?"

"I was just in the neighborhood …" I said, hoping to earn one of her smiles.

"Why didn't you tell me you were coming? I could have picked you up at the airport."

For a moment she seemed truly happy to see me. Excited that I had walked back into her life. It was the reaction I'd longed for. I stepped closer, overwhelmed by the sight of her. She had cut her hair. I was surprised by a sudden feeling of sadness, a realization that I'd missed so much of Jenny's life to my own selfishness.

"I had to see you. I have a lot to tell you, but…" I gestured toward the receptionist, signaling a desire for privacy.

"Let's go to my office," she said. "Staci, could you hold calls?"

I dropped my luggage, and we walked a narrow hallway back to her office. We passed two men laughing in a small conference room and a woman talking on the phone in the office across from Jenny's.

Jenny sat at her desk, and I took the seat across from her.

"Jack, I can't believe you're here. So … why *are* you here?" she asked.

"I don't know how or where to begin. There's so much to tell you. I've been on a plane for fourteen hours, so I'm a little wired, or maybe I mean tired, but either way, I'm finally here, and you look great. Amazing, actually."

"Slow down," Jenny said. "Why didn't you tell me you were coming?"

"I just wanted to ... Look, Jenny, it's taken a year for me to realize this, but ... I want to do whatever it takes to win back your trust. I get it now. I want to be with you."

Jenny continued to smile but shifted uncomfortably in her chair. She looked at her watch.

"Jack, I have a feeling this conversation could take awhile. I don't want to hurry through this. I can sense something significant is happening in you. But"—she looked at her watch again—"unfortunately there isn't time for us to talk right now. I just remembered I have to meet someone for dinner, and there isn't time for us to talk. Do you have time tomorrow?"

This was the first time since I'd known Jenny that she wasn't willing to drop everything for me at a moment's notice.

"Tomorrow? Couldn't you cancel your dinner date? This is important to me ... and I don't—"

Jenny shook her head. "What were you expecting, Jack? To walk in here and sweep me off my feet, and everything would be the way it was?" She smiled as she spoke, but it was an uncertain smile.

I didn't respond.

"Oh, Jack, you *were* expecting that. I don't know what ... I mean ..."

Jenny stood, took a step toward me, then stepped back, collected her jacket, and started walking back into the hall. I followed.

"How late is your thing tonight?" I asked.

"My thing, Jack, is going to go pretty late."

"Maybe I can see you afterward? I've been traveling all day, and I'd like to talk."

"Jack, I have some things to tell you, too." She stopped and turned around suddenly. I nearly ran into her.

"I'm engaged."

"What? No … that's not … But I thought you said …"

I reached out to touch her face. She turned her head and walked determinedly to the front door.

"His name is Murphy Bryant, and we've been seeing each other for nearly a year. The wedding is in two weeks, Jack."

She held the front door open. My cue to leave. I walked to the door in a daze.

"When can we talk, then? Is there anything …?"

"Jack, not now. Let's not get into this now. I can cancel a lunch appointment tomorrow. We can talk then. Meet me here at one. I'm sorry to dump all this on you so suddenly. But you didn't give me any choice."

I stepped outside into the darkening night. Back at street level, I turned to see Jenny standing in the doorway.

"You could have called, Jack." Jenny's expression was new to me. There was sadness there, but something else, too. Pity, perhaps.

She shut the metal door and locked the deadbolt.

I spent the night in a youth hostel a few blocks from the mission, sharing a dark, unventilated room with five strangers. I fell asleep fully clothed, with the strap of my backpack laced through my arms for fear of it being stolen.

I was jarred out of a restless sleep when the hostel rang its wake-up alarm the next morning at seven.

At one o'clock, Jenny and I left the Heart of the Savior Mission together and went to a sandwich shop. We sat at a tall pub table inside. A raised awning running the full length of the restaurant wall made the space open and airy.

"You look better rested this morning."

"I'm rested ... Not sure if I'm better."

"Your visit took me completely by surprise," Jenny said. "I'm sorry if I came off as brash or uncaring."

"Always apologizing. That's what you did when we first met."

She smiled, but it was a pained smile, one that wore heartache in its corners and old hurts in its creases.

"I should be the one to apologize," I began.

As if on cue, the waitress arrived with lunch plates and dropped them off without speaking.

"I want to tell you what's happened with me, Jenny. I've changed. I've thought a lot about you. About us. I think what I have to say is important."

"Not to me," she said. "Not anymore."

"Jenny, I'm sorry." I took hold of her hand and felt its unresponsiveness. Her face was cordial but reactionless. "Please, let me just say it. A year ago you were in love with me, but I was running. I ran to Chicago and lost Mitchell. I ran to New Mexico and nearly lost my life. Now I'm in England. I don't have a penny to my name, but I finally know what I want, and it's worth the cost of getting here. It's you, Jenny. I want you."

She withdrew her hand from mine.

"What words can I say to fix things, Jenny?"

"There aren't any, Jack." Her eyes filled with sympathy. "I'm sorry, but there aren't."

It was all calm and polite. We were angels sitting on a cloud. She would remain in heaven, but I would return to Earth.

"I did love you, and I would have done *anything* to make you love and want to stay with me. But you didn't want me, and that's the part you need to remember, Jack. You had the choice then, but you didn't want me.

"Let me tell you about the year I've had," she continued. "I cried for you, prayed for you, asked the Lord to help me forgive you—and allow me to forget you. He has been so gracious to do that. I finished my senior year without you. At Mitchell's funeral, I pleaded, begged you to come back with me to Providence. But you weren't finished breaking the hearts of those who loved you. The only thing you were sure of back then was that you didn't want me."

Tears came to Jenny's eyes, only these were the tears of a good angel who had been scarred. She wiped them off quickly.

"You went away to self-destruct, and I went on with my life. I didn't come here looking for your replacement. I didn't think there'd ever be one, but Murphy loves me. He wants to be *with* me."

"Jenny, what we had was special. Rare. It wasn't a fling ..."

"No, we weren't a fling, Jack. Trust me, I wouldn't have been dragged through this for a fling. But you're a little late in realizing this. You left, remember? I had to get on with my life, and I did. I wish I could change this for you, I really do, but I can't."

Jenny got up from the table and left for the bathroom. I sat alone for a moment, feeling the weight of the world crashing down on me. Then I got up from my chair, grabbed my bag, and started to leave. My heart ached, and I felt destroyed. Jenny came out of the bathroom as I headed toward the door.

"Jack," she said, "what are you doing?"

"I'm making it easier for you to forget me," I said in a daze.

She caught up with me on the street. "What's gotten into you? Why are you acting this way?"

Jenny stood in front of me, grabbed my arms, and stopped me in my tracks. I shook free of her hands and kept walking. "Jack, please stop a minute." She pulled me from the pedestrian walkway and sat me on a bench.

"Jack, you're scaring me. I want you to calm down. I want you to be okay."

"I don't know if I'll ever be okay. I can't cope with this." I was bleeding inside.

"I'm sorry, Jack. If there was any other way but to cause you pain."

"I have to go." I stood.

"Where?" Jenny asked.

I tried to summon a response, but there was none. I walked away and didn't look back. I left Jenny sitting on a bench in London without an answer. I didn't know where I was going, but she knew exactly where she was heading. In some strange, heartbreaking way I knew this was the way it had to be.

I kept walking along the bank of the Thames. All the running I'd done in my life had slowed to a broken crawl. A steel door had closed that I couldn't open. I wished I could change it all back, but I couldn't. That hopeless hope coursed over and over inside my mind.

I had let her go; I had lost her forever.

I collapsed in despair beside a moorings buoy, broke, broken, and friendless. I had reached the end. Life's clock had ticked down to zeros. I closed my eyes and turned to the only One left to call on, the God who had been calling on me all this time.

"Jesus, Jesus … are you there?" I said aloud. "Don't you see me? Don't you care? I'm an utter failure. My life is in ashes, worth nothing. Will you take my nothing and make it something? Do with me whatever you want. Will you come into my life? Please come into my life … and save me."

I cried tears of surrender. There was nothing left for the conqueror to seize.

"Lord Jesus, I'm a sinner and a stupid man. I'll give you the rest of my life, if you'll have me."

I hadn't cried all the tears I would for Jenny, maybe I still haven't. But a narrow band of hope appeared beyond the pale sky and gave me a sudden urge, a nudging in my heart to shed everything I had known, everything I had been. To start fresh, be cleansed. I got up and lifted my pack up over my head and tossed it into the river to the confused stares of bystanders.

I was, and still am, a man twice broken. Once by the loss, and again by the gain. I watched the bag float downstream, quickly taking on water, then disappearing, sinking underneath the strong current.

I walked to the bus stop, leaving behind everything but my passport, a one-way ticket to the United States, and forty-eight dollars in cash. When the jet took to the air out of Heathrow, I was alone, but not alone. Completely broken and poor, but finally able to mend—and richer than I could possibly imagine.

~ Thirty-four ~

I can see your face in the mirrors of my mind.

—Julian Lennon
"Valotte"

In the late afternoon I returned to Providence feeling I was close to wrapping up the book, surprisingly ahead of schedule. All the stories I wanted to tell had been told, either written down or recorded onto cassette tapes. I'd made peace with my mom. I'd stood next to Mitchell's grave on Christmas afternoon in a gently falling snow, told him about the last twenty years and how I missed him, how I missed all of us laughing and enjoying life together before the world fell apart.

How tragic that the four of us should be swallowed up by my sins, broken apart and scattered to the four winds. Standing graveside until my feet were numb from the cold, I had apologized again, still wishing it would've been me who died that night instead of Mitch.

I dropped a collection of minicassettes, the latest chapters of my story, into an overnight UPS delivery box addressed to Bud. Arthur would have his book soon, all the wild-running nits tucked snugly in their beds.

After a long, hot shower and a shave, I heated up a bowl of tomato soup for dinner. Around ten o'clock, I went into my office to write. I didn't type a word. Instead, I loaded two paper grocery sacks of clothing and small appliances and took them to the Norwood donation center. I was asleep by eleven and didn't awake until daylight the next morning.

The phone rang sometime midmorning while I sat at my desk paying bills. I glanced at the caller ID window and saw the number for the Providence Police Department. It seemed like an odd time for their annual benevolence request.

"Hello."

"Is this Jack Clayton?"

"Yes, it is."

"Mr. Clayton, this is detective Sandra Carter of the Providence Police Department. We arrested a suspect earlier this morning in Providence on an aggravated assault charge. When we picked him up, we ran his name and found he has a long history of priors and an outstanding arrest warrant for drug smuggling."

"Sounds like outstanding police work, detective, but what's all this have to do with me?"

"Mr. Clayton, the suspect's name is Carlos Garcia. Does that name mean anything to you?"

"No, should it?"

"Well, he's been asking for you. He probably just got your name from the newspaper or somewhere, but he insists he's in town to see you."

"To see me? Why would he say he wants to see me?"

"Who knows. We didn't suspect that he knew you personally, but he's waived his right to make a phone call and keeps saying he's here in town to see you. So you don't know him?"

"His name doesn't ring a bell."

"Well, he's probably figured out by now just how much trouble he's in, and he thinks using your name will help him in some way."

I racked my brain trying to remember if I'd ever met someone named Carlos Garcia. Could he be someone from Norwood? Someone we'd helped? Or was he some kid like Justin Duroth who'd worked with us in the ministry like hundreds of other student volunteers.

"Is he being held in city jail?"

Any crime perpetrated ten feet outside city limits was county jurisdiction, and Carlos would have been sent to the Jefferson lockup.

"Yeah, he'll be here awhile. He's being arraigned before the judge later today.

"Would I be allowed to come and see him? It's possible he's one of the students we've worked with over the years. Maybe I'll recognize him." I'd been down to the city jail a few times before as part of a local ministry run by Paul Allen from Christ United Methodist.

"Garcia will be allowed visitors at some point, but I wouldn't advise it. He's not exactly what you'd call the student type." The detective paused. "But if you wanted to make a pastoral visit, I can arrange something. If it turns out you do know him, we'll expect you to share that information with us. It might help with our investigation."

"*If* I know anything about him."

"Can you come by the jail after four o'clock?"

⁂

At four-thirty I entered the PCPD on Fifth Avenue. The exterior is like any public building in Providence from the courthouse to city hall, but not the inside. Nothing else is as wretched as what you experience stepping foot inside the doors of a jail. Visitors must walk through a metal detector. A corrections officer—that night it was a no-nonsense woman with a well-matched last name, Debra Payne—slides a plastic basket across the table and asks you to empty the contents of your pockets into the basket, where they're kept during your visit. Under bright fluorescent lights and surrounded by surveillance cameras, I removed my watch and waist belt and dumped all the change from my right front pocket.

Officer Payne took the basket and stowed it behind her work desk. Then she walked up to me with a metal-detection wand, and I was scanned and cleared to continue on to checkpoint two. Here rules govern every aspect of your personal identity. You're told where you can and cannot be, when you can come and go, and what you can and cannot possess. Here you move slowly and quietly, ever aware the officers and guards are watching you. The guards feed, supervise, and transport prisoners, a job that can be as simple as closing a patrol-car door behind an inmate or as dangerous as what happened in this entrance hall three years ago.

A handcuffed inmate named James Frank Norman

bucked like a mule, somehow ripped a gun from a state officer's holster, and got off four rounds in under two seconds, hitting one guard in the shoulder and another in the leg before being "taken out" in a shower of return fire. Norman's other two bullets ricocheted off the brick walls. The marks are still there; Paul Allen pointed them out to me once.

I signed in, stated the purpose for my visit, and told the supervising officer, Red Forrester, the inmate I was here to see—Carlos Garcia. Red wasn't in a talking mood, and I can't say I've ever seen him in one. Behind bulletproof glass, he pushed the red security button on the wall, and the two-inch-thick doors slid open. As they did, sounds of hollering inmates poured out, the bouncing echoes of a pickup basketball game in the gym, and the smell of mop bleach.

I thanked Red, and he responded with a token nod. On the other side of the door, I met Sergeant Bill Baines, who escorted me through the long labyrinth of cold institutional hallways. One more sliding door, and finally I was led into a room with a square folding table and two black plastic chairs. Above us in the ceiling, the obligatory bright fluorescent lights.

I hadn't been in this part of the jail before. When I'd been here with Paul, we'd always set up chairs in the gym for an evening service. This wasn't like what you see in the movies, a row of cubicles split down the middle by a wall of bulletproof glass, where you pick up a phone to speak to a prisoner. Carlos and I would sit face-to-face.

I stood in the empty room listening to an annoying hum in the lights. A key rattled in a second door, the door opened, and in waddled a handcuffed and leg-shackled Carlos Garcia.

His head was bowed, and his eyes remained fixed on the floor. And even though his black hair was shorter and speckled with silver, I knew him instantly. It was *him*. The man I'd last seen standing over me with a gun. He sat down across from me on the other side of the metal table.

"Who are you?" he asked in a voice as dry as sand. His eyes cracked open slightly. "Who sent you to see me—*the devil?*" He laughed like his lungs were filled with smoke.

I took in the sight of a shackled Carlos Garcia looking subdued and controlled in his orange jump suit.

"Don't you recognize me, Carlos? You said you wanted to see me."

"I'm here on business, preacher, but I won't be here too long, so take a good look. The sun comes up tomorrow, and the bird flies away back home."

He laughed again. A sickening mixture of emotions flooded my consciousness. At my core was molten anger—a raw fever that makes you afraid because you aren't sure what you're really capable of—and obscene pity at the loathsome and wretched reptile Carlos was. I felt my pulse drumming inside my cheek. My mind flashed scenes from an arid morning in a New Mexico desert.

"What business is that, Carlos?"

"I'm here returning a motorcycle." I felt the quick piercing of silver rage penetrate my anger. Here was the man who'd swaggered through my camp, brandishing the power that came from his firearm. Another face from my past, another reminder of something I once was.

He'd gotten what he wanted, Mitchell's bike. Now what was he here to take?

A silent prayer rose from my soul for spiritual direction. If this was a divine appointment, then why were we here? I was a follower of the Prince of Peace, so how could I be filled with so much hatred that I wanted to take Carlos by the throat and beat him to a bloody pulp? I prayed again, wanting to hear the clear voice of God granting me direction. And then there it was. Clarity. No audible voice, but a clearness of vision. I saw Carlos Garcia as he really was, a dying degenerating wretch.

His shriveled and powerless act masqueraded as control, but all his conceited crowing was empty. His strength was his weakness. Age, time, and the law had caught up with him. The power he'd held over me that day years before was gone, and then it dawned on me: so was the power of the past that tried to haunt me. It too was nothing more than a toothless phantom, just like Carlos Garcia.

"You know who I am, Carlos. You remember me." I said.

"I remember I killed you. Now what are you doing in my face, dead man?"

"The Lord spared me that day. He turned your bullets into handcuffs. I'm alive, and you're in chains."

He laughed, trying to sound fearless. "Don't preach at me with your religion! You're the one who's wasted. I will kill you again and finish the job this time!"

"No, you won't," I said. "Your time, your chances, and your freedom are all gone. You traded your soul, Carlos, for nothing. And my God isn't a religion; He's a Redeemer. He saved me from your bullets, then He saved me from myself."

"Guard!" he shouted.

In an instant the guard's keys turned in the lock.

"Good-bye, Carlos."

"Yeah, good-bye to you, too. I will see you again to kill you."

"No, you won't. I suspect you're going to spend the rest of your life in prison. My anger for you is gone, and all that's left is pity."

The guard pulled the door closed behind Carlos, and I was alone again in the sterile, windowless box. I took a deep breath and sat at the table closing my eyes to pray.

"Lord, forgive Carlos Garcia. He's lost; for now he's lost. I was once lost too, and yet You saved me. I forgive him just as You've forgiven me."

I left through the door I'd come in and walked back down the long corridor. Officer Payne was holding my wallet and car keys. As I drove away, I knew God had brought Carlos and me together so I could forgive him, so I could be free. Yet there was something more I needed to do. But what?

~ Thirty-five ~

Whatever road you choose
I'm right behind you, win or lose.

—Rod Stewart
"Forever Young"

After my mind-blowing encounter with Carlos Garcia, I drove along the winding Redstone River Drive to Aaron's place. It was more than half past nine. The bright three-quarter moon lit the sky enough to highlight the smoke lifting off the chimney and the twinkling snow on the rooftop. From the lights inside his house emanated the kind glow of Christmas.

"We don't see much of you these days, Jack. How are you?"

Aaron and I sat in front of red glowing embers in the fireplace. Aaron threw two splits of wood onto the fire. Soon they sputtered, and the glow in the room deepened. He rocked back and forth in his chair, looking like a fat Saint Nick with his trimmed white beard.

"The book's coming along. You were right about

this time of reflection. It has been good—not easy but fruitful."

I sat across from him on a comfy red-plaid sofa, enjoying the first real rest I'd had in weeks. I drank in the warmth of the room, the crackling fire, the American Indian rug beneath our feet, the framed paintings of Cheyenne on horseback. The frenetic heartbeat of life was finally winding down.

"I'm proud of you, Jack."

"For what?"

"I dunno … lots of things. Taking on the project, for one. I know it was the last thing you wanted to do." He doubled his newspaper and tossed it on the fire.

"It's been uncanny the people who've dropped into my life since I started writing."

Aaron brought our conversation to a point. "So what's on your mind tonight, Jack? You didn't come up here to give me a writing report."

"No, I didn't. I came to tell you I'm resigning from CMO," I said.

He offered no reaction.

"Do you know when you'd like to do this?"

"Effective immediately, if possible."

Aaron closed his eyes and continued rocking in tempo with the slow crackling fire. He'd seen this coming, probably before I did.

"God brought you to CMO for a purpose, Jack, but I think you're right. That time is probably over. He has something else for you to do now."

Light and shadows danced across the walls, flickered on the bookshelves lined with photos and mementos. I came to CMO a dozen odd years ago. I remembered sitting across from Aaron in his cramped office at the Urban Missions Board for my interview. He'd told me his dreams for Norwood.

Not old soldiers yet, still we were aware of being further along in the journey. The days ahead of us shorter than those behind.

"Jack, do you remember Conolly Airsdale?"

"He wanted so badly to be on the team," the memory bringing a smile to my face.

The two of us began to chuckle, then the chuckles became laughter until the bursts came out with tears. "Bought all that nice blue paint for Mrs. Waters' house and went up to Norwood to get the job done."

We both knew the story all too well. It had been told a dozen times. Only the barest details were needed to spill our laughter.

"Took his own car." I said.

"Took his own car and beat the crowd up there by a good two hours."

I doubled over on the red-plaid sofa, unable to even pause the laughter. It was another minute before Aaron could finish what we both knew was coming.

"Shame he got the wrong house."

I let out the raucous holler of a man who needed a good laugh. A laugh that could only be shared by old soldiers who'd fought the battle side by side in the sunny days of May, when the women of Norwood planted marigolds in their flower boxes, and through the frozen pipes of January, when the hearts of our fellow men sometimes seemed just as frozen.

We said our good-byes for the night, and I showed myself to the door, leaving Aaron to stir the dying fire.

I slept in Providence that night, then got up early the next morning to drive to Indianapolis. Arthur had asked me to come and spend the morning with his staff. And he needed me there for a photo shoot. The media firestorm Bud Abbott ignited in December had cooled. I ran into the occasional photographer when I was in Chicago, but whether or not those photos ever went to press, I couldn't say. I don't read the papers. But apparently, enough press was generated to suit Arthur.

"I should reimburse you for your hotel stay," Arthur smirked. "You brought us more face time on television than two million dollars can buy."

There were lots of new staffers at ARP, and all treated me with kindness. A new hire and recent grad of Providence, Jan Clouden, brought me a bottled water—the new status perk for VIPs. She was cute with her youthful glow and gregarious personality. She proudly showed me her engagement ring. I was envious of the exciting adventures in front of her.

Arthur introduced me to everyone in the conference room and retold his practiced pitch about the new book, one he'd honed in a million sales meetings over the past six months. I met with Judith in her office to see how my editor was faring with the pages Bud and I had been sending. Yes, she'd been getting them; yes, they were great; no, she couldn't think of anything else she needed, but if we could put them in chapter form … I told her we'd try.

After the few brief meetings, Arthur drove me to a photo studio. I was given a haircut, makeup, and a change of clothes before sitting with a photographer, who shot dozens of pictures of my face and dozens more of me standing in various positions in the studio. I'd imagined the photo was for the inside cover, but Arthur was insisting on a full-color *cover* photo.

After the photo shoot, we cruised downtown for Mexican food. Arthur had spent most of the morning on his cell phone talking out of earshot. If a face can tell a story—and sometimes it tells the *only* story—Arthur Reed was stressed. Like a clay vase tossed in an earthquake, each phone call brought jarring tremors.

I'd heard him say, "I didn't say I'd have it on Friday; I said I *might* have it on Friday," when we were still at the studio. At the restaurant Arthur left the table before ordering and climbed back into his car, where he stayed on the phone until we'd finished eating.

"He's never totally here, Jack," Carol Phillips, ARP's publicist, confided.

"What do you think it is?"

"I don't know. I think it has to do with money, but I can't understand why. I know the figures on your book. You've known him longer than I have. Has he always been so obsessed with money?"

"I wouldn't say obsessed. Lured by it, perhaps. It's important to him."

"I haven't worked with him long, but everyone thinks he's acting odd."

"How so?"

"He's in the office for a day, then gone unexpectedly for two or three. One Friday he missed signing paychecks. You can imagine how that went over. He wasn't back in the office until the following Tuesday."

"I know he's been erratic."

"That's not all. He's bounced some checks too. My

assistant Beth banks at Indiana National where ARP has its accounts, and last week they wouldn't cash her check due to insufficient funds."

"You've got to be kidding?"

"No. That's why she didn't join us for lunch; she's looking for another job. I've talked to Margaret in accounting. She hasn't come right out and said it, but I don't think Beth's was the only check made of rubber."

"That doesn't make sense at all. ARP should be swimming in dough."

"More like swimming in debt."

Arthur walked up to the table as the waiter cleared away our dirty dishes.

"Sorry, everyone. Business calls."

We drove back to ARP with Arthur talking production chitchat while Carol "uh-huhed" him from the backseat. I wondered if she was thinking of joining Beth in the job hunt.

After saying my good-byes back at the office, I took off for Chicago. Bud and I had another writing day ahead of us. The next morning I had breakfast delivered from the fifth-floor deli. Fresh bagels, cream cheese, black coffee. Bud was in by eight thirty, and we caught each other up on the story between bites and sips.

"I read through the pages you sent. I'm also transcribing the tapes. Looks like you had a productive holiday." Bud rolled his squeaky office chair over the Berber carpet. He set a thick stack of printed pages on the coffee table, a visible sign of the progress we'd been making.

"Jack, right now what we have is a lot of stories. I've started assembling the data, trying to think like an editor." Bud took a bite from his bagel and chewed while he spoke. "I'm seeing a couple of holes I think we need to plug up."

I noticed a change in Bud's commitment to the story we were working on—my story. Maybe his opinion of me would change too.

"Like what."

"Like this Brian Aspen guy from Chicago? I had a buddy of mine down at first district run his name through their police computers."

"And?"

"Well, the guy's dead."

I looked up.

"How'd he die?" I asked. "And are you sure it's the right Brian Aspen?"

Bud reached for his yellow legal pad and flipped through the pages. "He's the Brian Aspen who never left Chicago other than two years of college in Indiana. He went to Chicago University for a while, dropped out, worked at XN-tricity on Ellsworth, was busted for drug possession 1987, busted for trafficking in 1990. It's him."

Bud pulled out a fax photo the CPD had sent him. It was Brian.

"The kid kept busy. But he DUIed into a cement embankment doing about sixty. Not good."

I hadn't seen Brian since the night he'd left me at the hospital with Mitch, but I felt sympathy for him.

Bud continued. "Anyway, if I can talk to some of these people you mention in your stories, then we can get a little more perspective on things. I think that's necessary."

"Who do you want to talk to?" I asked, dubious.

He rolled the chair back to his computer bag and pulled out a smaller notepad. "For starters, there's Erin Taylor. Any idea where she is?"

"No, but wherever she is, I doubt she'd want to do an interview for the Jack Clayton story." I could see where this was going.

"And Jenny. I take it she's still in England, but your readers are going to want to know what's become of her, as well as the other people who are key to your story.

"She's been a missionary in England. That's what became of her."

"I don't mean we guess, Jack. I mean we find out for certain." Bud took his mug to the kitchen for a refill. "Plus, it would be interesting to learn what they think of your success as a writer. We need to wrap up the story somehow."

"I don't know how that's going to help with the book, Bud."

"You asked for my help. This is my help. Besides, you're going to have to get permission from everyone you mention by name before we go to press."

"These people are dear to me. We're not going to contact them for the first time in twenty years for a 'What do you think of Jack Clayton?' quote."

"Would you rather the copy editor call them all?" Bud looked back at his notes. "I also think we should find out what we can about these two goons from out west. Did you ever find out their names?"

"Just one."

"Well?"

"Carlos Garcia. The triggerman. He showed up in Providence this week and was picked up by the cops for starting a brawl."

Bud turned my direction with a puzzled look on his unshaven face. "What was he doing in Providence?"

"He was here to see me. That's what the police detective said when she called. Of course, neither of us knew his actual identity until I saw him at the jail."

"Wait, wait, wait—you went to see him at the jail?"

"Yes, I talked with him. Our conversation didn't last long. There wasn't much to say."

"Well, Jack, you've lived quite an interesting life for a low-rent campus pastor." Bud booted the laptop.

I thumbed through the chapters he'd printed out. Two hundred pages of life.

"Why was he coming to see you?"

"I don't know," I said, setting the papers back on the coffee table.

"Maybe he recognized you from all the press. You are getting a little, shall we say, 'overexposed' these days."

"Yeah, for some unknown reason, I've had my picture in the paper recently."

Bud grimaced a "Don't bring that up" look.

"Maybe he came here to finish the job."

"Who knows," I said. "It doesn't matter. He's in jail and will be there a long time. Turns out he's wanted on all sorts of charges."

"Right."

"But now I'm wrestling with what I'm supposed to do now that I know where he is."

Bud gazed up from the computer screen. "What do you mean … like revenge? That doesn't sound like you."

"Not revenge. I mean I'm wondering what God would want me to do about this. How far to reach out to him."

"You're kidding, right?" Bud asked. "You want to go save this guy's soul? You're out of your gourd, Jack! That guy'd rather kill you than spit."

"You might be surprised how much danger we've faced in Norwood. Peter was mugged at gunpoint, Aaron had his car vandalized, my Jeep was broken into. We've all been threatened, but we didn't leave. And who was threatening us? Sometimes people we were trying to reach. People who'd rather kill us than spit."

"I get it, Jack. You're going to go take a picnic lunch and a Bible down to this creep and turn him into your best friend, then save his soul. I'm sure that's what he's hoping for. It'll give him another chance to kill you."

"Bud, listen to me for a second. I'm not going to get on a soapbox, but I will say this: The faith I have is real, and I live by it. I honestly believe my life is not my own. God loves Carlos Garcia, and He may want me to tell him that."

"The guy he tried to kill."

"Maybe. Can you think of a better messenger?"

Bud didn't reply. He was shaking off my words, letting them fall into the crazy bin. I prayed silently for Carlos and Bud, that they'd both see the Light.

"There's more to life than a best-selling book, Bud. Or having your picture on a magazine cover. A man who shows love to his enemies does something far greater."

Erin Taylor was on my mind when I left the building to grab dinner. Sometimes we regard our former friends as a kind of diminished hologram. A hazy picture obscured by time and distance. Or as characters who no longer exist once the chapters we shared have ended. The pictures I had in my head of Erin, Mitchell, and Jenny may have been locked in time, but not their influences on my life. Their friendships had taken up permanent residence in me, shaping me even now.

I ducked into Melvin's for a burger and took my regular seat near the back. I'd caught the happy-hour crowd, and the place was lively with people, the floor covered with peanut shells. The jukebox pumped out another eighties track. I gave the waitress my order to the sounds of Simple Minds' "Don't You Forget about Me."

Erin and I had never been friends in the same way as, say, Mitch and Jenny, but she'd been an integral member of the quartet. I lost all contact with her in the months that followed Mitchell's death. We didn't speak at the funeral, except when I told her I was sorry. By the time I got back from out west, Erin was gone. Like Jenny, she'd moved on to start a new life somewhere.

I wondered how I would even go about trying to locate Erin. She might be listed in the Indianapolis phone directory, but even so, her last name would probably be different. I checked anyway. Nothing. I needed to find someone who knew Erin, someone who might have stayed in touch with her all this time. Jenny would probably know, but calling her was out of the question. Howard and Angela might know too, but I wasn't ready to go into a long explanation of why I wanted to contact her. I thought about whether Mitch's mom would still have her number. She was another person I hadn't spoken with in years. I was too ashamed, too condemned by what I'd done.

When Mitch and I were school kids, she'd claimed me as her other son, letting me stay overnight, feeding me, even washing my clothes once in a while. Her greatest gift to me was not saying, "How could you do this to him?"

I dialed the McDaniels' house and waited until her voice replaced the ringing.

"Hello?"

"Mrs. McDaniels? It's Jack Clayton."

"Hi, Jack. How are you?" Her tone was friendly and casual. I was relieved.

"I'm well. I'm actually up in Chicago right now, and I thought to call you. I'm trying to get in touch with someone, and I wondered if you might be able to help me."

"Who are you looking for?"

"Erin Taylor," I said.

Instantly there was silence on the other end of the line. It lasted two or three long seconds.

"I don't know if that's such a good idea, Jack. I don't know if she'd want me to give you her number."

"I understand why you'd be hesitant. But this is really important."

She let out a long sigh as if the story couldn't be told in a short version, and it was a story she'd rather not tell in any version.

"She … Erin's married, Jack. She lives in Virginia now. We still exchange Christmas cards, and she's doing great. But I don't know how she'd feel hearing from you. For the longest time, the only way she could deal with Mitch's death was by blaming you for everything."

"Do you blame me, Mrs. McDaniels?"

A long pause. Another sigh.

"Yeah, I guess I do, Jack. I know you've suffered all these years too, but you were a very stupid young man. But it's all over, Jack. You can't bring Mitch back, and neither can we. If you're asking me if I blame you, the answer is yes. If you're asking me if I forgive you, that's a different question. But yes, I do."

Tears welled up in my eyes. Something had been unlocked in my soul. Those words, simple words. *"If you're asking me if I forgive you … yes, I do.* I didn't know how much I wanted to hear them until they'd already been said.

I let out the uncontrollable cry of a man freed from a prison of his own making—a prison he'd been locked up in for twenty years.

"I'm so sorry …" I said after a minute or more of crying. "I've felt so much heavy guilt."

"Jack, you loved Mitchell, and he loved you. I don't think he would want you to suffer anymore."

"He was coming there to help me." I cried again. Another strongbox opened, another razor-sharp piece of the black puzzle was tossed into the fire.

"What if it would have been you?"

"I wished it would have been," I said, sobbing like a baby, saying things I wished I would have said years ago.

"I wish it would've been me."

"If the roles had been reversed, what would you have wanted Mitchell to do with the rest of his life?"

I thought for a moment, the cries ceasing like the break in a rain shower.

"I'd want him to get on with it," I said.

"Even if it was his fault." It wasn't a question. She already knew my answer.

"Yes." I knew what she'd say next. If that's what I'd want for him, it was probably what he'd want for me. Freedom *was* possible. It opened before me like a thick curtain.

"Jack, there's been enough suffering. We miss Mitchell every day, but he's in the hands of the Lord. You're still entangled in grief, and I think it's time for you to let go."

"I don't know if I can."

"Why not?"

"Because I'm still here."

"You're still here because God wants you here. Don't you think some good has come out of your life, Jack? With the books you've written and the people God's touched through the work you do? The whole country's more aware of the needs of the poor because of the way God has used you. Maybe the grief you experienced was what prepared you to do this work. But, Jack, no matter what good you've done, it isn't good works that set you free. It's forgiveness. Forgiveness frees us, Jack. And Hank and I forgive you."

I felt suddenly calm. It was as if the spirit of guilt had left me.

"I still wish I could take it all back, Mrs. McDaniels.

I'd do it all differently."

"You can't, Jack." Her words reminded me of something Howard had said. Perhaps I just had to hear them a dozen times before they would stick.

"I've done what I thought the Lord wanted me to do, day by day, step after step."

"And He made a way for healing, Jack—day by day, footstep after footstep."

I thanked Mrs. McDaniels for her kindness and asked again for Erin's number. A minute later she returned to the phone.

"Erin's husband is Donald Harrimore, and they live in Virginia." She gave me their number. "Tell Erin I gave it to you, Jack, but please use wisdom, and don't push things if she doesn't want to talk to you."

"I won't, and thank you."

"Jack, I'm glad you called. There's a part of us, Hank and I, that's proud of you. In some ways we feel like part of Mitchell lives on in your work. There are traces of the past still present."

"Yeah, I know."

"We lost two sons that day, Jack. Getting one back wouldn't be such a bad thing."

"I'm trying," I said.

"Keep trying, Jack."

I lay prostrate on the floor crying out to God in deep resolute worship. Mitch's parents had forgiven me a long time ago, but I needed to hear it again. I needed to hear it so I could take yet another step toward forgiving myself.

~ Thirty-six ~

Bring me a higher love
Where's that higher love I keep thinking of?

—Steve Winwood
"Higher Love"

The liberating conversation with Mrs. McDaniels stuck with me for days, two days to be exact. That's the amount of time it takes to drive from Chicago, Illinois, to Annandale, Virginia, following the speed limit and piloting for long hours with the radio off. I'd given the operator Erin's number and asked her what city I was calling. "Annandale," she said. "Outside Alexandria."

When I arrived in Alexandria, I checked in at the Holiday Inn and moved my things into the hotel from the trunk of the rental car (the Jeep would never have made it). I hadn't yet called Erin. If she would see me, I wanted that meeting to be in person. If she refused, I was prepared to turn around and go back.

The next morning I called Erin's number. It was a Friday. I wondered if she'd be working, or even if she was home at all between holidays. I hadn't thought very far ahead. I didn't know what sort of message I'd leave on the machine.

"Hello."

It took me a moment to respond. It had been a lifetime since I'd heard her dulcet voice.

"Hi, Erin … It's Jack Clayton," I said.

"Jack, hello," she said, giving away nothing.

"Hi. I didn't know if I'd find you home."

"Are you in Alexandria? The caller ID says Holiday Inn."

"Yes, I am. Got here yesterday. Mrs. McDaniels gave me your number. I came down hoping we could have coffee together or something."

"Is that why you're calling?"

"Yeah."

"You came all this way just to have coffee?"

"Yes. I've been working on this new book—it's sort of a memoir—and I've been thinking a lot about the past. I wanted a chance for the two of us to talk."

I heard a blast of nervous laughter from the other end of the line. Erin covered the phone for a moment to muffle the sound. "I'm sorry I'm laughing, Jack. It's just that this is what I've been praying for."

"I don't understand."

"Me, either, but are you free today?"

"Yes."

"I'm not usually home during the week, but with the holidays, Donald and I have family here, so I took a few days off."

"Oh, I'm sorry. If you have guests, we can make it another time. I have a habit of showing up unexpectedly."

"No, it's okay. Why don't you come over here? Let me give you directions. Do you have paper?"

I jotted the directions on the Holiday Inn pad by the phone.

"It's a large brick two-story with a small fountain and garden in front. Just pull in the horseshoe drive."

"Sounds beautiful."

"We like it. Can you be here for lunch around eleven thirty?"

"Yes. Are you sure it's all right? I don't want to intrude on you and your family."

"You won't. I'll see you 'round eleven thirty."

"Erin," I said. "Thanks for seeing me. I guess I wasn't sure what to expect."

"Well, Jack, this certainly is a surprise, but life is full of surprises, isn't it?"

"Yes, it certainly is." I said and hung up the phone. Life had been full of surprises, she was right about that.

I pulled in the drive at 2816 Bellpark Lane a few minutes early. The house was a beautiful two-story French Colonial with a large fountain surrounded by a colorful landscape of shrubs and flowers and stone. It brandished regal-looking brass light fixtures on either side of the front door, and clinging trumpet vines climbed up the brick exterior. It reminded me of a scaled-down version of Lillian Hall.

A silver Mercedes with Virginia tags and a blue Pontiac with an Enterprise rental sticker were parked in the driveway. I got out of the car and crunched over the pebble drive, listening to the pleasant gurgling sounds of water from the fountain. The glass storm door opened, and Erin peeked out, her eyes smiling, her face framed in blond hair.

"Welcome to Virginia, Jack."

I didn't respond to her right away, just content to see her again. I felt like crying and laughing at the same time. So many memories.

Time had been kind to her. She looked just like the young woman my best friend was going to marry all those years ago. She came down the steps, and we embraced, a grasp that started as a friendly hug between old friends but switched quickly into an "I'm sorry; it's been too long" hold.

"It's good to see you."

"I'm sorry, Erin. I'm so sorry." It didn't feel right to wait any longer to say those words.

"I know, Jack. You don't have to apologize anymore," she said. Her eyes expressed an understanding of suffering and an ability to recognize it in others. "It's time to put it in the past."

A healing rain poured down along with a flood of memories. We shared a love for the same person, and a similar sense of loss.

"I don't know where to begin," I said.

"Jack, it's okay … Really, it is." She gave my arms an amiable tug. "Whatever you came here to say, consider it said and done."

I smiled, and for the first time comprehended how the past can be folded away. Not stuffed into slivery crates and nailed shut. But washed over in a cool sea of forgiveness, or the softened eyes of an old friend. I took another giant step toward forgiving myself.

"Your home is beautiful, Erin. You know, in a weird way it reminds me of Lillian Hall. The way it's designed, the fountain, the front doors."

"I've never thought of it that way," she said. "But I guess you're right." Erin laughed, like she did the first time in the apartment. Probably just after Mitchell had said something funny.

"It reminds me of the day we all met in front of Lillian. Do you remember that?"

"When you and Mitch were jogging?"

"Yeah." I smiled. It was nice to remember with someone who'd been there.

"Mitch and I had already known each other for a while. But I met you for the first time that day. And that's when you met Jenny."

I nodded. "Yeah."

"Do you remember what it felt like when you first saw her?"

"Yeah, it's burned into my memory."

"Did it feel anything like this?"

I turned and saw Jenny standing in the doorway.

I had no words.

She walked outside, a slow, purposeful gait. I met her on the stairs, and without thinking, picked her up in my arms, holding her for what might have been a minute but felt like an eternity. I thought I heard the cheering of unseen angels and the sounds of workmen wheeling out the last of the scattered boards from old, busted memory crates. Or maybe it was the sound of the Spirit, whirling freely like the wind through uncluttered chambers of the heart.

"What are you doing here?"

"I'm back from England. We decided to fly into DC first and see Erin before we return to Indiana."

"But I saw your dad. He said you wouldn't arrive until February."

"We sold the house before Christmas, and the woman who's stepping in knows more about mission work than I do. The boys and I decided to start the new year in America."

Jenny wore a pair of blue jeans and an English-style white wool sweater. Her hair was redder than I'd seen before, highlighting her natural brown.

"What are *you* doing here?" she asked.

"I don't know," I said, laughing. "I sure didn't have any idea you'd be here."

"You mean you just happened to pick today to come to Annandale for the first time in your life to see a friend you haven't spoken to in twenty years?"

"Something like that."

Erin's Christmas tree was trimmed with strings of popcorn on its evergreen limbs, and a young child's painting of the nativity decorated the refrigerator. While she prepared chicken salad, we stood in the kitchen talking about everything and nothing, and I found myself lost in this moment. Every word Jenny and Erin spoke was music. Every gesture as fresh as it was familiar. The scene was sublime.

"Jack, do you think you could stay for dinner?" Erin asked. "I'd love for you to meet Donald."

"Yes, I'd love to stay, if it's not too much trouble. I know I sort of invited myself."

"I don't think so, Jack." Both girls laughed. "This one was a little over your head."

"So, where are the boys?"

"They went into DC this morning with Donald. He works with the Park Service and is giving the boys a tour."

After lunch Erin went upstairs to check on Baby Claire, and Jenny and I sat on the leather sofa in the front room, where sunlight was streaming in through the windows. We sat quietly in the airy room, content with the day's events.

"So. What's new?" Jenny jested. It had only been a lifetime since our last day together in London.

"Not a thing," I said, the two of us smiling like idiots.

"You know, if we keep grinning like this, Erin's going to think we're lunatics."

"Quite possibly," I said. "I may actually *be* a lunatic, though, so I'm bound to be found out sooner or later."

More quiet. The rustle of electricity humming around us made me feel alive. At last, words spilled out like water flooding over the rim of a cup.

"Jenny, however this day was laced together, I want to say for the record, I can die now. This has been an amazing day."

"It's been a very good day."

"Jenny, you know I didn't know you were going to be here, don't you?"

"I know," she said.

"When are you leaving for Indiana?"

"The day after tomorrow.

"Nate and Andrew, right?

"Uh-huh."

"I saw their pictures at lunch with your folks. Nice-looking boys."

"Thanks."

"I'm … sorry about Murphy."

"Yeah. Me, too. He was a great man and a wonderful father to the boys. They miss him."

"You must miss him too," I said, hoping she would be comfortable saying she loved him.

"Yeah, I miss him," she sighed. "Murphy was the man I always hoped I'd marry. I loved him very much. He was a great provider, and we had an amazing marriage. We were partners in every sense of the word, and when he died, the boys lost their father, and I lost my best friend."

Her lips closed tight. There was more, but it wasn't for me to hear. It was only for her and Murphy.

She turned the conversation to me. "How is it you escaped the bonds of matrimony all these years? I thought women would beat themselves senseless trying to snag a hot author like you."

"Funny you should ask. I actually have piles of senseless women stacked up outside my door in Providence. I'll have to clear the walkway if you ever come for a visit."

"You may have to do that," she said.

"I heard you read my book."

"Yes, I did. Jack, I liked hearing about what you'd been doing in Providence. I knew you could grow into that person."

"What person?"

"The person who would care more about other people than you cared about yourself. As I listened to your words—I had the book on tape—part of me was cheering on the ministry, but another part of me was really just happy about the person you've become."

"It took a long time," I confessed. "A long time and a lot of hardship ... But God changed me."

"I see that now." Jenny gave me the warm acceptance of her smile. "So how does it feel to be a best-selling author?" she asked, both teasing and flattering me.

"Honestly, I'd rather talk about you. The book, all the attention surrounding it, it's all about God—His doing. It has meant a lot to the people in Norwood. Did you recognize the project as an extension of the work you and Dr. Holland were doing?"

"I think it's much different than what we were trying to do. The fact that you're doing it to serve the Lord makes it better."

The phone rang. Erin answered it upstairs.

"You can put Band-Aids on people's lives, but they're only temporary fixes. If they can find the Spirit of the Lord, they're changed for good."

Erin walked into the room. "Donald just called. He said they should be back home by four. I told him you're here, Jack, and he says he's looking forward to meeting you."

For the next two hours the three of us talked about Mitchell, Providence College, and how the Lord had been working in three different lives over the past twenty years.

When Donald, Andrew, and Nate returned home

at four, I recognized the boys from their photos. I saw a little bit of Mitchell in Donald—his astuteness and athletic pose were reminiscent of my best buddy.

I prepared to leave for the hotel room around eight. The kids needed to get to bed, the baby needed a bath, and Erin and Donald needed their home back.

Jenny walked me to my car.

"I'm glad we got to see each other today, Jack. I truly am."

"Me, too. Although it was the shock of a lifetime."

Much had changed. The thick iron door that stood between us in London had melted away into nothing.

"So, you're heading back the day after tomorrow?" I asked.

"Yes, I think that's the plan. How about you?"

"I don't have any plans. My life these days is a testament to planlessness."

"Hmm. And you drove down?"

"Yeah, in a rental."

"Why don't I give you a call in the morning. Maybe you'll want to join us for breakfast." Jenny smiled.

We said our good-nights, not our good-byes, and I drove back to the hotel. When I lay down to sleep, I giggled like a kid whose father has just given him Christmas.

~ Thirty-seven ~

I'll be back in the high life again
All the doors I closed one time will open up again
I'll be back in the high life again
All the eyes that watched me once
will smile and take me in.

—Steve Winwood
"Back in the High Life Again"

The next morning I telephoned Bud to tell him I wouldn't be coming back to Chicago. My writing days were over. I told him about the previous twenty-four hours, though I wasn't sure he'd believe me.

"You're right, man. I don't believe it."

I told him everything while he took notes. He wanted to include all the new developments in the book, and I told him he should.

"Let me ask you something, Bud. Do you think it's possible God orchestrated the events that happened yesterday, or was it all just a coincidence?"

"How would I know?"

"I'm trying to make sense of what's happened in my life over the past month. I guess I'm wondering what you see. How you would explain all this."

I wanted Bud to see God's faithfulness. He'd been reading page after page of my life. He'd come in during the middle of my movie and then got to watch the ending unfold right before his eyes. I prayed that seeing how God was working out what I couldn't do myself might set Bud's own heart beating for God's wondrous grace.

The surprises kept coming.

Jenny called and asked if I would consider driving back to Indianapolis with them. "The boys have never been stateside before, and it's been a long time since I've driven on this side of the road. We *are* both going the same way."

I rested on my hotel bed with the shades open, the sun filling the room with more incredibly brilliant light.

Thank you, God, for all You've done …

At six o'clock on a chilly morning, we loaded her car with a surprisingly small amount of luggage and two sleepy boys still in their pajamas. Jenny and I said goodbye to Donald and Erin, returned my rental car at the airport, and took to the open road in Jenny's rental.

"How are we going to explain to your parents why I drove you and the boys home?" I asked.

"We'll just say it made sense for us to be together."

We made it back to Providence in a single stretch

of driving, with plenty of snack breaks along the way. The four of us took in the sights and sounds of our cross-country trek as if the United States were a strange new world being explored for the first time. Indeed, for Nate and Andrew it was. The boys were amazed at the size of the country, the number of minivans on the highway, swiping a card to pay for gas at the pump, and the dizzying array of stuff for sale in our stores. We played road-trip games and license-plate bingo, counted cows, and made one another laugh with jokes and silliness.

It took some getting used to, hearing English accents from Nate and Andrew, but it must have taken a lot more for the boys to get used to me. In quieter moments I would catch Andrew's stare from the backseat in the rearview mirror. At times I felt a connection, like during the footrace I lost to the boys at a rest stop, and the hysterical laughter we all shared upon finding a nine-foot-tall plastic chicken guarding the front of a Southern-style restaurant. Other times I sensed walls going up, distancing meant to protect, I suppose. Like when Nate saw the now-old issue of *Time* magazine on the counter at Cracker Barrel and asked, "Are you famous?"

"I used to be," I said, wishing that part of my life was behind me.

I saw Jenny studying me too sometimes, watching me interact with her boys. Wondering, perhaps, how I might have been Murphy had circumstances been different. Or how nice it was seeing the boys play and laugh in the country that was now their home. Or how much she wanted the boys to have a father.

"I didn't know you were such a natural with kids," she said, threading her arm through mine as we entered yet another Speedy Mart in search of snacks.

"You've raised a couple of awesome boys, Jen," I told her. "So what's it like to be a parent?"

I asked because the woman who'd played the starring role in all my memories was a twenty-something single college student. The real Jenny is a forty-something widow with two young children.

She gave the question due thought. "It's like having every important thing in the world wrapped up in two vulnerable and innocent little guys you would give your life for. You focus every day on everything you can do to make their lives happy and complete, while at the same time marveling at just how spectacular they already are as individuals."

"So you like them," I said, smiling.

"You could say that. So what's it like staying single all these years?"

"It's like living in a big mansion, and you know that behind a certain closed door, there's a room, a part of you that you can't access because the door is locked and you can't open it on your own. Still, you know the room's there, and every once in a while, you pass the door, and you wonder what's inside, and whether or not the door will ever be opened."

"That sounds terribly lonely."

"Yeah," I said. "It's been lonely. I just kept pushing on, doing the things I knew to do, trusting that God would do what He wanted, and not really thinking about the outcome."

"Jack, do you believe God cares about the outcome?

That He cares about you and what happens in your life?"

"Yeah, I do. I mean … I'm seeing it. You're here, Jenny. I didn't know if I'd ever see you again, but now you're here, standing next to me. We're talking again, and it feels so comfortable. Sort of like we shared all those years ago, and every time I …"

I stopped talking and lowered my gaze. I needed to stop saying so much. This wasn't a conversation to have in line at the Speedy Mart while waiting for the boys to come back from the bathroom.

"Every time you what?"

I lowered my voice and moved a step closer. "And every time I look at you, I praise God for allowing me to know you. I know in my heart there's no one else on earth like you. I am in awe of you."

Jenny was looking at me, *into* me, like she had so many years before. I recognized that smile, but there was something new in it as well. A sense of peace. The cashier rang up the Cokes and chips as the boys ran up behind Jenny to tell her all about the automatic air freshener that surprised them by misting in the bathroom.

Jenny and the boys dropped me off in Providence and drove on to Indy. Two days later I called and asked her if she wanted to spend a day with me in Providence. The following Saturday we met for lunch at Oscar's. I was there early to greet her at a quiet booth in the college sandwich shop, half empty on the weekend.

"Wow, this place brings back memories. It's hardly changed. I didn't realize so much of the town would still look the same."

"The students are always changing, but Providence … not so much. A lot of things are just like yesterday."

"Which do you care most about, Jack, yesterday or today?"

"Today. But that hasn't always been my answer. I've unpacked all my yesterdays and sorted through them. Everything's in order now. The past and present have caught up with each other and are getting along just fine. Though they do have a lot in common."

We sat at the cozy booth, breaking our focus on each other only when the server came for our order.

"So, are you going to let me read this new book you've been working on?"

"You know what it's about, right?"

"Yes, the Jack Clayton story. How you went from college dropout to the cover of *Time* magazine in twenty short years."

"Wow, you could work in marketing. It's something like that."

"Does the book have a happy ending? Does the boy get the girl?"

I didn't answer right away, but her good-natured question was inflating with importance every second we remained in the quiet.

"That chapter's still being written," I finally said.

Jenny smiled, and after the waiter returned with our food, we settled into long, slow conversations about London, Jenny's parents, my mom and her new life, and CMO.

After lunch we stepped outside. The sun was perched in the middle of the sky, warming the air, inviting us to take a walk. We wandered casually up the street, window-shopping like we'd done years before as money-stretched college students.

"You know what would feel perfect right now?" I asked her.

"What?"

"Me picking out a gift for you. A 'Welcome back to America' gift. You know, I do have a little money now," I joked.

"Oh, so you have money now, huh? Is the Lexus dealership open? We need to put those best-selling author dollars to work!"

"Dear, you're thinking too small. I'm talking about getting you something really nice. What's the nicest gift I ever got you?"

Jenny thought for a minute. "What was the nicest gift … probably the locket. Do you remember the locket?"

"The one you gave back to me."

"Yes. Sorry … I mean, yes. It was the right thing to do at the time. Do you still have it?"

"No, I hocked it when I wanted to forget you, back when I still thought that was possible."

"You sold my locket? I can't believe it!"

"Yeah, I got twenty-five dollars for it."

"You stinker." She laughed.

"You know, I could buy you a big diamond now."

"I'll have to think about that."

On Bush Street we approached the front window of Baxter's Jewelers and peered into the glass display case. The small boutique presented a beautiful array of diamond rings and watches, colored stones and bracelets, earrings and gold jewelry, all set out on posh jewelry boxes on a plum-colored sash.

"Oh my gosh!" Jenny blurted out.

"What is it?"

"They've got one of those lockets like you bought me!"

I looked in the window. On the top glass shelf, in the center of the window display, rested a little silver heart-shaped necklace on a chain. Across the heart the words *Love Is Forever* were engraved in a graceful script.

"You know, I think you're right."

Jenny turned to me, her mouth gaped open in mock shock.

"Unbelievable! Let's go in and see how much they want for it," I said.

"Last time it was fifty dollars; this time it'll be fifty thousand."

The clerk lifted the locket from the display window and placed it in Jenny's hands.

"This is a classic silver heart-shaped locket," he said. "It once belonged to a young couple, very much in love, but beyond that, I can't tell you much. Lockets hold secrets. If you look at the back, you'll see it's tarnished, and there's no longer a key to open it."

"You don't need a key for these," Jenny said. "I used to have one just like it, but I lost my key days after I got it."

Jenny pulled a hairpin out of her purse and stuck it in the keyhole. Instantly the locket sprung open, and there inside were two heart-shaped pictures, one of

Jenny and the other of me. She turned to me and stared, disbelieving what her eyes were telling her.

"I brought it down yesterday, Jenny. I never sold it."

She smacked me on the arm and huffed. "Just for that, I'm keeping it now," she said, both put out and delighted by the trick.

I smiled at the manager, who gave me a wink, and Jenny and I left the store with the keepsake wrapped inside a jeweler's box.

"Jack, do you really believe love is forever, or is that just childish sentimentality?"

"I think it lasts forever," I said.

Jenny was quiet as we walked back up Meadowgreen toward the campus. I thought of going to CMO since it was nearby, and the weather had gotten considerably colder. When a sudden burst of arctic wind hit us out of nowhere, we raced up the street and into Marilyn's Bakery to escape.

Inside Marilyn's it was cozy and warm. A recent renovation had opened one wall, connecting the bakery to a cozy bookstore next door. Modern life was well represented by several people sitting in plump, oversize chairs, sipping coffee, their laptops connected to the bookstore's Wi-Fi.

We made our way to two comfy wingback chairs in a section of the store decorated with an eclectic mix of colorful contemporary art and twentieth-century antiques.

"It's getting cold out there," Jenny said, opening her coat to let in the warm air.

I made my way to the counter for hot chocolate to accelerate her warm-up, and to collect coffee for me.

Jenny wrapped her hands around the ceramic mug and thanked me for the hot chocolate. "And thank you for the necklace, too. That was really a sweet gesture, Jack. I'm still trying to soak in what it means."

"What's next for you and the boys? I asked.

"I'm going to enroll the boys in a private school at Mike and Tessa's church in Indianapolis, help my mom and dad get situated, and give the kids plenty of opportunities to get to know their cousins."

"What about you?" I asked. "Who's taking care of you?"

Jenny set the mug on a table. "Jack, can I change the subject?"

"Sure," I said.

Jenny ran her thumb across the jewelry box in her lap. "I've only loved two men in my life. One of them, I lost, because the Lord decided to take him. It was abrupt, it was painful, and it's been a long process of grieving to get to where we all are now, which is finally a good place. The other man I loved once, I also lost. I lost him to his own youthful immaturity. That, too, was abrupt, it was painful, and it took a long time to get over. I can't compare you with Murphy, and thankfully, I don't have to. However, I do have to do what's right. Things have to make sense."

Jenny stopped. For once it seemed she didn't quite know what to say. Or how to say it. When she finally spoke, her words were tender and intimate, her pauses confessing a deep vulnerability.

"I guess what I'm trying to say is … Can you tell me if this is special to you, Jack? Tell me if there's a part of you that remembers us. Do you still have any feelings for me, or is this all just my imagination? And are these old feelings or new feelings? I feel like I've come home to something I remember. It's more than just being back in the States. It's … bigger than that, but I just can't put it all together yet. I guess I'm a little … I don't know … overwhelmed? Uncertain? Both?"

"Jenny, I think there's a story you need to hear. I've been wondering all along why God would want me to go through all that's happened these past months. But I see now that this is the journey I needed to take. I mean, it couldn't have all happened any other way."

"What do you mean?"

"My friends suggested there was some big important reason God wanted me to write my story. My friend Aaron said that while many people had benefited from *Laborers of the Orchard,* maybe God wasn't finished with *me* yet. You're asking me if I still have feelings for you, aren't you?"

"Yes … I mean, that's part of it. I mean, yes."

I collected the brown parcel I'd been toting around and handed it to her. "Jenny, this is the manuscript for my book, the answer to your question."

She pulled the white-lace bow and opened the tan wrapping, revealing a pile of white papers, the result of my memory excavation. I secretly thanked Bud for staying up late, putting this together with me the past two days.

Jenny ran her fingers over the title. "Am I in this story?"

"You have no idea. I started writing this story back when I didn't know if I would ever see you again, when I didn't even know *why* I was writing. I just wrote to be faithful, but now it's something more. This book is your answer. And mine, too … to so many questions."

The rest of the afternoon, Jenny sat on the large sofa in my living room, with her back against the cushioned arm and her feet resting on the middle cushion. I brought her drink and food as she poured over the double-spaced pages, the pile on her lap shrinking as she delved deeper and deeper into my story.

As sunlight slipped and dimmed in the silent house, I switched on the floor lamp at the end of the sofa and the reading light behind her. She took a break around 4:30, curling up to take a nap. I took the quilt from the foot of the bed in the guest room and covered her up, watching her sleep awhile before heading upstairs for my own nap.

I awoke from a peaceful dream into an even more peaceful reality. Jenny was sitting on the edge of the bed.

"I just finished your book."

I pulled myself upright and rubbed the sleep from my eyes. "Any good?"

Jenny just nodded her head, reaching for my hand and squeezing it. "Jack, I asked you this afternoon, but I want to ask you again. Do you think love is forever?"

"Yes, I do. I know it is."

Jenny was holding the small silver locket. She opened her hand and stared at the photos. "I remember those times," she said, a slight tremor in her voice. She looked at me with a sense of wonder about everything that had happened. "Jack, what are we going to do about all this? I'm forty-two years old, with two children and parents who need me. I can't live in the past. But that's not where we are … is it? What exactly am I to do with this? I mean … with you?"

"Why don't you let me take you to dinner?"

"Jack, I'm serious."

"So am I—I'm starving."

Jenny let her body fall against mine, and I held her there.

"It's all happening so fast," she said.

"Yes, just twenty years in the making."

"Do you really believe this is twenty years in the making?"

"No, I don't think everything that's happened has been designed to bring us to this moment. That would devalue what we've lived between then and now. I just believe that every right thing we've done by faith has made a moment like this possible."

Jenny sat up and wiped a tear from her eye.

"I can think of three important questions to ask you, but I think I know the answers to at least two of them."

"Okay … ask," I said.

"Do you love me?" Jenny looked at me with the serious expression of an adult woman, not the college girl I once knew.

"Yes, with all my heart."

"Do you care for my parents, my family?"

"I love them, too."

Jenny wiped another tear from her eye. I'd seen her cry many times. These were tears of joy.

"I watched you on the trip, spending time with the

boys. Do you think you could love them? Would you add to their lives, give them all the things that young boys need? Could you do that, Jack?"

"I would make it my life's work if given the chance, Jenny."

Jenny broke out in tears and laughter. She melted into my arms. This was where I wanted to be forever, wrapped around Jenny, wrapped around hope. I was trying to figure out if she'd asked two or three questions when she spoke again.

"Well, then I guess there's only one thing left to ask."

"What's that?"

"What do you want to have for dinner?"

Bud Abbott delivered my book well ahead of schedule to a very relieved and very broke Arthur Reed. Two weeks earlier he'd confessed to me, his employees, and his wife how he'd gambled away a staggering ten million dollars. As I write this, Arthur is in the process of selling his publishing company to Burrows in New York for an undisclosed sum. My book will be the last publication with the ARP logo on the binding.

Carlos Garcia was sentenced to thirty years to life in the Puttington Correctional Facility. He has one regular visitor—a humbled man who first saw him on the other side of a gun; a man who took seriously the call to pick up his cross and follow Christ.

Bud and I still talk on the phone every so often. He's been down to visit on several occasions, bringing his lovely wife, Katie, and their little boy, Josh. He even came to church with us once, twice if you count the wedding.

Jenny and I were married on June 14th by Aaron Richmond in Providence Chapel. It was a small wedding attended by Jenny's parents, of course, and my mother and her new husband, Frank; Erin and Donald; Andrew and Nate; Raymond Mac and Mrs. Hernandez; and Peter, Nancy, and many of the students who've worked with us over the years at CMO. Arthur wanted to hire a publicist to service a photo to the press … Like *that* was going to happen! Erin was the matron of honor; Peter and Donald were my best men.

This is my last book. My life isn't about putting words on paper, as noble a pursuit as that may be. My life is about serving God, loving Jenny with all my heart, and caring for those two boys.

I sat with Raymond Mac for a while at the reception.

"That's a good girl you got yourself, Jack. You gonna treat her right this time?"

"Yes, sir."

"You gonna do her right or you gonna do her wrong like you done last time?"

"No, sir, she's my girl."

"That's good, you learning." He laughed, an old man's laugh. "You're doing all right, son. You're doing all right."

... a little more ...

When a delightful concert comes to an end,
the orchestra might offer an encore.
When a fine meal comes to an end,
it's always nice to savor a bit of dessert.
When a great story comes to an end,
we think you may want to linger.
And so, we offer ...

AfterWords—just a little something more after you
have finished a David C. Cook novel.
We invite you to stay awhile in the story.
Thanks for reading!

Turn the page for ...

- An excerpt from ***A Beautiful Fall***

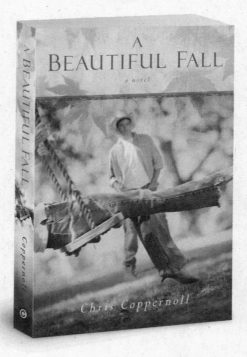

~ ONE ~

Pretty woman–
You look lovely as can be
Are you lonely just like me?

—Roy Orbison
"Pretty Woman"

At 5'8", Emma Madison would have described herself as too tall. That's why she rarely dressed in high heels. She wore her dark auburn hair past her shoulders, something she'd done since childhood, thinking the length gave balance to the rest of her body. Emma looked beautiful that morning in the downtown Boston courtroom although she would never describe herself that way. She stood near the mahogany plaintiff's table, beyond the waist-high wooden railing lawyers call "the bar" separating the area for official court proceedings from the spectators' galley. Even though she hadn't left the city since June, her face retained a trace of a summer tan, and her skin looked so clear and soft she could have passed as a model for skin cream. Emma's eyes were her most striking feature—two brown orbs that somehow made her seem vulnerable and strong all at the same time. Their color appeared so dark it overshadowed her pupils, making the windows of her soul a deep pool to look, or fall, into.

To jurors, the thirty-four-year-old attorney for the plaintiff had been captivating to watch over the long August trial, but not for mere beauty alone. Emma expressed an intense passion for her client's case that had in turn induced strong emotions in the jury. They'd been swept up in the drama of her client's sympathetic story and felt themselves standing in Anna Kelly's shoes, wondering how they'd feel in her circumstances, and knowing somehow they'd feel good about Emma as their attorney.

Her body language conveyed an easy openness when she cross-examined a witness. On good days, the jury grinned along with her good-natured humor. On difficult days, Emma displayed courtesy and grit; confident and comfortable in her own skin. She was clear and honest when she spoke, articulate in matters concerning the law, and always upbeat in spirit.

Emma's client was a young, fair-skinned woman named Anna Kelley. Anna had approached the law firm of Adler, McCormick & Madison months earlier when her Northeast health-care provider, Interscope Insurance, dropped Anna from coverage without explanation during a difficult battle with breast cancer. Eventually it was revealed that Interscope had instituted a controversial new profit-making policy called "Retroactive Review." Even though Anna had been approved for coverage and had been paying premiums with her employer for over two years, Interscope cut her coverage, claiming there were "inconsistencies" on Anna's application after the hospital began submitting bills. As it turned out, there were inconsistencies on *lots* of customer's applications—inconsistencies discovered by Interscope only after one of their clients got sick.

On the final day of the trial, twelve earnest jurors watched from the jury box, listening to closing arguments from defense attorney Kenneth Blackman. In the end, the jury trusted Emma, agreed with the evidence she'd presented in her case, and returned from deliberation with a favorable verdict, and ultimately, a seven-million-dollar award.

"I didn't know where to turn," Anna confided to her after the trial. "I felt so hopeless and didn't think there was anything I could do. I felt so small, you know? Like these were the big guys. They could do whatever they wanted."

The courtroom bustled. Dismissed jurors headed back to the jury room, Judge Brown stood and collected papers from his bench, and Kenneth Blackman briskly exited the courtroom. Emma reached across the table to touch Anna's sleeve.

"But you *did* do something, Anna. You stood up to those big guys, and you won."

Anna smiled with the realization that all they'd set out to do had been accomplished. She leaned over and gave Emma a hug.

"Thank you."

"I'm proud of you," Emma said. "You could have run away, but you didn't. That's what most of us do when we have to face a giant."

In the hallway, her colleague Colin Douglas congratulated Emma with a cordial embrace. Colin represented the new breed of smart, young, and hip Northeastern lawyers: the man in the Kensington suit with a racquetball-thin and money-clip-thick physique.

"You were incredible," he said to her in a near whisper, letting Emma slip back out of his arms, the space between them returning to a more professional distance. "This calls for a celebration. What would you say to dinner tonight at 33's? You've earned yourself a night of extravagance."

"Frankly, I'd welcome any diversion from the endless stacks of depositions I've been reading."

She smiled at Colin. "How come you always make me feel so special?"

"Because you are," he said.

Emma tried to read his expression, but wasn't quite sure where the smooth lawyer ended and the intriguing friend began. Colin was a man who drove too fast in his BMW and thrived in the accelerated pace of a seventy-hour workweek. She imagined him guarding his Sundays for tennis at a private country club or three-day weekends at Martha's Vineyard.

They were both up-and-comers in Boston city law. His star shone a little brighter, though Emma suspected her Interscope victory might raise her own status a notch or two. Did he picture the two of them together? Could she?

"Then it's a date," he said. "I'll make a reservation for seven thirty."

"It makes me nervous when you use the word date. You know I think of us as just friends, don't you?"

Colin reeled back on the heel of his Allen-Edmonds dress shoe.

"Emma, can I help it if only one of us has seen the light?"

"Maybe we should put dinner on hold until one of us changes his light switch."

"Congratulations, counselor." Robert Adler stepped into their circle and patted Emma on her shoulder. "I can't tell you how much I enjoyed seeing Kenneth Blackman crushed this morning."

The seventy-five-year-old senior partner of Adler, McCormick & Madison crowed at the taste of sweet victory.

"He had a tough case to argue," Emma said. "Interscope shouldn't be dropping clients just because they become ill."

"Blackman's the one who's going to be ill when he sees the repercussions of losing this case," Adler smirked. "I expect news of your victory to reverberate through courtrooms and cocktail parties all over Boston and New York."

"Robert's right, Emma. This morning you slew Goliath," Colin said. "To the victor goes the spoils. All Blackman can expect to walk away with is a headache."

"Before long," Adler continued, "we can expect some of those clients who've been hiring Blackman & Lowe to come knocking at our door."

Robert Adler pressed his right eye shut in a slow, wrinkled wink. He turned to walk back down the courthouse's cold marble hallway, leaving Emma and Colin alone again outside the courtroom doors.

"Well, my boss seems happy, and Anna's gotten a verdict she was hoping for. Today has all the markings of a great day."

"I couldn't agree with you more," Colin said, now walking beside her down the corridor. "Now that Anna has what she wants, and the firm's getting what it wants, what about you, Emma? What do you want?"

Emma stopped and pursed her lips as she thought about the question. Colin watched Emma's face intently.

"Oh, I don't know, a vacation. Time to just slow down, relax, and dream awhile." She sighed. "It's the scourge of the age I guess. Too much stress and not enough time to dream."

The thought of a stress-free getaway pleased Emma. Colin picked up on it right away.

"Listen, I have a friend who owns a beach house in Costa Rica," said Colin. "Why don't we fly down there this weekend—just as friends, of course—and get away for a while."

"Now look at who's dreaming," Emma quipped. "And by the way, how did you manage to play hooky and be in court this morning?"

"Officially, I'm not. I was scheduled to be in court downstairs. One delay from Judge Stalling later, and I was on my way up to see you spike the ball. And for the record, Emma, I'm no dreamer. The plans I make are very practical. When I see two things that go together—like your elevated stress levels and a private beach chair in Costa Rica for example—I move in to close the deal."

Colin's cell phone buzzed. He glanced down at the number on the screen.

"Sorry, Em. Gotta take this."

Colin stepped away from Emma, placing his cell phone against his left ear and covering the right with the palm of his hand.

Emma understood. She watched him as he walked away, knowing all too well the practice of law and its demands on attorneys to create billable hours.

Colin's call reminded Emma it had been more than an hour since she'd checked her own messages. She reached in her attaché and retrieved a sleek, charcoal-colored cell phone. Emma powered it up with the push of a button, and stared at the blue backlit screen. Two missed calls. Two messages. The first number she recognized from the firm. The other was unfamiliar except for the area code.

803.

The call was from a place as far away from Boston as you can get. Or as Emma once thought of Boston, a place as far away from Juneberry, South Carolina, as one can go. But who had called her?

She tucked the thin cell phone under her chin the way she sometimes did when deep in thought, trying to solve a riddle her skillful mind could sort out given enough facts and time. She pushed the message button.

"Hi, Emma? It's your cousin Samantha. I have news about your dad. Please call me back right away."

Emma wandered around a large, marble pillar while she listened to the message, then stood in the rainy daylight of a paned-glass window overlooking a landscaped city park.

Emma felt a cruel lump of fear choking out her breath. Her hands shook as she flipped up the lid on her phone, scrolled down to the mystery number, Samantha's number, and pushed Send.

Pick up, pick up.

The phone rang once, twice. Then she heard a woman's soft Southern accent on the other end of the line.

"Hello?"

"Hello, this is Emma. Samantha, what's going on?"

She meant for her voice to sound calm and controlled, but it had cracked as she'd said the word *on*.

"Emma, I know we haven't talked in a while, but I had to get in touch with you. I have some bad news."

Emma suddenly felt as cold as the marble columns in the alcove.

"It's your father. He's had a heart attack."

Emma froze.

"How … how is he?"

"We don't know, honey. An ambulance came to the house this morning and took him to Wellman Medical. The doctors have him in surgery right now."

"Oh my gosh."

"I'm so sorry, hon."

Emma turned and looked for Colin. She found him on the other side of the crowded corridor near the banister overlooking the first floor. He was standing with his back to her, still talking on his cell. In a room filled with people, she'd never felt so alone.

"Are you able to come down here?" Samantha asked.

"I'd have to move some things in my schedule," she said. "I'll call the airport right away."

"Emma, he's in surgery right now. There's a chance he won't make it. Please, please hurry."

"I'll reserve a seat on the next flight out," she promised. Going back home to Juneberry wouldn't be easy, but what choice did she have?

"Let us know when you think you'll be arriving, Emma. We'll send someone to meet you at the airport."

It was a short conversation, their first in forever. The cousins said their good-byes and Emma dropped her cell phone back into her bag. She accepted the disturbing news with an unnerving mixture of calm resolve and blind panic. Her world had been knocked off its axis.

She stirred from her daze to find Colin standing directly in front of her struggling to interpret the troubled look on Emma's ashen face.

"What's going on?" he asked.

"My father's had a heart attack. I need to get home right away," she said. Her voice sounded lifeless, and her body felt numb. Colin's reaction was decisive. He placed his hands on her shoulders.

"What can I do to help?" he asked.

"I don't know. I need to book a plane ticket. I'll need to call my office."

"Listen, you call your office. Tell them what's happened. I'll contact the airlines and see how quickly we can get you out of the city. At least let me do that much."

Emma nodded and Colin escorted her from the courthouse to the parking garage. As they walked in silence, she whispered a prayer, something she hadn't done in half a lifetime.

"God, please let him live."

The next hour was a blur. She managed to drive her car out of the parking garage and to her Back Bay townhouse without crying or getting stuck in midday traffic. She'd considered making a brief stop at the office to let her partners know she was going out of town for a couple of days, but instead decided to forgo everything else and get home as quickly as possible to pack.

Colin called her at home from his car to say he'd booked Emma a flight on United Airlines. He told her he would arrive in thirty minutes to take her to Logan.

Her father's heart attack had cracked Emma's world like the edge of a knife striking the hard shell of an egg. Her mind raced with fears of returning to Juneberry only to find she'd missed her chance to say good-bye, her chance to say how much she loved him.

Emma wheeled her large black travel bag out the front door of the three-story redbrick townhouse. Colin's silver BMW pulled up out front, double-parked, and Emma began pulling her bulky suitcase down the dozen front steps. As she reached the sidewalk, Emma's cell phone rang. She tilted the phone to glance at the name. CHRISTINA HERRY. The name toggled back and forth on the screen. Emma pushed the Call button.

"Hello?"

"Hi, Emma—it's Christina. I'm *so* sorry. I don't mean to intrude. Samantha just told me about your dad and that you're flying out. I just felt like I needed to reach out and contact you."

"No, no, it's fine, Christina. I … it's nice hearing your voice again. I just don't know where to begin today …"

"I know, I know. You don't have to say anything, but I just wanted to call and say if there's *anything* we can do, please let us know."

"Thank you," Emma said, comforted by another voice from another world she'd allowed time and busyness to erase. "I really do appreciate it. I'm just in a whirlwind at the moment."

"I know, and I'm praying for you and your dad. That's all I wanted to say."

"Thank you," Emma said, then both women said good-bye.

Colin sprung open the small trunk to load Emma's carry-on bag. The larger luggage he stashed in the space behind the seats.

"Any news?" Colin asked.

"No, that was a friend, an old friend from back home just calling to check in on me."

Colin nodded his approval.

"Nice to know you've got friends when you need them."

Colin didn't say anything else. He roared the BMW to life, accelerating into busy midday traffic on route to the airport. Emma leaned her head back into the leather headrest, closed her worried eyes, and prayed a second prayer.

God, please let him live. Please let me talk to him again.

In record time Colin pulled curbside at Logan and helped Emma with her bags. The temperature had fallen, and the sky looked like it was about to rain.

"Thank you, Colin, for being here for me today," she said. "Sorry, I don't know what else to say. I just feel numb." A uniformed police officer blew his whistle, commanding Colin to move his car. Colin opened his mouth to say something in the rushed moment, words of consolation perhaps, but all he could think to say was "Call me." He climbed back in and gave Emma one last wave through the passenger window, then disappeared back into the river flow of airport traffic.

A cold blast of wind hit Emma as she wheeled her suitcase to the outside check-in. She walked through the automatic sliding doors, patiently stepped through the paces of airport security, and finally made her way down the concourse, dragging her black carry-on bag to the gate. Somewhere on her long walk through the concourse, between the bright lights of the Hudson News & Books and warm aroma of the Pizza Hut, the irony of her trip finally dawned on her. She was rushing back to Juneberry, a place she hadn't wanted to set foot in for the past twelve years.